WHO WAS SYLVIA?

Also by Judy Gardiner

THE QUICK AND THE DEAD

WHO WAS SYLVIA?

Judy Gardiner

ST. MARTIN'S PRESS
NEW YORK

 For information, address St. Martin's Press, 175 Fifth Avenue, New York, N.Y. 10010.

Library of Congress Cataloging in Publication Data

Gardiner, Judy, 1922—
Who was Sylvia?

I. Title.
PR6057.A627W4 1983 823'.914 82-17048
ISBN 0-312-87030-2

First published in Great Britain by Severn House Publishers Ltd.

First U.S. Edition
10 9 8 7 6 5 4 3 2 1

While the setting of this story is fact,
and as accurate as memory will allow, the
characters portrayed are purely fictional.

J.G.

1

Who was Sylvia? The more I think about her the less I know, but sitting alone in this over-heated hotel bedroom it's not surprising that I keep seeing her like a ghost, like a dream. She appears through the wallpaper, her cream linen dress blending with its oatmealy texture, and when I look towards the doorway she's standing there too. Wherever I look she appears, filling the barren waste between bed and dressing-table, window and wardrobe with her shining authenticity.

'Sylvia . . . '

She looks back at me, her dark blue eyes alight with laughter, her curly blonde hair tied up in a bit of blue ribbon, but when I put out my hand to touch her she disappears; extinguished like a candleflame.

'Sylvia, I've come to find you . . . '

Silence, except for the keening of a distant tram. The room feels heavy and oppressive and I'm suddenly assailed by homesickness. I've never been so far away before, at least not on my own, and I long for a sight of all the old familiar things.

But tomorrow you're going to see Sylvia.

Yes, I know. And now that I'm here, the thought fills me with terror.

It's the waiting that's getting you down. So forget about Sylvia until tomorrow morning and occupy yourself with something sensible. Write a letter home.

There's a thick pile of hotel writing paper and envelopes on the little desk opposite the door. I find my pen, light a cigarette and sit down. The lamp throws a warm pool of light on the waiting paper.

Darling,
Just a brief note to let you know that I've arrived safely and that I'll be seeing her first thing tomorrow.

Pause. What else can I say? The hotel's comfortable, the flight was uneventful? But even as the trite sentences form in my head, my hand starts writing her name.

Sylvia Coryn. Elder daughter of William and Dorothy Coryn of Barnard Castle in the county of Durham.

And it's no use. The room overflows with her presence and once more I'm lost in a reverie that culminates in the same old question: beneath the beauty and the laughter, what was Sylvia really like? And what made her do the things she did?

They say that the closer you are to a person the less you know them, but I still swear that in those early childhood days I knew Sylvia more deeply, more intuitively, than anyone else, and whatever happened afterwards must surely have had some sort of tenuous thread leading from our childhood.

I look up, and there she is again. Not the Sylvia I'm expecting – with terror, even now – to see tomorrow, but the young glowing Sylvia of before the war. And as the questions crowd in, and the endless speculations begin again, I slowly crumple up the letter to my husband and drop it in the waste-paper basket.

Still staring at her, I take another sheet of hotel writing paper and as if by its own volition my pen traces the words *Who Was Sylvia?*

Yes, indeed – who was she? And what was she? It's nine o'clock in this silent, foreign hotel and I've got until tomorrow morning to find out. Stay with me, I need the company.

Sylvia was – why do I say *was* when I mean *is?* – my sister, and my first memory of her is as a child of ten dressed in a bedspread and a crown of buttercups and daisies.

'I'm the Queen,' she said.

'No, you're not,' I told her, six years old and stolidly in favour of prosaic fact.

'Oh, yes, I am,' she said. 'Because I say so.'

Even after all this time I can still remember how lovely she looked with the suffused summer light coming down through the apple tree boughs and touching her with fingers of gold. She was tall for her age, and I remember very clearly that although I was so young her beauty filled me with a strange and inexplicable melancholy, a sort of yearning to protect her from something I didn't understand.

'I'm the Queen, and I'm married to the King,' she said, holding out the bedspread skirt, 'and on Friday nights we go to supper dances at the Masonic Hall.'

And suddenly I believed her. The fact that she'd said she was the Queen was sufficient to banish all doubt.

'Okay,' I said, and curtseyed.

She inclined her head in regal acknowledgement, then began to giggle as the crown of buttercups and daisies slipped drunkenly over her forehead, transforming her from a vision of beauty into a music hall clown. She grabbed at the crown and the bedspread fell open, disclosing her interlock vest and knickers. Her giggles increased, and it was impossible to remain unaffected by them. I began to laugh too, and bunching the bedspread round her knees she seized my hand and began to run with me through the sun-speckled orchard to the end of the garden and the drystone wall that divided us from the rolling Teesdale countryside.

'I'm the Queen – the Queen – the *Queen*!' she sang, and collapsed in a panting, laughing heap. I collapsed beside her, dizzy with happiness, and hit my knee on a sharp bit of stone lying half-buried in the grass. Blood gathered on the raw surface and I began to howl.

'Oh, Kit – ' she exclaimed. 'Oh, you poor thing! Here, let me look . . . '

The bedspread discarded, she bent over my wound and then groped up her knickerleg for her handkerchief. She dried my tears with it, then smoothed it out and tied it gently round my kneecap.

'Poor little girl . . . does it hurt much? Can you walk?'

Her beautiful child's face was tender with concern, and I looked at her through a haze of loving tears.

'You've lost your crown.'

'Oh, blow that,' she said briskly. 'I'm not really the

Queen, I'm a nurse.'

From which you will see that it was something of a problem to identify the real Sylvia right from the start.

There were just the four of us – Ma and Pa, Sylvia and I – and we lived in a stone house not far out of Barnard Castle. Pa was a grocer (although he always referred to himself as a provision merchant), and the shop had been in his family for three generations. He took it all very seriously, and travelled to and fro in a high black Austin van with WM. CORYN & SONS written on the side, and underneath it in smaller letters FAMILIES PROVIDED. He was a quiet, sallow, and rather pompous man with a long top lip and a way of elevating his chin and staring down his nose which made him resemble a camel.

He worked a hard six-day week, and when he was at home expected to be waited on with deference. He provided Sylvia and me with a comfortable lower middle-class background and a High School eduation – it had to be paid for in those days – but I don't remember him ever hugging us or playing with us. Families Provided, but only from a sense of duty, as it were. Perhaps he was disappointed because we weren't sons, and the stuff of which future provision merchants are made.

And Ma was the perfect partner for him. Thin and apprehensive in neat crêpe de Chine, she ran the house and trained a succession of local girls to do the rough and answer the door. I never remember her raising her voice in anger or in pleasure, but in her own insidious way she was as repressive as Pa. Whereas he said don't jump down the stairs or be late for meals or bring friends home because it disturbs my peace and quiet, Ma had a less direct approach. She forbade us to do this or that because of the awful consequences entailed. Don't play with the children from the cottages because you'll catch their fleas; don't sleep with the cat on your bed because it will use up all the oxygen; if you swallow orange pips they'll lodge in your appendix and if you tell lies no one will love you. And so on.

Once I asked whether she did in fact love me and she said yes of course, don't be silly. And with that I had to remain content.

As well as the cat we had a spaniel called Trix, although I can dimly remember her predecessor, a black and witchlike pomeranian that bit people. Trix was large and lethargic, and didn't mind being adorned with bits of cardboard armour when we played Crusaders, or being trundled about in a pram when we played Babies. Sylvia told me that she learned about menstruation because of Trix, and to begin with took it for granted that at certain times she too would have to be closely confined in case men leaped the garden wall to get at her (for what precise reason, however, Ma declined to explain).

And so inevitably we get back to Sylvia. Whenever I think of anything funny or happy or lovely in our home, Sylvia was always at the heart of it. Without her, my childhood would have been drab and meaningless beyond description. And of course, being four years older than I was, she had this extra sort of glamour so far as I was concerned. Hers was the glamour of having a fountain pen when I was only at the pencil stage: of having lace-up shoes when I was only in strap-and-button. She had a grown-up tennis racket when I only had a toy one, and in due course she blazed the puberty trail with effortless ease. No acne or puppy fat or blues in the night for her; she just seemed to grow naturally and gracefully, like a flower reaching up to the sun, with that fair curly hair tied back with a bit of blue ribbon and long swift legs ending in high-heeled shoes that she sometimes used to let me wobble around in.

She was just sixteen then, and once when we'd been to see a film with Alice Faye in it I wrote to Twentieth Century Fox in Hollywood enclosing a snap of Sylvia and telling them that she was the dead spit of Alice and would they kindly send the fare for her to go to Hollywood for a screen test. They replied thanks very much but we only pay the travelling expenses of actors and actresses already engaged by us. And as they only engaged actors and actresses after they had been to Hollywood for a screen test it was difficult to work out the next move on my sixpence a week pocket money. When Sylvia came across the letter in a library book she roared with laughter and said oh Honeybee, can you imagine Pa's face if he found out that one of his little girls was on at the Odeon?

She always called me Honeybee . . . .

Oh Lord, how the memories spill out once I start looking back to those early days, and to Sylvia the lovely, lovable laughing sister who taught me the Lambeth Walk and the Palais Glide, who ate walnut whirls in the bath and played rounders in the rain and who could listen to Henry Hall on the wireless and help me with my homework (only it was called prep. in those days) and help Ma with the supper all at the same time. Oh Sylvia, what happened? What went wrong?

I loved you so much all the years I can remember trotting along holding your hand, trying to take strides as big and brisk as yours, and trying to pretend that I was a ten-year-old girl in Miss Summerday's form instead of only a six-year-old one in Mrs Pye's. I remember your hockey stick (which I afterwards inherited), and your big leather satchel stuffed full of Latin and Chemistry and Indian ink maps of the Midlothian coalfields. I remember your big white cookery apron, and the time you made a Swiss roll in Domestic Science and we wolfed the whole lot between us on the way home through the park . . . I remember you being made a prefect, and then head girl, and I remember you on Speech Day, airily addressing the assembled school and the governors and parents in sixth-form French which you afterwards confessed you didn't understand the half of.

And while I was small and adoring and dun-coloured in wrinkled gym stockings and crushed-down velour po-hat you were laughing and vital and beautiful with a newly springing bustline and a complexion like roses and cream. Even your regulation po-hat was so much less po than mine . . .

But it's no use rambling on like this. I've already covered three sheets of writing paper and I don't seem to be getting anywhere. If the idea of writing down the Sylvia story as I've uncovered it so far is to help my understanding of her – is to help me when I finally meet her tomorrow – then I've got to arrange the facts in chronological order and cut out the nostalgia. So – bearing that firmly in mind, we'll proceed.

Sylvia left the High School when she was close on eighteen and took shorthand and typing at Heat & Dawes (known to us as Teeth and Drawers), an establishment run by two fragrant old maids who turned out competent secretaries with machine-like precision, and on my fourteenth birthday she bought me a copy of *Three Men in a Boat* out of her first week's wages at the Gas Light & Coke Company, where she was junior.

We took turns in reading it aloud, sitting up in the attic which we'd recently converted into a private sanctuary, and when we'd giggled ourselves to a standstill Sylvia would wind up the old portable gramophone.

My God, how we punished that poor old machine; we must have got through a box of needles a week. When Pa was at home and demanding peace and quiet we played it either up in the attic or down at the bottom of the orchard, and now when I look back the whole time is drenched with the sound of the Palais Glide, the Lambeth Walk and, finally and most poignantly of all, the record we both played day and night: 'The Donkey Serenade', sung by a chap called Allan Jones.

We played it and played it. As other people rush home and put the kettle on for a reviving cup of tea, so we rushed home and put on 'The Donkey Serenade'. Me first, out of school at four fifteen, and then Sylvia, released from the Gas Light & Coke Company at six o'clock. We loved it so much that it became as necessary as air. I did my prep. to it, Sylvia washed her hair and mended her silk stockings to it; we danced to it and sang to it, and the last thing I generally remembered before drifting off to sleep at night was the sound of it – muffled by a silk scarf tucked down the soundbox – coming from Sylvia's bedroom next door.

And borne on the wings of 'The Donkey Serenade', Mr Chamberlain flew off to Munich and signed a non-aggression pact with Herr Hitler. The year was 1938.

Because Sylvia was so important to me I was shattered when she ran away.

It happened so suddenly – on Friday night she was there as usual, laying the table for supper while I got ready to cycle over to Eggleston to spend the weekend with a schoolfriend. She saw me off at the gate, and whereas Pa had said good-bye and don't be a nuisance to anyone, and Ma had said remember to thank them for having you, Sylvia gave me a hug and said: 'Here's a couple of bob, Honeybee. It's not much, but have a lovely time.'

She stood waving and smiling until I'd turned the corner and that was the last I saw of her. When I got back on Sunday night she'd gone.

'Gone?' I said. 'Gone where?'

Ma was sitting, pale but apparently composed, with a basket of mending by her side.

'To London.'

'But how long's she gone to London *for?*'

Ma hesitated, then said; 'I suppose you'll have to know sooner or later. She's run away.'

Aghast, I watched her thread a needle with fingers that trembled slightly. 'But she can't run away – we've got to go after her!'

'There's nothing we can do,' she said.

Her stoicism drove me wild. 'We've got to find her! We can't possibly be without her — '

Rushing into the hall I collided violently with Pa. He staggered and put out his hand to save himself. Through a haze of scalding tears I implored him to get Sylvia to come home again. 'We *can't* be without her – nothing'll be the same!'

'I've told her that if the home we've got to offer isn't good enough, she'd better make her own arrangements,' Pa muttered. 'And that's what she's done.'

I couldn't understand why Sylvia had run away, but even less could I understand how they managed to remain so calm. Ma, pale and tight-lipped, continued with her mending while Pa in his neat house slippers shut himself up in the dining-room with his account books. The only sound to break the silence of that dreadful, baffling Sunday evening was the whimpering of Trix chasing rabbits in her sleep.

I was convinced she'd be home by bedtime. I lay reading for a long while, then went into her bedroom and drew the curtains and turned the bedclothes down ready. Her clothes had gone and the dressing table was bare, but the place was still full of her. It was crazy to think that she'd really gone. I filled her hot-water bottle and pushed it down the bed where her feet would be.

I didn't go to sleep for a long time after I'd heard Ma and Pa's bedroom door close, and towards dawn suddenly woke up with the terrible thought that Sylvia might have come home and found the front door locked. I crept downstairs, and sure enough the heavy iron bolt was firmly in place. I eased it back, unlocked the door and peered out into the dim, frosty garden.

'Sylvia, come on in – it's only me . . . '

A blackbird mumbled in the hedge, but that was all. I went back to bed.

As the days passed I began to grow accustomed to the idea that Sylvia had really gone, and waited anxiously to get a letter from her. Surely she'd write and explain? Surely she'd send her address, so that we could at least keep in touch? But no letter came, and I was faced with the hurt realisation that she didn't write to me because she didn't trust me, any more than she trusted Ma and Pa. In her eyes I was evidently part of the enemy, part of whatever it was she had run away from. Perhaps it had always been like that; perhaps the closeness between us had only been a sham, and I'd been fooled by it. I couldn't believe it, although the tears flowed again.

I tried and tried to get Ma to tell me what had happened that weekend I was away, or even to talk about Sylvia in general terms, but I never got anywhere. I was too young to realise the power of lower middle-class respectability and the solace of wounded dignity borne in silence.

The nearest approach to a talk about Sylvia took place one afternoon after school. March had set in cold and damp and Ma and I were sitting in front of the fire making toast. This time I chose the words very carefully, and even did my utmost to imitate her own little expressionless thread of a voice.

'I still miss Sylvia quite a bit.'

'Yes. I daresay.'

A pause. The firelight flickering on our faces. We kept our gaze resolutely averted.

'I often wonder what made her go.'

'Look, your toast's burning.'

'It's only the crust.'

I removed it from the long-handled fork and impaled it the other way round. I waited with decreasing hope for her to say something more.

'Life often seems very simple when you're young,' she remarked eventually. I wondered whether she was referring to Sylvia or to me, but didn't dare to interrupt. 'We very often find as we get older that people aren't what they seem.'

Did she mean that she and Pa had found out that Sylvia wasn't what she seemed? Or that Sylvia had inadvertently stumbled upon some awful truth about Ma and Pa? For the life of me I couldn't ask.

We continued to stare at the bread suspended from our toasting forks.

'Will she come back?'

'I really don't know.'

'Why don't you know, Ma?'

For a moment it seemed as if she were on the point of telling me something I could grasp hold of and examine, but in the end all she said was: 'You'll understand more when you're older. Be careful, you're getting butter on your gym-slip . . .'

About this time Pa developed what was to become known as his Gastric Trouble, bouts of pasty-faced irritability that were on no account to be exacerbated by such wicked thoughtlessness as banging doors, romping with Trix or answering back. Mealtime conversation between the three of us became pegged to a level of almost preposterous inanity and it became increasingly difficult, and finally impossible, even to mention Sylvia's name without the risk of incurring a dangerous Gastric Attack. I learned to keep out of his way and I think Ma did too, although loyalty prevented her from ever saying anything.

Looking back, I remember that the misery of life without Sylvia gradually settled down into a glum resignation. The sharp anguish of bereavement dulled, and the time came when I could sit on her bed and play 'The Donkey Serenade' without crying.

From the upper fourth onwards, school became more absorbing; to my own and everyone else's astonishment I won the Junior Croxley Prize for English Literature and came third from top in the summer exams. I asked Ma if I could have my pigtails cut off and she said no, but if things are still normal next year you can go off to camp with the Guides.

Wondering whether the reference to normality might be in some way connected with Sylvia, I asked her what she meant.

'Your father thinks Hitler's after Poland. If there's a war there won't be any Guides, or anything else; the Germans will see to that.'

'Oh?'

People were always talking about Hitler and Mussolini on the wireless, but I'd never considered that their activities might seriously jeopardise my own.

'If there's a war,' Ma went on, 'we'll all have to wear gas-masks, not just the troops. The Germans are horrible, terrible people and no one can trust a word they say.'

It's funny, but for the life of me I can't remember whether I went to Guide camp or not, but I do recall the feeling that summer and peace were both running out hand in hand – that we were all sliding helplessly towards some sort of dark unknown. Some girls' fathers joined the ARP and there was talk of evacuees from Liverpool and Manchester being billeted in our area. Pa laid aside a large stock of bismuth powder to see him through the duration of hostilities, and kept his assistants behind after the shop was closed in order to fill sandbags and cover the windows with criss-cross strips of sticky brown paper.

'More people will be killed by flying glass than by being blown up,' he told me with gloomy relish. 'One sliver of glass can cut a man into thin gammon steaks.'

That Sunday night after Chamberlain had told us that we were at war with Germany I leaned out of my bedroom window and looked out over the quiet skies and sleeping trees. I felt rather excited, and contemptuous of Ma's furtive tears.

For the first time for weeks I thought about Sylvia. I wondered if she was still in London, and if it was true that the Germans were going to start bombing all our major cities any moment now. It was getting on for a year since I'd seen her and I wondered if she still wore her hair tied back with a bit of blue baby ribbon. It was rotten of her never to have written, and because time was doing a good healing job I wasn't too sure that I'd speak to her if ever I did see her again.

I'd no suspicion at that point that Ma's tears were caused not only by the onset of war, but also because she had in fact received a letter from Sylvia.

In 1941 I passed matric., and that September followed in my sister's footsteps and enrolled for a secretarial course at Teeth & Drawers. They remembered her, of course, and asked me how she was. By this time I was able to say oh fine – still living in London, with genuine carelessness.

'What a pretty girl she was,' they chorused. 'And so full of life!'

I was used to this too, and quite accustomed to the knowledge that my rounded face and homely teapot-brown eyes could in no way compare with the memory of her dazzling gold beauty. And it was the same story when we came to personalities – for although I didn't identify with Ma and Pa's small-town vacuity, I realise now that quite a lot of it had rubbed off on me. The common round of study interspersed with solitary walks and occasional visits to the cinema filled my life quite happily, and if ever I looked back to the old Sylvia-days it was to wonder what on earth we were always giggling about. I was still fond of her, of course, and she was still inescapably close, if only because each year I'd inherited her school textbooks. But at that period I wasn't particularly involved with anything or anyone but myself (not even the ex-Grammar School boy who kissed me on the way home through the park where Sylvia and I had eaten her Swiss roll. His mouth tasted of wine drops and I remember telling him to shove off).

All I can say is thank God I was saved from total priggishness by getting conscripted, and by the decision to go into the services.

Ma saw me off on the train for Shropshire and the WAAF intake camp. I stood at the open window and looked down at her pale face and into the pale apprehensive eyes, protected nowadays by a pair of crystal-framed spectacles.

'Well, good-bye, Ma.'

'Good-bye, dear. Don't forget to write.'

'No. I won't.'

We smiled aimlessly and the engine let fly with a burst of steam. Carriage doors crashed.

'Have a good journey.'

'Thanks, Ma.'

'I hope you won't feel homesick.'

'I'm sure I won't. But of course — ' a quick dutiful smile, 'I'll miss you and Pa, naturally.'

'We'll miss you too,' she said, with equal lack of conviction.

The guard's whistle shrilled and as the train began to move she suddenly opened her handbag and thrust an envelope towards me. Our fingers touched fleetingly.

'You might like to have this . . . ' she said.

I watched her grow smaller and smaller, and when I couldn't see her any more jerked the window shut with a bang. there was no one else in the carriage and I sat staring at my suitcase on the luggage rack opposite. This was the first long train journey I'd ever taken on my own and I wondered whether the Royal Air Force would send someone to meet me at Bridgnorth station.

Before settling down to read I opened the envelope Ma had given me. Expecting to find a little note with perhaps some money tucked inside I was startled when I suddenly came face to face with Sylvia. It was a photograph I'd never seen before, taken in our garden when she was about seventeen. She was wearing a striped blouse and a dirndl skirt, and she was the most luminously beautiful, the most radiantly sparkling girl who ever laughed into a camera's lens.

I stared at it for a long, long time, and we were almost at Wolverhampton before I started wondering what strange and inarticulate motive had impelled Ma to give it to me.

They did come to meet me at Bridgnorth, in an Air Force blue truck with heavy canvas curtains at the back. Among the scattering of passengers on the platform were a dozen or so other girls, all lugging suitcases and all trying, like me, to give the impression that joining up was a matter of the utmost triviality.

The RAF corporal who watched us handing in our travel warrants (no more civilian nonsense with tickets) herded us outside and then indicated that we should get into the back of the truck.

'C'mon,' he said. 'Wakey wakey.'

Although we all appeared to be young and reasonably athletic, it wasn't easy. The first contestant put her suitcase through the curtains and there was a sound of tearing cotton dress as she attempted to spring in after it. She tried again, then disappeared abruptly within the dark interior as the corporal walloped her on the backside with a heavy hand.

'How *dare* you?' she demanded, sticking a ruffled head through the curtains.

'Stand to attention when you address a non-commissioned officer,' said the corporal equably. 'C'mon, who's next?'

One by one we leaped in, fell in, rolled in, and in my case executed a sort of desperate nose-dive. It was the last girl, with short bobbed hair and pearl earrings, who asked in tones of the utmost politeness whether it would be possible to lower the tailboard.

'What a simply wizard idea,' declared the corporal. 'Fancy none of us thinking of that before.'

With exaggerated deference he released the bolts and the girl sat down and then swung herself decorously inside.

'Thank you, Corporal,' she said.

My memories of Bridgnorth are disconnected but very clear; there was a lot of concrete, and we slept in wooden huts on black iron bedsteads with grey blankets, roly-poly straw pillows and khaki mattresses in three separate sections which were known as biscuits. We were also issued with coarse stiff sheets that crackled like ships' sails.

And we discovered that in the eyes of the Royal Air Force there was something deeply distasteful, nay, something verging on the downright decadent, about the sight of a bed made in the conventional manner, that is with the blankets tucked under the mattress and the top sheet folded down below the pillow. From now on, authority dictated that the moment the occupant had risen from it the whole thing should be pulled ruthlessly to pieces, the blankets folded in a certain way and made into a sort of sandwich with the sheets and then placed on top of the three biscuits piled at the head of the bed. The pillow went on top. Stacking our beds was the first thing we were taught, and it was made abundantly clear that approximate neatness was not sufficient. The innards of the sandwich had to be identical in measurement, the pillow had to be placed with exactitude, and the whole lot located in the precise centre of the top biscuit. Failure to achieve this high standard of bed-stacking was regarded as sloppiness, and sloppiness – a word we soon learned to dread – indicated shortcomings far more serious than mere negligence.

Sloppiness stood for inferiority of mind and body; for moral deterioration and feeble acceptance of second-rate values. Long hair and long fingernails were sloppiness personified, and Hitler, we discovered, would never have come to power if it hadn't been for sloppy thinking on the part of the German electorate.

The purveyor of much of this information was the WAAF corporal in charge of our hut. She had a thin sausage of hair rolled round her head and she slept in a little cubicle up at the far end. Every morning at six thirty she marched down the length of the hut with blue dressing-gown over striped issue pyjamas and a sponge bag and towel over her arm, on the way to the ablutions.

'Morning, all!'

'Morning, Corporal,' we would chorus, and looking round at the other girls in varying stages of waking up I would try to guess which of them I had heard weeping during the night. Quite a few seemed to weep, presumably from home-sickness, but I only remember hearing of one who ran away.

In retrospect, the few days at Bridgnorth seem to have been spent in endless bouts of form-filling, and when they weren't asking us for our names, religion and next of kin they were examining us for lice. Then we were issued with our uniforms and I remember the languid RAF tailor who checked them for correct fitting saying in a small quiet voice *Dear God in heaven, if I see one more blasted woman today I'll scream the place down* . . .

Being kitted out took the best part of a day and involved queuing in various buildings for various bits of paraphernalia which included two sorts of knickers, a thick white china mug and a knife, a fork and a spoon, a tin hat and a respirator. We were also given a cunningly contrived piece of equipment which doubled for a groundsheet and for a rather unbecoming mackintosh cape which buttoned under the chin. They gave us a lot of clothes and other things as well, including a little khaki pouch containing field dressings and a little white pouch containing needles and thread. It was rather exciting receiving all this booty at once, and we bore it home to our respective huts where we were instructed to mark it all in indelible ink with our name and the serial number by which we would henceforth be identified; mine was 2010057.

No sooner had we marked all our possessions than they had to be laid out for kit inspection by the WAAF adjutant, and if stacking one's bed was an anxious, arduous business, it was nowhere in the same league as setting everything out on a clean issue towel on that part of the bed not occupied by biscuits and blankets. Every garment had to be meticulously folded, shoe laces tied in bows whether your feet were in the shoes or not, and knife, fork and spoon placed with scrupulous exactitude between the mug and the stick with a slot in it which was to be used for cleaning uniform buttons.

No one could have described the hut corporal as a tyrant, but somehow she managed to inject the atmosphere with sweating terror at the thought of the adjutant's approach; the arrival of God in all His majesty couldn't have presented a more daunting prospect, and we stood by our beds with our hats on, raking our careful little exhibitions with harassed eyes. I was about to shift my field dressing a quarter of an inch to the left when we were called to attention and the adjutant made her entrance with two WAAF sergeants a deferential pace behind. Our corporal saluted violently, and accompanied the slow procession down the linoleum which we had all polished in readiness.

They reached my bed.

'Where is your hose?'

Flung into panic by the knowledge that everyone had been issued with a length of hose but me, I stammered that I wasn't exactly sure.

'What d'you call this?' The adjutant indicated a small pile

of dark grey lisle half concealed behind two shirts.

'Oh . . . well, stockings — '

'Address an officer as ma'am,' said one of the sergeants.

'Stockings, ma'am . . . '

The adjutant gave me a flinty look and I spent the rest of the day glooming over the fact that I was obviously going to make a lousy WAAF.

But I made friends with the girl who had asked the RAF driver to lower the tailboard of the truck; her name was Moira and she slept in the bed next to mine, and on the last morning of our stay at Bridgnorth she said she'd overheard that we were going to have a paper raid.

'What's that?'

'God knows. Sounds like a sort of cross-country running.'

'Will we have to wear our shorts?'

'You'd think so, but now I'm getting to grips with service mentality I wouldn't be surprised if it was gas capes and respirators.'

Great therefore was our jubilation when we learned that the event planned to take place at 14.00 hours precisely was in fact a pay parade.

Once again we all put our hats on, and with shoes and buttons well polished stood to attention while the accounts officer (also in his hat) sat with his minions behind a trestle table covered by a blanket and prepared to dish out the little mounds of money that had been laid out on it. But in order to qualify as a recipient you had to wait until your name and number were called, then cry *'Sir!'* in suitably ringing tones, step forward with the left foot, come to attention before the table with a smart bang of the feet, salute him with the right hand, take the money with the left one, perform an about-turn (which involved a tricky pivoting action), and then march back to your place in the rank. The awful business of reversing to face front again tended mercifully to be cloaked by the next candidate presenting herself.

Having received no more than minimum instruction in the art of square-bashing, it was very easy to make a mess of it. To step off on the wrong foot, to salute with the wrong hand, to drop some of the money, and then, glazed with embarrassment, to be unable to locate one's own little gap in the rank of stiff blue uniforms. But I suppose we managed because I remember Moira and I, armed with our precious few bob, making a dash for the NAAFI.

We bought mugs of coffee, thick Spam sandwiches and some slabs of cake, then a flight sergeant I had never seen before stalked across to us and said that we had no business to be wearing our hats in the NAAFI. Sheepishly we took them off, only to be ticked off again on the way back to our hut because we hadn't got them on.

The Air Force seemed to be greatly obsessed by the wearing or non-wearing of hats. You could keep them on in shops, but not sitting down in cafés. They were not to be removed while on public transport or in the street in case you met a commissioned rank and had to salute (to salute in a state of bareheadedness was considered too ludicrous even to contemplate). But you weren't supposed to wear them in houses or cinemas, and I remember a later occasion when a girl was given fourteen days' extra duties in the cookhouse for being found at a drunken party wearing her hat and nothing else. Technically she was insulting the king's uniform. I'd been in the Air Force for ten days before I awoke to the fact that they were called caps and not hats.

After a few days at Bridgnorth we were sent up to Morecambe, and Moira and I managed to keep together. Instead of being in huts we were billeted in a series of boarding houses which had been commandeered for the duration. The lady who ran ours told me that she was a retired soubrette – a word I had to look up in order to discover that it meant a singer of light songs – but she was very nice to us when our injections for typhus made us feel ill and after we got better she didn't mind if we came in late at night.

But oh, those cold north winds sweeping across the flat expanse of Morecambe Bay. We spent hours drilling on the deserted promenade – *ay-bout turn – left right left!* – and we marched through spiteful rain to requisitioned church halls where we sat damp and disquieted through lectures on poison gas and tried to remember which one smelt of musty hay. They also told us about VD and the importance of clean living, then we went on to incendiary bombs and how to deal with them with the aid of a stirrup pump. Yet it wasn't a bad time; very like school, except that they still kept searching us for nits and body lice.

While we were there I got a letter from Ma saying she hoped I was all right, so I sent her one back saying yes thank you, I was. Already I was beginning to think of home as some remote and rather nondescript place I had visited briefly, a long time ago.

On the last day at Morecambe we were assembled in yet another church hall and given our postings, and although Moira and I stood hopefully together it was no use. She got sent to Filey in Yorkshire and I got sent to Swillingham in Lincolnshire. We swore we'd write to one another and that we'd meet up when the war was over, but of course we never did. In fact I'd forgotten all about her until I started scribbling this.

And I don't remember all that much about Swillingham, either; something to do with time drawing a merciful veil perhaps. But I certainly hated it there, stuck fast in a paralysing dullness that was in no way alleviated by the WAAF commanding officer's despairing attempts to get up a concert party or the padre's series of lectures about life after death. Even the weekly off-duty sortie into Gainsborough, the nearest town, was only made memorable by its dismal failure to achieve any kind of real social contact with anyone. Drearily we ambled round the streets, looked in the empty shop windows, ate Spam and chips in greasy cafés, then with a sigh of thankfulness sank into the stuffy darkness of the cinema where drab reality could be swopped for a couple of hours of Hollywood make-believe.

We slept and worked (I was in the WAAF admin. office) in Nissen huts, but ate, for some reason, in a converted hangar two miles away. Marching with our mugs and knives and forks through a chilly dawn we sometimes used to see the Lancasters coming back from night raids over Germany, but were too peevishly intent on breakfast to get much of a patriotic kick out of them. Even the war itself seemed to be in the grip of inertia; the drama of the blitz and if possible invasion had long since passed, and if ever I contemplated peace it was with the dismal knowledge that in order to achieve it the Germans had first to be driven out of more countries than I had fingers.

I went home on leave in the following February, when a slow thaw was peppering holes in the snow and the first lambs of 1944 were bleating out on the hills. I found Pa propped up in bed recovering from a gastric attack and offered him the block of chocolate for which I'd saved my sweet ration. He dismissed it with a tired shake of the head. 'Give it to your mother. I haven't eaten chocolate for years.'

'I'm sorry, I hadn't noticed.'

'I hardly expected that you would.'

His striped winceyette pyjamas (not unlike WAAF issue), were buttoned to the neck and his skin had a yellowish tinge. I couldn't help thinking that it would do him a power of good to wrap up well and go out for a walk. We sat in silence.

'I see they've started bombing London again,' he said finally. 'What are your lot doing to stop them getting through?'

'I don't know,' I said. 'I work in the WAAF guardroom, sorting mail and stamping late passes.'

He shuffled the bedclothes irritably. 'And what about the Second Front? When are they going to start liberating Europe?'

'I don't know that either.'

'Do you realise,' he demanded, 'that they're putting chalk in our bread? And that the cheese ration is likely to go down to two ounces a week?'

'No,' I said. 'Stuck out in the middle of Lincolnshire we don't get to hear much news.'

He snorted, and looking down at his pinched and petulant face I wished I could love him more. Most of the girls back on the camp seemed to love their families from the way they spoke of them and had their photographs pinned up over their beds. Away from home, I'd almost succeeded in kidding myself that I loved mine too, and had felt a genuine glow of pleasure at the prospect of being reunited with all the old familiar faces and places. But within ten minutes I knew that it wasn't going to work. Swillingham, by comparison, seemed a place of marvellous exhilaration.

Ma tiptoed in with a dose of bismuth in a medicine glass.

'Here, you'd better eat this.' Pa gave her the chocolate.

'Where's it come from?'

'Kit brought it.'

'Oh, that's very kind. Now sit up, William, and I'll see to your pillows.'

She plumped them up, and, grimacing, he disposed of the bismuth.

'I've brought a little present for you, too,' I said to her.

'Oh. There was no need to, dear;'

'I know there wasn't. I just wanted to.' I thought perhaps she'd ask what it was, or express some form of eagerness to receive it, but of course she didn't.

'Apparently,' Pa said, lying back on the pillow, 'the RAF is unaware that London is being bombed – and by that I mean the fragments of London that remain from previous enemy attacks – and appears furthermore to have little interest in the prospect of liberating Europe from the vile clutches of that Nazi lunatic – '

'Now, don't start getting upset, dear,' Ma said. 'Leave the war to Mr Churchill while you have a little nap. Shall I refill the hot water bottle?'

He said no, so we tucked him up and left him.

Because of the fuel shortage the main rooms downstairs had been shut up, and Ma and I huddled close to the kitchen fire while Trix snored under the table.

'I worry about your father,' she said in her little faded voice. 'He's not well at all.'

'And I don't think you're well either,' I said, looking at her. 'You're so pale and thin, you should look after yourself more. All you do is run after other people.'

'I have to nurse him when he's ill.'

'Yes, but you've made him your whole life, Ma. You ought to get out more, meet people, invite them here — ' I looked round the neat, gloomy kitchen. 'The place could certainly do with a bit of livening up.'

'It's the winter,' she sighed. 'And the war.'

We sat staring at the fire, and it occurred to me that if Pa was declining into an irascible old man, Ma was becoming even more quietly indefinable with the years. Each time I saw her it was less easy to imagine the emotions that lay behind her fawn-coloured exterior.

'Ma,' I said abruptly, 'what made you give me that snap of Sylvia when you saw me off on the train?'

'I don't know. I just thought you might like to have it.' She spoke quickly, evasively.

'Have you ever heard from her?'

She hesitated, then said: 'No. We don't expect to.'

'Did she run away because she was pregnant?'

She drew her breath in sharply, but instinct told me that it was because she was shocked by the suggestion and not because I had stumbled on the truth.

'Good gracious, no. She ran away because . . . '

'Because?'

I waited, but in the end Ma passed her hand across her forehead and said almost pettishly: 'Oh, I don't know. How much do we ever know about other people?'

'She was your daughter. Not just another person.'

'Young girls get strange ideas, and Sylvia apparently thought that she had some sort of – of — '

'Destiny?'

'That's rather a grand term for it.' Her voice had resumed its expressionless, threadlike quality.

I remembered my first memory of Sylvia standing in the sun-dappled orchard telling me that she was the Queen.

'But all the same,' I insisted, 'something must have happened that weekend to make her pack up and go. I don't believe that she planned it weeks in advance.'

Ma got up from her chair and filled the kettle for tea. She began to set out the cups and saucers.

'Why did she go that weekend?'

'I don't know.'

'You do.'

I watched her fill the milk jug, then tip a couple of spoonfuls of precious sugar into the sugar bowl.

'Tell me. I've got a right to know.'

She turned round from the table, folding her arms across her thin chest. 'She had a quarrel with your father. They never got on very well because of her irresponsibility, but we always tried to hide it from you. After the last upset she said she would leave home and he told her that it was a good idea, in the circumstances.'

'What circumstances? And why did you try to hide it from me?' My lips felt dry and stiff.

'We didn't want her to be a bad influence on you.'

'A bad influence? On *me?*' The staggering unfairness of this appalled me. 'For God's sake, Ma, don't you realise that Sylvia was the only person who made life worth while? Who made this place bearable?'

'You'll see things very differently one day — '

'Sylvia meant everything to me when I was a child – she gave me the only warmth and affection I ever knew, and now you dare to say that you were afraid she'd be a bad influence — ' I rushed on, choking with angry, vicious tears, 'Well, all I can say is that if you'd both given her a bit more love and understanding she'd still have been here, and this place would have been less like a damned morgue to come home to!'

'You're being extremely impertinent,' Ma said, a bright red spot burning in either cheek.

'I'm telling the truth!' I shouted. 'You both drove Sylvia away because you were too small and narrow to appreciate how beautiful she was, and how intelligent and full of life. You let her go because you were too *stupid* – ' I stopped when I heard a banging sound overhead. It was Pa, awake now and banging for his tea.

'Here, take his tray — ' she almost shoved it at me, 'and ask about his hot water bottle — '

'But I tell you one thing, Ma.' I took the tray over to the door, then turned round to face her. 'I'm going to find Sylvia. Sooner than you think.'

'You won't find her.'

'I will. I'm going to spend my next leave in London.'

She began to speak, then changed her mind. 'Take your father's tea up to him,' was all she said finally, 'before it gets cold.'

I went, still raging at the chill bigotry that had driven Sylvia away.

The rest of my stay with them passed quietly and uneventfully, however, neither Ma nor I referring to the row we had

had. The day before it ended Pa came downstairs for the first time and sat, small and hunched, by the kitchen fire. His dressing-gown looked far too big and there was a dingy white stubble on his cheeks.

'What else do you do in the WAAF guardroom,' he asked, 'besides sorting mail and stamping late passes?'

'Collect shoe repairs. Make out the fire picquet roster. Quite a lot, when you come to add it up.'

He grunted, and said something about frittering the country's money.

'Look,' I said, 'if they gave me a gun and sent me to Berchtesgaden to shoot Hitler I'd be very frightened, but I'd go. I'd have no option because I'm under martial law. So it follows that if I'm bored to death with the trivial work I'm given to do, I've got to put up with that as well. I've no alternative.'

I felt tempted to say something about his own inadequacies, not least in the role of father, but didn't. And so my leave crept to an end and I got back into uniform.

I kissed them both good-bye, and Ma gave me a little parcel containing a home-made soda cake and a quarter of tea.

'Don't forget to write.'

I promised. 'And I'll let you know when I find Sylvia.'

She shook her head. 'You won't find her.'

'You're not by any chance,' I stared hard at her, 'trying to tell me that something – something's *happened* to her, are you?'

'No. Of course not.'

'In that case I'll find her,' I said from the gate. 'You see if I don't.'

Travelling back to the dismal mud of Lincolnshire I calculated when my next leave would be, and told myself that nothing would be simpler than to book in at a London YWCA while I set about finding my sister. Two weeks should be ample, and I could probably start the proceedings in advance by writing to the various organisations that I was rosily certain existed for the prime purpose of tracing lost persons. My spirits brightened with every mile.

I got back to camp determined to ignore the grey tedium

inseparable from the next few months, but as things turned out, there was no need.

'Get your things packed, ACW Coryn,' the WAAF admin. sergeant said. 'You've been posted.'

'Oh Lord, Sarge. Where to?'

'If you get your clearance chit signed in time, you can catch a lift with Transport down to the station.'

'Thanks, Sarge. But where am I going?'

'Eh? Oh – a place called Regent's Park. It's somewhere in London.'

Five hours later I arrived at King's Cross, and heard for the first time in my life the sepulchral wail of the air raid siren. I suddenly felt very small and helpless.

'Oh God,' I said. 'Please God, if you're up there and listening, don't let me get killed before I've found Sylvia.'

2

It was all fantastically different from Swillingham.

To begin with, in place of Nissen huts we were billeted in requisitioned luxury flats and the WAAF admin. office was in Holme House, a small Georgian mansion of elegant proportions and idyllic setting on the other side of the Park. There was no mud, the weather was mild, and the streets glowed with colourful uniforms the like of which I'd never seen before. Free French officers in round hats, Free Poles in square ones, Czechs, Dutch, Norwegians and Belgians all proclaiming their motherland on their shoulder flashes, and there seemed to be hundreds of American GIs loping about feeding popcorn to the pigeons and chewing gum to the girls.

But there was a darker side, too. If the howl of the air raid siren had chilled my blood as I stepped off the train, I remember that when the great London barrage opened up with its earsplitting chorus of gunfire I thought it was the noise of bombs. With my kitbag bumping at every step I fled down into what I took to be the Underground only to make the harassed discovery that I'd taken refuge in a men's urinal.

'Don't get fright, darlin',' comforted a large sailor. 'They say lightnin' never strikes twice and King's Cross's bin hit at least four times while I bin standin' on it . . . '

I thanked him, backed away up the steps and eventually found my way to Prince Albert Road where the WAAF hostel stood facing the Regent Canal and the dark mass of the Park. The roar of the guns had diminished although searchlights were still probing the sky, and the all-clear sounded as the duty corporal was making a note of my arrival.

'ACW Coryn, you say? What number?'

'2010057.'
'Where from?'
'Swillingham.'
'Trade?'
'Admin.'
'Ah, you'll be working with us, then.' She gave me an appraising look. 'I'm Corporal Phillips. It's not a bad set-up; the CO flaps a bit sometimes – she's Squadron Officer Gilby and was a sculptor or something in civvy street – but everyone else is okay. The only one you've really got to watch is Flight Sergeant Cutter.'
'Oh?'
'Dead sold on discipline and everything being done according to the book, so unless you're one hundred per cent efficient keep out of her way.'
I said that I wasn't so I would, whereupon the corporal grinned and told me that there was an empty bed in flat 10 room 4 and that the NAAFI was on the other side of the courtyard.
'So report back here for duty tomorrow morning at 08.30 hours.'
'Yes, Corporal.'
'Anything else you want to know?'
'Yes, Corporal. What does a bomb actually sound like when it's coming down?'
'It whistles,' she said. Then added. 'But if it's got your number on, they say you don't hear anything at all. Which is a relief, isn't it?'
'Yes. Thank you, Corporal.'
'Don't worry,' she said kindly. 'We've only had five girls killed in two years.'
Flat 10 was reached by a circular stone staircase from which the carpet had been removed and the lift dismantled for the duration of the war. I found room 4 at the end of the corridor with its own luxury bathroom attached, after which all pretence of pre-war degeneracy ended. Scrubbed floorboards, twill black-out curtains, bare electric light bulbs and three regulation iron beds – two of them vacant. By the side of each stood an ex-ammunition box which did duty as a bedside table, and any final hint of pre-war lush living had

been resolutely stifled by the smell of Sunlight soap.

A thin girl with a sharp ferret face was sitting on the bed under the window, polishing her tunic buttons. I introduced myself, and she said that her name was Maisy Page. She had a strong accent which I identified as Cockney, and after indicating the vacant bed opposite her own, continued with her polishing.

I unrolled my gas cape and hung it up with my tin hat and respirator in the regulation manner. I unpacked my little clock and put it on the ammunition box together with a couple of books. I made the bed up with the two clean sheets that Corporal Phillips had issued to me, and then to complete the brave home-from-home illusion stuck the photograph of Sylvia on my portion of wall with the aid of a bit of stamp paper.

'Proper smasher,' commented Maisy Page. 'Film star, is she?'

'No. My sister.'

'Cor stone me.' I was aware of her quick dark eyes appraising my homely features. 'Well, I mean — '

'I know what you mean,' I said. 'And she's so nice that I've never been jealous.'

She finished her tunic buttons and began on her cap badge. 'Where's she now?'

For a moment I was tempted to tell her something of the story as far as it went, then thought better of it. I didn't know her well enough.

'She's in London,' I said. 'And I'm going to see her.'

'There's a phone box in the road outside. Ring her up.'

'Yes. I might . . . '

'Go on,' she prompted. 'And in ten minutes I'll treat you to a drop of rosie down the Naff.'

'Rosie?'

'Gorstrufe – *tea!* Where you bin brought up?'

'Oh – sorry.'

'Go on, then. Got tuppence, have you?'

I nodded, and departed with reluctance, feeling annoyed that I'd allowed myself to be trapped in a stupid situation. If I had to tell lies, I should have had the presence of mind to say that my sister wasn't on the phone.

The phone box was empty, so for want of anything better to do I went in and in the dim light started peering down the list of Coryns in the London directory. There were seven of them and only one had the initial S, so I dialled it and it turned out to be a Samuel who said well, well, in a dark gurgling voice, if you're young, willing and able come round for a drink. I began stumblingly to decline, whereupon he banged down the receiver without even saying good-bye.

That's sophisticated London for you, I thought.

Going back through the gloom of the courtyard I began to wonder for the first time exactly how I was going to accomplish the task of finding Sylvia. I had airily assured myself that there were numerous organisations only too keen to help trace missing persons, but where were they? What were they called, and how did I get in touch with them?

Incredible as it may seem, it also began to dawn on me for the first time that Sylvia would in all probability be married by now, so her name would no longer be Sylvia Coryn. (Oh God, supposing it was Jones or Smith?) By now, she could just as easily be in Taunton or Edinburgh — or even back in Barnard Castle, although I didn't think that that was very likely. But one way and another it began to seem a little less certain that I'd fulfil my arrogant boast to Ma about finding her elder daughter. Depression set in.

'Get her okay?' Maisy Page bought me a mug of tea at the NAAFI counter and we sat down at one of the tables.

'No.'

'Out somewhere?'

'Suppose so.' I wished we could change the subject.

'What part of London's she living in?'

'South,' I muttered.

We sipped our tea in silence, and I couldn't help noticing how many girls passing our table paused to smile and say *Wotcher, Maze!* Everyone seemed to know her.

'Is she married?'

'Who?'

'Your sister.'

'No. Yes — '

'Livin' in sin?' Her pointed ferret face lit up with a quick grin.

'What's it got to do with you?' I tried to keep my voice amiable although I could feel my temper rising.
'Nothing, mate. Just friendly interest, that's all.'
The NAAFI manageress turned on the radio and the place filled with the homespun voice of Bing Crosby.
'Get on well with your sister, do you?'
My God, she was at it again. I didn't answer.
'I mean, some sisters is real close, aren't they? Go everywhere together, tell each other everything . . . '
'Maybe,' I said through set teeth.
'Why don't you get a late pass and go and see her tomorrow night?' she suggested, and my temper snapped.
'Why don't you mind your own damn business? It's got nothing to do with you when I go and see my sister — '
I saw the colour leave her face. She looked sick, as if I'd just hit her.
'Okay,' she said, and pushing back her chair walked out. I went on sitting there, listening to Forces Favourites while I stared at her half empty mug of tea. I didn't like her, and wished that I didn't have to share a room with her. Perhaps I could organise a transfer in a day or two.
I stayed in the NAAFI until closing time, then went back to flat 10 room 4. I took off my tunic and sat down on the bed. The girl they called Maze was reading *Picture Post*.
'I'm sorry,' I said. 'I was very rude.'
'S'okay.' She appeared engrossed.
I wound my clock and then took off my shoes, telling myself that I ought to clean them ready for the morning, but tiredness, plus the knowledge that the polishing things were down at the bottom of my kitbag, prevented me. I thought I'd go and have a bath instead, but it was too much bother to move. I just went on sitting there, staring at her narrow profile and thin frizzy hair.
'You see,' I heard myself say, 'it's a bit complicated, really . . . '
And suddenly I was telling her all about Sylvia, haltingly at first, then with the eager words falling out faster and faster as I described her looks, her special kind of warmth and the lovely laughing quality that had shone a beam of light down all the early years with humourless, colourless Ma and Pa.

I told her everything, exactly the way I've told it here on these eight sheets of hotel writing paper.

Eight sheets, closely written on both sides. No wonder my hand aches. I put the pen down and close my eyes, listening to the muted sounds of the hotel; hot water chuckling through the pipes, the creak of a floorboard outside the door and the soft rattle of the lift gates at the end of the corridor.

It's only ten o'clock, far too early to think of sleep. I'm not sure that I'll be able to sleep at all, now that I've stirred up all these memories. So I go over to the phone and haltingly order coffee and sandwiches, and while I'm waiting for them to arrive lie back on the bed and think about Maisy Page.

Maze, with her sharp-angled limbs, her pointed old-young face and her quick city wits. Time and again the word ferret comes to mind in trying to describe her, but it troubles me to use it because it sounds derogatory. Most people fear and dislike ferrets, but I only think of their nimbleness, their intelligence and their courage. Qualities which Maze shared in full, particularly the last two.

I remember how she sat crouched on her bed, staring down at the grey blanket and listening with a strange kind of hungry intentness while I told her about Sylvia, and I also remember the ignominious twinge of self-satisfaction when I saw her furtively wipe her cheek on the back of her hand.

My God, if only I'd had the modesty even to suspect that her tears might be for something far more terrible than my pathetic little tale of self-pity. If only I'd had the courtesy to ask about her own family, for instance . . .

The coffee and sandwiches are brought by a blond young man in a white jacket. We smile at one another, then he goes out, closing the door behind him. I pour some coffee – there's enough for at least three cups – then start on the sandwiches, which turn out to be liver sausage.

And then, brushing the crumbs away, reach for another sheet of writing paper.

The RAF station at Regent's Park was the preliminary assembly point for newly recruited aircrew, and a couple of hundred would arrive at a time, crumpled and anxious in their civvy suits, to be marched by bawling NCOs up and down Prince Albert Road and Park Road in the course of being kitted out and then subjected to the long tedium of medicals, psychology tests and so forth. Having satisfied the Air Force that they possessed sufficient aptitude to become pilots and navigators they were then sent on their way to undergo training. A lot of them went to Canada and Rhodesia.

A good many places in the area of Regent's Park had been requisitioned by the Air Ministry; Lord's cricket ground, part of the zoo, several blocks of flats, and a big garage which had been converted into equipment stores. Barbara Hutton the Woolworth heiress even lent us her parkside mansion, and once when I filled in for someone as duty clerk I had a bath in her bath. (It was made of onyx, and had what everyone swore were solid gold taps; not that you came out any the cleaner.)

I worked in the WAAF admin. office, which as I've said was in the white Georgian dream-house on the other side of the Park. I think that our room on the top floor had once been part of the nurseries because of the Mother Goose tiles that surrounded the empty fireplace.

Squadron Officer Gilby's room was next door, and it was part of my job to type the stencil of the daily details, a communication which was supposed to issue direct from the WAAF commanding officer herself, but which was more often composed by Flight Sergeant Cutter.

'It has been drawn to my notice that airwomen are fastening their hair in their cap bands,' the CO read with quiet amazement while I stood to attention, waiting for her signature. *'This practice is not in conformity with King's Regulations and must cease forthwith.* Did I really say that, Coryn?'

'I'm not sure, ma'am.'

Squadron Officer Gilby, who was a large, spreading lady, regarded me with gloomy eyes. 'How do they come to fasten their hair in their cap bands? Is it some sort of sexual fetish?'

'I don't think so, ma'am. It just means tucking your front curls in on either side to make them stay up. I believe the girls in Medical first started it.'

'And it's against King's Regs?'

'Apparently so, ma'am.'

'Hmm.' She brooded over the stencil while I gazed at the big blue dress ring on her finger.

'When we've won the war,' she said finally, 'it is my earnest hope that women the world over will be free to tuck their curls wheresoever it most pleases them. In the meantime, give me the whatsit — '

Sighing, she held out her hand for the engraving pen. I passed it to her and she scrawled her signature.

But she could be tough. Like the time shortly after my arrival when she sentenced a WAAF aircrafthand to fourteen days' scrubbing out the blitz bunks for hitting another girl with a bottle.

'If wilful violence and the infliction of pain upon others is morally acceptable to you,' she said, glowering across her desk, 'then I suggest that you are fighting on the wrong side of the war. And as it is impossible to change horses in midstream, I propose to do everything within my power to discourage you from the obnoxious bullying and contemptible intimidation of your fellow airwomen.'

Harsh words to a girl of lowly intelligence who had got drunk to anaesthetise the pain of her new husband's overseas posting, but that's how it was in those days; hardly anyone was doing the job for which nature and pre-war training had intended them, and when I went to an exhibition at the Tate Gallery not long ago, the sculptures of Eugenia Gilby were among the most acclaimed.

All things considered, she wasn't too bad as a CO either.

But Flight Sergeant Cutter was a very different proposition. Somehow I'd anticipated a horny-faced graceless female of muscular build, and I couldn't have been more wrong. She turned out to be tall and willowy and platinum blonde and she sailed round the camp on a blue issue bicycle.

As Corporal Phillips had advised, I kept out of her way as much as possible, but it wasn't always easy. She had an unerring nose for trouble, and eyesight that could spot a tunic button inadvertently left undone from a distance of fifty yards. A diamond engagement ring sparkled on her left hand and most of us pitied the unwary chap who'd placed it there.

And so I settled in at Aircrew Receiving Centre, Regent's Park, and after a dutiful letter giving my new address to Ma and Pa began devoting my off-duty hours to the task of locating Sylvia.

I thought, not very hopefully, of Somerset House, but its frowning formal exterior made me hesitant about going in to ask if they knew a girl who was once Sylvia Coryn but who might now be Sylvia anybody. And when Maze told me that Somerset House was only interested in births and deaths and that most of their records had been evacuated to the country anyway, I abandoned the idea.

I wasn't all that hopeful when I tried the station padre, either. As it happened the regular one was on leave and his locum – if that's the term – said that due to pressure of work he could only deal with matters of a spiritual nature.

I began, a little falteringly, to tell him about Sylvia and he asked if she was a regular communicant.

'I don't know. As I just said, I haven't seen her for five years.'

'In that case,' he said briskly, 'we must pray.'

I thought with alarm that he meant there and then, but when I saw him glance at his watch realised with relief that I was mistaken. So I thanked him for his advice, and he gave me a flashing smile and we parted.

The next choice was equally fatuous. I called in at the local police station and the sergeant on the desk listened with even less patience than the padre.

'So what d'you expect me to do?' he asked when I'd finished.

Taken aback with his bluntness, I could only stammer: 'Find her.'

With a sigh he drew a sheet of paper towards him and uncapped his fountain pen.

'How old is she?'

'Twenty-five.'

'What d'you say her name is?'

'Sylvia Margaret Coryn. I think.'

'You think.'

'Well, you see, she might be married.'

'And when did you last see her?'

'The second week in February 1939.'
'That's five years ago.'
'I know.'
'Has no one heard from her since?'
'No. At least, not at home.'
'And she said she was going to London?'
'Yes.'
'Why?'

I watched him draw a face on the piece of paper. Add eyes, nose and a small mouth.

'I don't know.'

He shaded in a small inky moustache. Hitler.

'But you must have some reason for believing she's still in London.'

'I haven't. But I've got to start by believing something, or I'll never get anywhere.'

The sergeant's pen nib hovered over Hitler's forehead, ready to add the famous cowlick. Then he paused.

'Looking for runaway girls in London is a waste of time,' he said. 'It's about as useless as trying to find a lost bus ticket. Worse, when you take into account her determination not to *get* herself found. Bus tickets can only lie where somebody dropped 'em – but girls have got legs and can nip from one place to another.'

'Yes, I know. But — '

'Look,' he said, laying down his fountain pen. 'In peace time the chances of finding someone who doesn't want to be found are roughly seventy-five to one against. Now there's a war on, the chances are far worse. People are shifting about all the time, in the services, directed into industry and all that. Then there's the bombing. I can't tell you how many people have been killed in London because it comes under the Official Secrets Act, but take it from me it's a lot. A terrible lot. You've only got to look at all the bomb sites.'

'So you can't help?'

'Put it this way,' he said. 'If a young lady calling herself – whatsername, Sylvia Coryn – comes in here and asks if I can trace her sister, I'll send her to the WAAF place up the road and tell her you're there. That do you?' He picked up his fountain pen.

'But supposing she comes, she mightn't ask for me — '

'Exactly. You've hit the nail right smack on the head, chummy. Because if a girl called Sylvia Coryn comes in here, I've got no power to make her get in touch with you unless she wants to. And it seems pretty obvious that she doesn't want to, doesn't it?' He leaned confidingly over the desk. 'Maybe she just doesn't like you.'

'She always used to . . . '

'Girls change,' he said wisely. 'And five years is a long time. She's probably got herself fixed up with a nice fella somewhere and she's living the life of Riley. Leave her alone, chummy. Don't interfere. If she wants to see you, all she's got to do is write home, isn't it?'

I nodded, silenced by his brutal logic.

'Okay. I see what you mean.'

'No hard feelings, I hope,' said the sergeant, and returning to the face he had drawn added a brisk bowler hat instead of the expected cowlick.

'Charlie Chaplin. Used to slay me when I was a nipper.'

After that I rather gave up trying to be practical about finding Sylvia, and in the evenings when I wasn't on duty took to wandering about where mist from the lake turned the empty Park a soft milky blue. I discovered the Nash terraces standing silent and withdrawn with their doors and windows nailed over and their gracious plaster faces cracked and disfigured by bombing.

My favourite was Chester Terrace, entered by a high triumphal archway, and facing the Park across its own little private garden. The whole place was empty and my footsteps fell softly on the grass-grown pavement. I felt like someone who'd come to the party a day late. The atmosphere lingered, but the voices and the music that I heard were no more than ghostly echoes. The guests had all moved on.

But for all I knew, Sylvia might have been one of them. Anything was possible for a girl like her.

Other evenings I used to walk to the end of Baker Street, and looking in Selfridge's windows would picture her hurrying through the departments in her high-heeled shoes with strings of parcels dangling gleefully from her fingers.

Sylvia rich, with a uniformed chauffeur yawning discreetly outside; Sylvia a poor typist, sacrificing her lunch money for a pair of new stockings. But Sylvia however she was, locked somewhere private in this huge city that lay with its magnificent face upturned to the hammer fist of war. Perhaps she was living only a stone's throw away. Perhaps I'd already passed her in the street somewhere. Somewhere . . .

The first breakthrough came from an unexpected quarter.

Dear Kit, (wrote Ma)

Thank you for your letter saying that you have been posted to London. It will make a nice change after Lincolnshire although I hope you are not suffering too much from air raids. Your father has taken a turn for the better and gone back to the shop. I don't think he ought to, but with the shortage of staff and the worries of rationing he gets very depressed sitting at home. Trix has had a funny place on her back leg and we had to get the vet to lance it last Friday. The crocuses are coming out by the front door but the sparrows keep nipping the buds off. I am knitting a cardigan in dishcloth yarn. I don't suppose it will look very nice but it is no coupons. No more news.

Love from Mother

P.S. Your Aunt Mitty Weston still lives in London as far as I know. I haven't seen her for many years but I believe she still lives at 75 Campion Road, W.9, if you want to call.

Not exactly heart-warming in its exuberance, and like the rest of Ma's letters I'd forgotten all about it within an hour of reading it. Then one evening when Maze was making up her long ferret face to go out to a dance it came in unexpectedly useful.

'Why don't you come too, mate?' she asked, licking her index fingers and smoothing her eyebrows with them.

'I don't really like dances much.'

'Might meet a nice bloke.'

'Haven't got a ticket.'

'Pay at the door.'

'Well . . . '

'Smashin' band,' said Maze, adding a bit more blue eye-shadow. 'And they allow jiving.'

'As a matter of fact,' I said, suddenly inspired, 'I thought of going to see my Aunt Mitty. She lives in W.9.'
'Maida Vale,' said Maze. 'Where all the tarts hang out.'
'My Aunt Mitty — '
'Okay, okay, I never said she was, did I?'
I watched her barm another layer of lipstick on her thin mouth then dab a circle of it on either cheek. She rubbed it in vigorously.
'How do I look, mate?'
'Like a technicolour sunset.'
'Bloody jealous, that's you,' she replied, unperturbed, and settled down to the task of balancing her cap on the wodge of tight frizz she had just released from a packet of pipe cleaner curlers.
'Don't forget your late pass,' I told her. 'And don't wake me up when you come in.'
She stood looking at me from the door, her shoes brilliantly polished, her uniform buttons ablaze and her sharp face a riot of pink and red and thunder blue.
'It'd do you good,' she said, 'to come and have a bit of fun.'
'I know,' I said. 'I'll come next time, promise.'
'Rita Hayworth's honour?'
'Rita Hayworth's honour.'
'Okay. Ta-ra then, mate.'
I listened to her footsteps going down the bare boards of the corridor. They sounded a bit lonely, I thought.
Twenty minutes later I was on a bus that went along Oxford Street and down the Edgware Road, and got off at a place called Clifton Gardens. It was a sad, seedy area with paint peeling from the big ramshackle houses and old newspaper soggily afloat in a static water tank. Like everywhere else in London it was almost devoid of traffic.
I found Campion Road, and when I went up the steps of number 75 there was a card with *Mrs Mary Weston* printed on it next to the second-floor bell-push.
I began to think she wasn't in, then heard a window open above my head.
'Who is it?'
'It's Kit Coryn, Aunt Mitty. From Barnard Castle . . . '
'Who?' The voice sounded sharp and peremptory. 'What

d'you want?'

'I'm Kit Coryn. Your sister Dorothy's daughter . . . '

Peering upwards I could just make out the shape of a head and shoulders in the spring dusk. I began to feel stupid and despairing, and when the window suddenly shut with a bang I walked away down the steps.

Then the front door opened, and a voice cried: 'Dorothy's daughter? Not – *Sylvia?*'

I turned, and there she was, standing poised on the top step with her arms wide open. And I watched them fall very slowly to her sides as she looked at me.

'You're not Sylvia.'

'No, I'm Kit. The younger, plainer one.'

She began to smile again, but not before I had read the disappointment. 'Well, well,' she said kindly. 'So this is little Kit.'

I walked back, and slowly ascended the steps again.

'You're an ATS girlie!'

'A WAAF, actually.'

'Of course,' she said. 'I really must get the names right. I expect it's very important.'

She led the way in, and up the dark stairs to her flat where we stood in renewed contemplation of one another. I saw a little, agile woman with an old-fashioned kiss-curl stuck to either cheek and a small Cupid's bow of a mouth drawn in bright red. She was wearing a loose kimono and a pair of men's socks.

'We haven't met since your christening,' she said. 'How time flies!'

'And quite honestly, I'd forgotten that I'd got an Aunt Mitty until Ma sent me your address!' I began to laugh, suddenly pleased I'd found her.

'You're not plain,' she said, still studying me. 'You're really rather pretty in a tawny, elfin sort of way.'

'Thank you very much.' Naturally the pleasure increased.

She told me to sit down while she made a cup of tea, and I watched her potter off behind an old red curtain to what was presumably the kitchen area.

The room I was in was large and shabby, with a worn Turkey carpet and an immense sagging sofa. It was very untidy in a comfortable kind of way, with clothes and papers and photographs all over the place. In one corner I noticed an old-fashioned gramophone with a horn on top, and on the divan under the window a black cat lay suckling a litter of kittens.

It was no more like Barnard Castle than Aunt Mitty was like Ma.

She reappeared from behind the curtain with a tray containing a silver teapot, two odd cups and saucers and a milk bottle.

'Now,' she said, 'tell me all about yourself. Have you got a sweetheart?'

'No,' I said, and wondered fleetingly how Maze was getting on at the dance.

'Oh well,' she replied, pouring out the tea, 'there's plenty of time, I daresay. Although I must admit that I had dozens when I was your age. Milk and saccharine, darling?'

'Just milk, please, Aunt. You mean you had lots of boyfriends in Barnard Castle?'

She laughed merrily. 'Heavens, yes! And one of them was your father.'

'*Pa?*'

'He was insane about me,' said Aunt Mitty happily. 'Brought me flowers every day and sobbed like a baby when I turned him down. Poor Dorothy snapped him up on the rebound – well, my dear, he was like *clay!*'

Fascinated by these disclosures I begged her to go on, until I discovered that Aunt Mitty needed little encouragement to spill out her memories; she gossiped as easily and spontaneously as a lark sings in April, and went on to tell me about her late husband, my Uncle Edgar.

'I've never heard much about him from Ma and Pa.'

'What with one thing and another,' she said, 'I'm not entirely surprised. Can I borrow your saucer for Queenie, darling? She wants a wee sip of milk and there's a crack in mine.'

I handed it to her, and watched the cat detach herself from the kittens and come towards Aunt Mitty with a pleased chirrup.

'Go on about Uncle Edgar.'

'A consummate gentleman,' she said with emphasis. 'Handsome, well-educated, amusing, adored by women – he played alto sax in a dance band. Such a *famous* band it was, they played at all *the* most exclusive night-spots – do you know a tune called "My Huggable Hide-away Girl"?'

I had to admit that I didn't.

'The darling wrote it especially for me – but perhaps it was a bit before your time.'

'What happened to him?'

'Drink,' said Aunt Mitty, clouding. 'He couldn't leave it alone. *Just another little Harry Sippers,* I can still hear him saying, *one more little drinkie and then we'll toddle off to bye-byes* . . . Of course, as you well know the entertainment world is very susceptible to emotional extravagance and to give my poor darling his due he was one of the golden boys of his era. Cannes, Monte Carlo . . . Oh, what ripping fun it all was — ' she lowered her voice, as if she didn't want the cat to hear, 'that is, until the last few months. He passed away in a Glasgow rooming house.'

'Oh, how awful — '

'Using his very last penny,' she fingered her kiss-curls, 'for the gas.'

I stared at her aghast. 'You mean, he . . . ?'

'Suicide. Although they brought in a verdict of death through misadventure, of course. Silver hair and a beard, a most *charming* man . . . '

'Uncle Ed?'

'No, no, the coroner,' she said impatiently. 'He took me out to dinner.'

We sat in silence as the luminous spring twilight deepened to darkness. On the other side of the room I could hear the soft rhythmic sound of Queenie washing her kittens.

'And then there was Paul,' said Aunt Mitty, rousing herself. 'Now I come to think of it, I'm wearing his socks.'

'What became of Paul, Aunt?'

'Oh, my darling,' she said, turning her face towards me in the last silvery gleam of light, 'what becomes of any of us? We're no more than moths fluttering together for a moment or two in the lamplight.'

There was such sadness in her voice that I instinctively

reached for her hand. It was much softer and warmer than Ma's.

'Aunt Mitty,' I said very quietly and carefully. 'When you first saw me this evening you thought I was Sylvia, and then you recognised that I wasn't. Does Sylvia come here?'

I waited a long time for her to answer.

'No,' she said finally.

'But you've seen her, haven't you?'

Again I had to wait. I felt her fingers twitch spasmodically in mine.

'Yes,' she said in a low voice. 'I've seen her twice.'

Abruptly she got up from the sofa and drew the curtains. When she switched on the lamp I could see that she was ill at ease, distressed almost.

'Where does she live, Aunt?'

'I don't know.'

'But is she still in London?'

My voice must have betrayed a state of tension because she pressed her hands against the two kiss-curls and said with sudden peevishness: 'I've just told you, I don't know where she is. Please leave it at that.'

I drew a deep breath. 'I want to find Sylvia,' I said, 'firstly because she's my sister, and secondly because I want to know why she ran away.'

'Didn't Dorothy tell you?'

'No. If you haven't seen Ma since my christening I expect you've forgotten her splendid gift for reticence.'

'Yes. Of course.' Aunt Mitty stood looking at me thoughtfully, doubtfully.

'But then, everyone's reticent about Sylvia. Wherever I go there's this conspiracy of silence – this determination not to help me. It makes me so angry — '

'Don't be so theatrical, darling.'

She sat down on the divan and scooped a tangle of kittens into her lap.

'There's no conspiracy of silence on my part, I can assure you. Sylvia called here one day just as you have done, and I was delighted. She had been no more than four or five when I last saw her, but I recognised her immediately. She had that same rare quality that I remembered – she was what Edgar would have called an absolute spiffer.'

'What we call a smasher . . . '

'She stayed to supper,' Aunt Mitty stroked the kittens reflectively, 'and we talked and talked.'

'Did she tell you why she ran away?'

'I don't remember that she said much about home at all. She spent most of the time telling me about the school where she was teaching — '

'Teaching!'

'In a rather unfortunate area, somewhere. Oh yes, St Ebenezer's, Bethnal Green. I must say I thought it a terrible waste – after all, there's nothing to stop *plain* girlies being teachers.'

'How long is it since she came?'

She screwed up her eyes in an effort to remember.

'A long time,' she said finally. 'Before the war. I think it was about April.'

'April '39? Not long after she left home. And then she came a second time?'

'Yes. After the first visit she promised to come regularly and I looked forward to seeing her – it wasn't long after Paul left and I was a teeny bit lonely – but she didn't come. And then she suddenly reappeared one evening just before the war began. I always associate it with the war because I had just been to collect my gas mask from the Civil Defence place, and there she was waiting for me when I got back. She was wearing a white summer dress and her beautiful hair was tied up any old how in a bit of blue ribbon.'

'Yes,' I said. 'I remember the bits of blue ribbon.'

'She looked absolutely radiant, and somehow I wasn't at all surprised when she put her arms round me and told me she was going to be married. Of course I immediately asked his name, but she wouldn't tell me. She said it was a secret, but could she bring him round to meet me on the following Sunday. Naturally I said I would be thrilled to death, and what about having a little luncheon party to celebrate? Just the three of us, but something special to eat and a nice bottle of wine . . . She seemed terribly excited in a strange, nervy sort of way, poor darling, and agreed to arrive with her mysterious fiancé at about midday.'

'So what happened?'

Aunt Mitty stopped stroking the kittens. 'Nothing. I bought some smoked salmon, made a salad, bought some fruit and cheese and wine, and nothing happened. The table looked absolutely ripping with the lace cloth and flowers, but she didn't come. I'd never asked her address so I couldn't get in touch with her. I just waited until evening, and then I lost my temper at the thought of her discourtesy and threw it all away. No, that's not strictly true – I gave the smoked salmon to Queenie.'

'But why didn't she come?'

'I don't know,' said Aunt Mitty, then suddenly cried: 'but ever since I've been haunted by a terrible feeling that it was my fault. That I let her down in some way.'

'I think we've all let her down.'

'But on the other hand, it may have had something to do with — '

'With what?'

'I forgot to mention,' she said, 'that the day they were supposed to come to lunch was the day that Chamberlain declared war.'

'Why should that have affected her plans?'

'As you can't ask her, I suppose you'll never know.'

'I'll ask her when I find her.'

My aunt sat gazing at the kittens in silence.

'Are you just one more person who thinks I never will?'

Almost imperceptibly she nodded.

'But why – *why?*'

'Because,' said Aunt Mitty in a little choking voice, 'I have a terrible feeling that she's dead.'

3

'Met a smashin' Yank,' Maze said, lying on her bed with her eyes shut. 'Corporal Sam Corbellini.'

'Seeing him again?'

'Rainbow Corner, tomorrow night.'

'Bet he won't turn up.'

To my surprise she took me seriously. 'No,' she said mournfully, 'blokes like him are too smashin' to be true.'

'What does he look like?'

'Robert Taylor. Only better.'

Getting undressed, I told her that I'd spent the evening with my Aunt Mitty.

'What's she like?'

'Funny. Nice. Not at all like Ma.'

'Did she know anything about Sylvia?'

'She's seen her twice. Once was before the war and the second time was just before it started. She arranged to take her fiancé round to lunch but they never turned up.'

'Why not?'

'Nobody knows.'

Maze contemplated the ceiling. 'So you're no nearer to finding her?'

'Doesn't look like it.'

I went to clean my teeth and when I came back she was smoking a cigarette. She asked what I planned to do next.

I told her about the school in Bethnal Green. 'I'm off duty all day on Thursday, so I think I'll call there. There might be someone who remembers her – come to that, she might even still be teaching there.'

'Have a heart,' retorted Maze. 'After all this time she could have five kids of her own. That is, if she didn't change her mind about the bloke, which could be why they didn't turn up at your auntie's.'

I switched the light off, then drew the black-out curtains. A small wind was rustling the dark band of trees over in the Park and a watchful searchlight probed the sky. I got into bed.

'Aunt Mitty said something about Sylvia seeming strange and nervy about taking her boyfriend there to lunch.'

'Love gets me like that, too.'

'I wonder what he was like . . . '

'Smashin' . . . '

From the tone of her voice I could tell that she was thinking about Corporal Sam thingummy and not Sylvia's fiancé.

Love, I thought, falling asleep. Everyone's in love except me.

Or if they weren't in love, they were intensely preoccupied with the idea of it.

Looking back, I remember how the whole WAAF billet seemed to pulsate with a romantic yearning that was none the less real for having largely been inspired by the world of films and hit tunes. The corridors rang with the songs of Crosby and the up-and-coming Sinatra, while the throbbing sentiments of Vera Lynn's ballads lingered weepily on the chill stone stairs.

Everyone sang about the glory of love and the even more glorious anguish of parting, and despite the harsh confines of uniform invariably did their best to look like Lana Turner or Rita Hayworth.

Maybe Hollywood was a tinsel culture but our generation was brought up on it, and it did at least indicate a reasonably simple path through the turgid confusion of wartime living, with courage and, above all, faithfulness coming out strongly on top. Practically all the WAAF at Regent's Park were sold on the idea of faithfulness in theory if not in practice, although I remember a girl called Godetia who blatantly swopped a flight lieutenant for a wing commander, and then ditched him in turn for a Polish count. Serve her right if she's now being called Comrade instead of Countess . . .

On the Thursday I was off duty someone gave me a complimentary ticket for a concert at the Royal Albert Hall, so I took it with me to Bethnal Green. Jerking along on the top of a bus I became aware that the further we travelled east the worse the bombing had been. The City was bad enough with the great holes torn in its illustrious streets, but the little soot-encrusted terraces of Bethnal Green had suffered even more. I walked down whole streets where the rubble still trickled under the temporary hoardings that hid the dead houses from view, and the warm spring air was heavy with the smell of damp plaster.

It didn't take long to find St Ebenezer's Infants' School because it seemed to be the only building intact in the street, its Victorian pomposity standing proudly against the desolate skyline. Walking across the broken asphalt playground I heard treble voices chanting tables from an open window and thought how funny it would be if I discovered Sylvia in charge of the proceedings. (Funny, and very strange; I wasn't sure that I'd know what to say to her.)

The main door was open and led into a cloakroom lined with small coats and hats. A tap dripped over in the corner. There was no one about, so I followed the sound of chanting down a short passage until I came to a square hall surrounded by partitioned classrooms. Everything I could see was treacle brown in colour, and very depressing.

I stood there listening to all the school-sounds and not knowing quite what to do next, then noticed someone looking at me through a broken pane in one of the classroom doors. She came out, a woman of about thirty in a sagging tweed suit and horn-rimmed glasses.

I said that I was sorry to be a nuisance, but could I see the headmistress if she wasn't too busy?

The woman smiled and said she'd see. Miss Mather had been examining Standard Three in spelling, but had probably finished before the bell went.

I thanked her.

'On leave?' she asked.

I said no, I was stationed at Regent's Park, whereupon she said how nice, and went off in search of the headmistress.

A few minutes later she showed me into a small dingy room

where a grey-haired woman sat behind a desk. She was writing when I walked in, and continued to write while I stood waiting. I began to feel glad I wasn't a pupil.

'Good-afternoon,' she asked, finally raising her eyes. 'And what can I do for you?'

'I wondered — ' I cleared my throat. 'I wondered whether you could give me any news of my sister. Her name was Sylvia Coryn and I believe she used to teach here.'

Miss Mather laid down her pen and placed the tips of her fingers together. They were thin and chalky.

'Sylvia Coryn? I don't recollect the name. When was she here?'

'Sometime in 1939.'

Miss Mather stared at me through small eyes. 'Who are you?'

'I'm her sister, and I do apologise for taking up your time — '

'Was she evacuated with us?'

I said I didn't know, and felt a fool for knowing so little, but even as I watched her expression began to change. She got up from the desk and went over to a wooden filing cabinet.

'I did have a temporary, unqualified teacher of that name,' she said, flicking her chalk fingers through a green folder.

My heart began to beat very fast. 'Can you tell me where she is now?'

Miss Mather swept her gaze over a page in the folder, then closed it with a decisive snap. 'No,' she said. 'I can't.'

She returned to the desk and picked up her pen. And once again I was back in the old conspiracy of silence.

'But surely you can tell me something about her?' I felt my voice begin to shake, and suddenly wished she'd ask me to sit down, or manifest some other token form of courtesy, however formal. But she didn't.

'I mean . . . do you remember what she was like, when she was here?'

Even as Miss Mather laid down her pen I began to wish that I hadn't asked; to wish that I'd just apologised for wasting her time and left it at that.

'My sole memory of Miss Coryn,' she said, 'is one of total

ineptitude. She was only here for a matter of weeks, but quite long enough for me to realise her complete unsuitability for the responsible post entrusted to her.'

I could only stand and blink at her, taking in the neat grey hair, the little eyes and the terrible chill composure.

'But she was very clever,' I managed to say. 'She was head girl at school and came second from top in matric.'

'I was not referring to Miss Coryn's scholastic achievements,' said Miss Mather.

'Well . . . '

'Suffice it to say,' she chose her words with care, 'that Miss Coryn had no aptitude for responsibility, and during the time she was here her attitude towards her pupils left a very great deal to be desired. I remember now that she was in fact dismissed.'

I managed to look away from her and found my gaze riveted to a bundle of canes standing in the corner. (Surely Sylvia hadn't . . . ?)

Desperately I sought the truth in Miss Mather's face but her head was lowered. She had returned to her writing and I was left in contemplation of the straight, stern parting in her hair.

Suddenly filled with rage I turned on my heel and walked out. The unseen children were still chanting tables.

Outside the school I took the wrong direction, and had plodded off into the borough of Hackney before I realised my mistake. Not that it mattered particularly. It was true that I had a free ticket to an Albert Hall concert, but I didn't feel much like going now. I'd no idea how to get to Kensington Gore, and it was easier just to keep trudging along without worrying about a destination.

So I kept going, an anonymous uniformed figure lost in its own gloomy thoughts, until I came to a café that offered cups of tea and some clumsy-looking cakes with imitation icing.

They tasted better than they looked, and halfway through a second cup of tea the old boy behind the marble counter suddenly said: 'Cheer up, kiddo, the war'll soon be over, then you can all pack up and go 'ome.'

'I'm all right here.'

'Smile then,' he suggested.

I sat staring at him while I sipped tea and continued to think over the interview with Miss Mather. Not only had it been unpleasant and disquieting, it still hadn't got me anywhere. The only clue Aunt Mitty had been able to give me had ended in a blank.

'Go on, kiddo. Givvus a smile.'

I put down my cup. 'I don't suppose you ever met a girl called Sylvia who used to be a schoolteacher in Bethnal Green?'

'Sylvia who?'

'Used to be Sylvia Coryn. Blonde, with blue eyes and looked like Alice Faye. She taught at St Ebenezer's in 1939.'

He shook his head. 'A lot's happened since then.'

'I know. Like the Blitz.' I said it for him, and got up to pay for the tea and cake.

'The only Sylvia I knew round here kept a fish shop off the Kingsland Road until she got bombed out. Woman of about fifty with a big nose. Had the best sprats for miles around.'

'I don't think that was her.'

'Gawd, what I wouldn't give for a plate of sprats,' mourned the old boy, ringing the money into the till. 'Sprats come in with the noo Lord Mayor, my ole mum used to say, and after we'd stood in the cold for hours to watch the procession we'd belt orf home to fried sprats and vinegar and bloomin' great doorsteps of white bread plastered all over wiv butter. Nothin' like it now. Gawd only knows how we keep alive at all.'

'Smile,' I said from the door.

'This Sylvia of yours,' he called. 'Shall I give her a message if she comes in asking for you?'

'No,' I said. 'She won't come. And even if she did, I don't suppose she'd think of asking for me.'

We smiled at one another with painstaking fortitude and parted.

And somehow I found my way to Kensington Gore. I was in fact beginning to get the hang of London's geography quite well; not through any systematic study of road maps or bus routes, but more because of a natural fondness for rambling round the streets in solitude, so that bit by bit the different areas began to connect in my mind and I started to develop an instinct for knowing where I was by the feel of a place rather than by its name. And although London was so shabby and bomb-racked, it had a haunting beauty that I've never been able to discover again since. Maybe there's too much traffic about now, or maybe I'm beginning to get old.

That first evening when I found myself outside the Albert Hall a violet-coloured haze was drifting up from Kensington Gardens while a thin young moon rode high above the barrage balloons. There was hardly anyone about, and I had a certain amount of trouble finding a way into the mammoth beehive building. I was tired and hot, and after I'd tried the third wrong door I felt inclined to give up.

But the fourth one proved successful, and I climbed the stairs to find myself outside a glass door in a dingy red-plush corridor.

The aged lady attendant who took my ticket told me to go in. 'But be quiet because it's started.'

I pushed the door open and for the first time in my life heard the incredible sound of a live symphony orchestra at work. The sound welled up from the floor of this vast circular dome, and climbing up past tier upon tier of seats poured its gorgeous torrent of sound over the gangway where I was standing with two or three other latecomers. They looked so small, all those men down on the platform behind the bank of ferns and the ragged ranks of music stands; even the conductor appeared no more than a matchbox marionette, but the soaring music that came from them overwhelmed me completely.

I'd had no idea it would be anything like this. Nobody had ever warned me about the powerful impact of a living orchestra on the uninitiated, and I began to cry, standing there with my cap in my hands while my legs ached with tiredness and my mind swam with the miserable disappointment of the trip to St Ebenezer's. All the terribleness of the war and the littleness of my own endeavours was being described by the beautiful, grave sounds that rose up to me until the whole scene dissolved in a million prickling pinpoints of light as the tears went on filling my eyes, over-flowing and then running down my cheeks.

It was crazy, the way I couldn't stop; almost as if all the

unshed tears of the last decade or so had accumulated and finally been released, thanks to the BBC Symphony Orchestra, in one long violent torrent.

Blind and choking I became aware of someone pushing a handkerchief into my hand and I raised it to my face, mopping the tears and then resting my burning eyes in its comfortable darkness. Resolutely ignoring the music and all thoughts of Sylvia enabled me to regain some sort of control, but after a minute or two another problem arose. My nose was running, and whereas it was okay to sop up tears on a stranger's handkerchief it didn't seem right to blow on it. Ma of course would have known the rights and wrongs of it, but the thought of her, small and meek back in Barnard Castle, merely promoted another gush of weeping. I wished I'd been nicer to her, and resolved that from henceforth I would even try to love Pa more.

Mercifully the piece of music came to an end, and as the applause thundered out I half fell into a vacant seat on the side of the gangway, and bit by bit managed to calm down. As for the handkerchief, it was already so wet that there didn't seem much point in not blowing on it, so I did, raucously.

And then looked round to see who'd lent it to me.

I couldn't tell, because the other late arrivals had also found seats and become indistinguishable from the rest of the audience. Not that I'd recognise them, anyway. But I kept on looking, and when an old lady in a Queen Mary toque caught my eye and smiled winningly I smiled back and mouthed *Thank you*. (And then started wondering how I'd get it laundered and returned to her, because handkerchiefs were rationed like everything else.)

The rest of the concert passed without incident, and with my emotions now firmly under control I could concentrate on listening and trying to follow the development of the music. The soldier sitting next to me had a pocket score, and I was envious of his ability to make sense of all those little bunches of grapes.

It ended with a march by Chabrier, and I thought the applause would never die; each time it dwindled someone would rekindle it, and the new blaze would bring Sir Henry

Wood back to the rostrum for a further genial acknowledgement.

'It's the young people in the services,' I heard someone explaining. 'They're sick of all that squalid jitterbugging.'

The crowds dispersed outside, and getting my bearings worked out I began to walk through Kensington Gardens towards Hyde Park Corner. It was a warm, still night and I didn't feel tired any more.

'They always say a good cry works wonders,' said a voice at my side. 'Feeling better now?'

A quick glance showed that it was a chap in Air Force uniform. And a second glance showed that it was a squadron leader, of all things.

'Yes, thank you,' I said. Then muttered: 'Sir.'

He continued to walk along with me. 'I thought the second movement of the Beethoven dragged a bit, but it picked up towards the end. I must say the old boy wears very well.'

Not knowing whether he meant Beethoven or Sir Henry Wood, I decided not to commit myself. A group of people passed us humming the Chabrier march.

'Go to many concerts?' The squadron leader was still there.

'No. This was my first.'

'Enjoy it?'

'Yes . . . ' I knew I should add *sir,* but it made me feel stupid. I wished he'd go away and bother someone of his own rank.

'I couldn't help noticing you,' he went on. 'But please don't think I was being officious.'

It suddenly occurred to me then that it was his handkerchief lying in a damp ball in my tunic pocket. I stopped under a dim, tree-shaded lamp to give it to him, then hesitated. 'Thank you very much,' I mumbled. 'Where can I return it to?'

'Keep it,' he said. 'With my compliments.'

'Thank you,' I repeated, and because we were standing face to face with our caps on I had to salute him.

'Not at all.' Gravely he returned the compliment.

I thought surely to God he'd walk away on his own after

that, but he didn't. And so we continued in silence until we'd passed the Albert Gate, then he asked me where I was stationed.

'Regent's Park. Sir.'

'ACRC? I was there in 1942.'

'On permanent staff?'

'No. As a palpitating cadet.'

So not only was he of commissioned rank, he was aircrew as well. I began to think he must have mistaken me for a WAAF officer, but couldn't imagine how. No self-respecting ma'am would burst into tears in the middle of the Albert Hall – and besides, their uniforms were much more distinguished.

'I thought it was an old lady,' I finally ventured when the silence was becoming awkwardly protracted.

'Thought who was an old lady?'

'You. I mean, I thought it was an old lady in a toque like Queen Mary's who lent me the handkerchief.'

'Don't think I've ever gone in for toques, although I've got a nice deerstalker at home. It belonged to my uncle.'

The conversation lapsed again, but as we were crossing Hyde Park Corner he asked if I was proposing to walk all the way to ACRC.

'Well, it's not all that far – just up Park Lane and then down Baker Street.'

'God help us,' he said. You should have been in the Infantry, not the Air Force.'

'You don't have to come too,' I retorted, then remembered that I was addressing a commissioned rank: 'sir.'

'In the absence of anything better to do,' he said, 'it gives me a certain amount of quiet satisfaction to restore a wandering airwoman safely to her billet.'

There was a pretty little Spanish-looking house in Park Lane that I always liked looking at, but this time I couldn't see it because the squadron leader was blocking it from view. We were well past the Dorchester before I thought of something else to say.

'I should have realised that an old lady wouldn't have lent me a man's handkerchief.'

'When my mother went to see Norma Shearer in a film called *Smilin' Through* I'm told she took one of my cot sheets with her.'

'Was it as sad as that?'

'Never saw it. But it apparently reduced Mother and all her sisters to a state of tear-sodden euphoria.'

'I've got a sister. Just the one.'

'Really?'

'I think it was her I was crying about. Her, and the war and everything.'

'What's her name?'

'Sylvia.'

'And come to think of it — ' he stopped abruptly. 'What's yours?'

Automatically I stopped too, and standing face to face with him became filled once more with the urgent compulsion to salute. After fifteen months in the armed forces the instinct was as blindly unreasoning as that of bird migration.

'If you don't stop doing that,' said the squadron leader, 'I'll put you straight on the next bus. So now.'

Truth to tell, I wouldn't have minded doing the rest of the journey by bus, because I was beginning to feel dog-tired after all the miles I must have walked during the course of the day. But something prevented me from saying so. Pride, I daresay.

We reached Marble Arch, turned along Oxford Street, where so many of the big shop windows had been refitted with cardboard, then went down Orchard Street.

'I asked you what your name was.'

'Kit Coryn. Aircraftwoman Second Class.' If he'd been an ordinary ranker I'd have asked him his name in return. But as things stood he'd only got one name so far as I was concerned. *Sir*.

'Are you stationed near here?' That at least sounded polite without being personal.

'Cambridgeshire.'

'Oh.'

'Rather cold and flat.'

'I used to be in Lincs. That's cold and flat, too.'

'Yes.'

'Are you in fighters or bombers?'

'Lancasters.'

'Oh. Bombers. We had them in Lincs . . . sir.'

'Yes,' he said. 'They crop up all over the place.'

Which got us to Baker Street Station. Drawn up at the wide intersection where Marylebone Road crosses Baker Street there was generally an old-fashioned coffee stall run by a man called Lofty. It was only ever there at night, and although I often seemed to be up and down Baker Street I never once saw it arrive, or, for that matter, depart. Maybe it was really there all the time but no one noticed it when it was shut up. A huge cumbersome box on little iron wheels, it couldn't have been easy to shift, but the mystery of its movements was all part of London's magic.

And come to think of it, Lofty himself had a certain magic too, because you only had to duck your head under the wooden awning that extended over the counter and you were in another world. With your elbows planted on Lofty's American cloth and your eyes adjusted to the dim blue light floating in steam from the coffee urn, you were part of an intimate London night-life where cab drivers and insomniacs swopped philosophies and debated the date of the Allied invasion of Europe; and Lofty in his white apron and black trilby dished out mugs of hot coffee and rock buns with currants like tin tacks and chucked the money in an Oxo tin.

'This your club?' enquired the squadron leader.

'Yes.'

'Very nice too.'

'I like it,' I said defensively. 'Better than the NAFFI or the Sally Army or any of those.'

In the blue gloom that rendered all things mysterious I could see that he had dark eyes and a dark lock of hair showing under the officer's cap that was now pushed back from his forehead. Most of the squadron leaders at ACRC were chairbound and old – dreadfully old with paunches and horn-rims – but this one was still quite young. But of course that was the way with aircrew; they never lived long enough to get old.

With his elbows propped on the counter in the approved manner, the squadron leader said: 'You come from the north, don't you?'

'How can you tell?'

'Neat clipped speech and an air of self-sufficiency.'

'I sound like Flight Sergeant Cutter.'

'Who's she?'

'The NCO in charge of the admin. section. She's wizard to look at, but not very nice.'

'Does she put people on charges?'

'Yes. If she gets half a chance.'

'Has she ever put you on one?'

'No,' I said. 'But there's still time.'

Which reminded me that it was getting very late. I had a late pass, which expired at 23.59, and there was a bare fifteen minutes to go. I drank down the rest of the coffee, turned to face the squadron leader and said: 'Thank you very much. I've got to go now.'

'Shall I come the rest of the way with you?'

'No, please don't bother. For one thing, I'll have to run.'

'I'm capable of running.'

'I know. I just meant . . . ' I just meant for God's sake let me go. If we stand here looking at one another much longer I'll get the saluting-thing again.

'All right.' He held out his hand. 'Good-bye. Been nice seeing you.'

'Nice seeing you too, sir. Thank you.'

Conscious of Lofty's impassive gaze from behind the coffee urn I shook the ends of the squadron leader's fingers, dropped them, ducked from under the wooden awning and sprinted towards the top of Baker Street. Half way along Park Road I remembered that I'd still got his handkerchief, and by the time I'd reached the WAAF hostel remembered that he'd told me to keep it. With his compliments.

After I'd been in the WAAF admin. office for a couple of months I found myself entrusted with the sacred chore of keeping the ration strength.

Theoretically this entailed keeping a record of every

WAAF on the station by ticking her name each day against the ration return slip which had to be submitted to us by the NCO in charge of every working section. The ration strength (in the form of a floppy foolscap exercise book) was then sent down to the station catering officer so that he might be enabled, in Air Force parlance, to take the necessary action.

Simple enough in theory, but in fact it often constituted an awful bind because of the various sections who didn't fill in the ration return slip, either through forgetfulness, carelessness, or in some cases sheer bloody-mindedness. It was my job to chase them, because if the ration strength wasn't received by the catering officer by midday at the latest he chased us.

On the morning after I'd met the squadron leader everyone seemed worse than usual at doing their returns and by eleven o'clock I'd still only got the accounts section, 54 Group, Equipment, Transport and the teleprinters' room. Medical & Dental were always inclined to take a scornful view of administrative form-filling, and the orderly room – who should have known better – invariably lost their return slip under a deluge of other papers.

So I rang them up, in between typing the daily details stencil and trying to pacify Squadron Officer Gilby who wanted her coffee before going to see the adjutant about Saturday night dances. (He wanted them every *other* Saturday night.) And when the time got to ten past twelve and I still hadn't had the return slip from the orderly room I suddenly got fed up, ticked the names anyway, and then set off with the ration strength book through the Park to the catering section.

It was a marvellous day with the scent of late wallflowers drifting across the lake and the grass growing lush and green, and when I'd delivered the ration strength I decided that it wasn't worth going back to the office before lunch. I'd look in on Maze instead.

Maze was an MT driver, and every now and then had to do a spell on duty ambulance down at Abbey Lodge sick quarters. It was very boring being cooped up in the duty ambulance driver's room waiting for the phone to ring and when I walked in she was lying on the bed, dozing.

'Look I've brought you some bluebells.'

'Stone me.' She opened her eyes. 'You get shot for picking flowers round here.'

'Nobody saw.'

'That's what you think.'

I sat down on the foot of the bed. 'If you don't want them, just say so.'

'Ah, shuddup.' Getting off the bed she filled a mug with water and arranged the bluebells lovingly in it.

'Heard from Corporal Corbellini?'

'I hear from him every day.'

'Must be getting serious.'

She didn't answer, but something about her told me that it was. She was still thin and ferrety but there was a sort of gleam about her.

'He's asked me to get engaged,' she said finally.

'Maze – how smashing! Are you going to?'

'Might as well.'

'After the war you'll have to go and live in America. What'll your parents think?'

The phone rang before she could tell me, and I left her lacing her shoes and cramming her cap on.

'Some soppy cadet with a nosebleed,' she grumbled. 'Nothing interesting happens these days.'

Sauntering back to the WAAF cookhouse for lunch I realised that she was right, at least so far as the war was concerned. The air raids of early spring seemed to have petered out and there was still no sign of us invading Europe. Sometimes I got the feeling that the war would go on for ever, out of sheer force of habit.

Turning into Prince Albert Road I saw a neat blue-uniformed figure skimming towards me on a blue issue bicycle. It seemed for one glad moment as if she was going to cycle on, then she placed a sparkling black foot on the kerb and waited for me to draw level with her.

'Is that an *issue* tie you're wearing, Coryn?' Flight Sergeant Cutter demanded.

'Yes, Flight.'

'Has it ever occurred to you to sponge and press it?'

I squinted down at it.

'Tonight's domestic night,' she said. 'So do it.'

'Yes, Flight.'

I thought she'd finished with me, but she continued to scrutinise me thoughtfully.

'Where have you been?'

'Delivering the ration strength, Flight.'

'Couldn't you find a runner to take it?'

'No, Flight. They were all busy.' Oh, the glib lies that fall from the lips of underdogs.

Flight Sergeant Cutter continued to stare at me, and I stared back, fascinated by the peerless skin overlaid by impeccable make-up and the dazzling platinum page-boy suspended the regulation two inches from her starched collar.

'If you've been to the catering section,' she said at length, 'then all I can say is that you're coming from the wrong direction. But we'll let it pass for the moment.' And she rode off.

Something in the warmth of the sun and the laziness of the breeze prompted me to think fleetingly about the squadron leader who'd lent me his handkerchief. He'd had rather a warm, lazy sort of charm, I supposed, but I still couldn't work out his preoccupation with a sobbing aircraftwoman second class. In the end I put him down as one of those people who derive whimsical enjoyment from ignoring the social barriers occasionally.

White clouds were massing over the Park when I walked back to Holme House with a group of other girls after lunch, but I didn't see it as any kind of omen until the admin. office door flew open with the first crack of thunder and Flight Sergeant Cutter, baleful as a demon king, made her entrance. She laid a piece of paper on top of my typewriter.

'The ration return slip,' she said. 'From the orderly room.'

I didn't say anything.

'They have just given it to me, with apologies for being late.'

'Yes, Flight.'

'Yet you took the ration strength over to Catering before lunch.'

'Yes, Flight.'

Outside, the rain fell in large harsh drops.

'Which can only mean that you deliberately falsified the book.' My God, she made it sound worse than gun-running.

'Well . . . ' I had to think quickly. 'Not exactly, Flight. I had to go down to the orderly room earlier on for something, and I — '

'Well?'

'I counted heads.'

She recoiled as if from a blow. *'You counted heads?'*

'Only the WAAF heads of course, Flight . . . '

The rain beat faster, and in the greeny gloom I saw her close her eyes. Moistening my lips I waited to hear that I was on a charge for neglect of duty, but in the end she contented herself with a long furious lecture about the folly of airy-fairy improvisations as compared with going through the proper channels which had been specifically laid down by members of the Air Council who, perhaps I would agree, ought to know what they were doing. She had gone on to ask me whether I realised that in doing what I did I was calmly juggling with the lives of merchant seamen when she was cut short by the frantic buzzing of Squadron Officer Gilby's bell.

'The trouble with you, Coryn, is that you have absolutely no sense of *esprit de corps,'* she said. 'And furthermore, get that tie sponged and pressed tonight and report to me first thing tomorrow.'

'Yes, Flight.'

She jerked her platinum head towards the door. 'Now go and see what's the matter with *her.'*

The rest of the afternoon passed pretty glumly, but shortly before five o'clock the phone rang with an outside call.

'Excuse me,' said a voice I didn't recognise. 'Is that Miss Coryn? Sylvia's sister?'

Surprised and faintly perturbed, I said that it was.

'My name is Simpson,' said the voice. 'Kay Simpson, and we met very briefly when you came to see Miss Mather yesterday at St Ebenezer's.'

Suddenly I remembered her. The woman in the brown sagging tweed suit and horn-rim glasses.

'Listen,' she said rapidly, 'Miss Mather told me why you'd come, and I wondered if we could meet for a chat. I'll be in the West End tonight, so perhaps we could have a drink somewhere?'

I said yes, of course.

She asked me whether I knew the Regent Palace and I told her that I'd heard of it, so we planned to meet in the lounge at seven o'clock.

'Did you know Sylvia?' I asked before she could ring off.

'Of course,' she said. 'I used to share a flat with her.'

I felt my heart thumping with excitement and wanted to go on talking to her, but she put the receiver down.

Filled with elation I hurried through the rest of the day's work, locked the door on the dot of six and rushed back to the WAAF hostel to have supper and make myself presentable for the Regent Palace and Miss Simpson.

But one step inside the guardroom and I came down to earth. I'd completely forgotten that it was domestic night, the one night of the week when all WAAF personnel without exception were confined to quarters to scrub their bedspaces, do their mending and so on. To try to sneak out without a pass was to court disaster at the hands of the military police who roamed London looking for deserters.

I trailed up to flat 10 and already the whole place was permeated with the melancholy inseparable from domestic night; the smell of wet floorboards and kitchen soap, girls in curlers and cold cream, the sound of scrubbing accompanied by the despairing wail of love songs . . . and when I thought about Miss Simpson waiting patiently in the lounge of the Regent Palace I wanted to lean against the wall and howl like a dog.

Then I decided that, pass or no pass, I was going anyway.

All I had to do was to get past the duty NCO in the guardroom with a trumped-up excuse about having to fetch some important papers from Holme House (NCOs from other sections were always very vague about what went on in the admin. world), so it would be dead easy.

Accordingly I changed my shirt and powdered my nose, and wearing a carefully preoccupied smile marched boldly into the guardroom. But unfortunately I hadn't checked on the identity of the duty NCO.

Which was a great pity. Because it was Flight Sergeant Cutter.

4

It was too late to retreat. Sitting at the table by the switchboard she saw me immediately.

'Well, Coryn?'

'I'm sorry, Flight, but I can't remember whether I locked the admin. office door before I left Holme House.' (Useless to try baffling her with lies about fetching important papers.) 'I came to ask if I could nip over to make sure.'

She eyed me narrowly. 'You're becoming increasingly inefficient, aren't you?'

'Yes, Flight.'

'And if you're not very careful, it's going to land you in trouble. Serious trouble. The Air Force has no time for slacking, Coryn, and one of these days you're going to find yourself remustered to aircrafthand. A spell in the cookhouse would do you a lot of good.'

'Yes, Flight.'

During the pause which followed I waited for a moment or two before saying, very gently: 'So had I better go over to Holme House, Flight?'

'Certainly not,' she said. 'I'll ring the guardroom and ask the SPs to check.'

Resignedly I watched her flick the switches and then frown into the receiver. She tried again, then slammed it down.

'They're engaged. All right, you'd better go, and I'll expect you back in ten minutes sharp.'

Outside, the air smelt of freedom but I hesitated for a moment before dashing off to the West End. Desperately as I wanted to meet this Miss Simpson there wasn't the slightest chance of getting there and back within the prescribed ten minutes, and I wasn't too happy about incurring the further wrath of Flight Sergeant Cutter. Our relationship had suffered quite enough for one day.

Perhaps I'd better make a token trip to Holme House – or even walk round the block – and then return to the guard-room with the glad tidings that the door had been safely locked all the time. But even as I decided to play safe, I took to my heels and ran off down the road towards Baker Street tube station. But when I got there I remembered that military police were very fond of patrolling the Underground (and Piccadilly in particular), so hurried past, and when an empty taxi turned the corner of Marylebone Road I nabbed it. I hadn't got much money, but speed and anonymity were of prime importance; besides which, I wasn't sure where the Regent Palace was.

It turned out to be on the corner of two narrow streets within a stone's throw of Piccadilly Circus, and when I'd paid the taxi driver I'd got exactly two shillings and fourpence ha'penny left. The lounge was a vast marble affair with palm trees and basket chairs, the plaintive sound of a small string orchestra punctuated by the rattle of drinks on glass-topped tables.

I stood in the doorway, warmed and exhilarated by the knowledge that I'd no business to be there, and when Miss Simpson waved to me from a nearby table I hurried over and seized her hand. She was wearing the same tweed suit but had knotted a bright scarf in the neck.

'I'm so glad you could come,' she said. 'Will you join me with a sherry?'

I accepted, and when it arrived on a silver salver tried to see how much it cost; I wasn't sure that two and fourpence ha'penny would enable me to return the hospitality.

'Cheers,' she said. 'Here's to Sylvia.'

I repeated the toast, then put my glass down. 'Where is she?'

'I only wish I knew,' she sighed.

'But I thought — '

'I haven't seen her since she went to the club.'

'Club? What club?'

'I think it was called the Beaver Club. She wouldn't tell me much about it except that it was a place for young people.' She smiled reminiscently. 'Sylvia was marvellous with children.'

'Miss Mather didn't seem to think so,' I said bitterly.

'She was jealous. Everyone knew that, except Sylvia.'

'But tell me about her – about sharing a flat with her, and where's this Beaver Club?' The questions fell over each other. I took another sip of sherry as a cure for incoherence.

'Sylvia . . . oh, Sylvia,' sighed Miss Simpson, shaking her head. 'There's so much, and yet so little, to tell.'

Glancing round the huge teeming room I wished she'd get a move on; it was very disappointing to learn that she didn't know where Sylvia was, but she must surely have a few helpful crumbs of information to give me.

'Why did Miss Mather sack her?' I asked. From behind her horn-rims Miss Simpson's rather sticky brown eyes regarded me sentimentally.

'Jealousy,' she said. 'Sylvia was the sort of person you either adored or were jealous of. I adored her.'

'Yes,' I said. 'Yes, of course. But what I mean is, when it actually came to sacking her, Miss Mather couldn't say I'm sacking you because I'm jealous of you, could she?'

'Oh, no,' Miss Simpson said vindictively, 'the real reason had to be wrapped up in a lot of waffle about being irresponsible and having no vocation for teaching – although I suppose that in some ways she was actually a bit irresponsible – but all I can say is that our kids adored Sylvia. They really adored her.'

'When I was a kid I adored her too. And that's why I want to know why she ran away from home without telling me.'

'History has a habit of repeating itself,' Miss Simpson said. 'She did the same thing to me.'

'You mean, she left your flat — '

'She promised to let me know as soon as she got this job she was after at the Beaver Club, then one afternoon when I got home from St Ebenezer's I found she'd gone. Her bedroom was empty. She hadn't even left a note. So I waited to hear from her but nothing happened. Of course it was all a long time ago now, but I've never forgotten her. I never, never will.'

'I know,' I said. 'That's the trouble. I can't forget her either.'

We sat staring at our empty glasses as the string orchestra finished playing its selection from *The Student Prince* and made a start on *No, No Nanette,* and I became conscious of a sense of enervation. I didn't like Miss Simpson all that much.

'Sylvia was damned rotten to me,' she said. 'There I was, convinced that I'd really found a close chum at last – we used to sing and dance and play the fool – and I'd never been so happy in all my life. Then without a word of warning it was all over. She'd packed up and gone without even saying good-bye.'

Her voice began to tremble and I knew I wouldn't be able to stand it if she cried.

'Have another sherry,' I said, and beckoned a cruising waitress. Then remembered about the two and fourpence ha'penny.

But it was too late to worry now. 'Thank you, madam,' the waitress said grimly, '*most* kind,' and swept the sixpence and twenty-two pennies into the palm of her hand.

'Not at all,' I told her, and triumphantly returned the odd ha'penny to my skirt pocket.

'The trouble is, I'm so lonely,' said Miss Simpson. 'It's not my fault that I don't like men very much, it's because they're so bossy and self-opiniated and of course they're only really interested in one thing. The happiest time of my whole life was when Sylvia shared the flat.'

'So you said. How long was she there for?'

'Only a month. But it was like drawing back the curtains and letting the sunshine in after a long dark night. Sylvia was always laughing . . . '

'I know. I remember.'

But this wasn't getting us anywhere. I hadn't sneaked out in order to reminisce; I'd come to glean a bit of definite information, which didn't however seem to be forthcoming. I glanced at Miss Simpson, who was gazing forlornly at a young WRN officer, then discreetly looked at my watch. Hell, I'd already been away for well over an hour. I began to feel worried and edgy.

'Look,' I said, 'I think I'll have to go. It's been very nice

meeting you — '
'Oh, please don't go yet — ' she said quickly, and took my hand. 'Please, let's be chums . . . let's talk about Sylvia — '
'But what's there to talk about?' I felt the sense of irritated disappointment growing with every minute. 'I'm just trying to find her, that's all.'
'I'll help you — '
'How?'
'You see, I'm so lonely — '
'Did you say it was called the Beaver Club? Can you tell me where it is?'
'I only know that it's somewhere in London. I tried to trace her there but it's not in the phone book . . . look, why don't you have another sherry?'
'I'd love to, but I really must be getting back. It's rather urgent — '
For a moment I considered telling her about skipping out, then decided against it. I detached my hand and stood up.
'Thank you very much indeed, it's been so nice — '
'You don't like me, do you?' she said.
Deeply embarrassed, I said that of course I did.
'You don't,' she said. 'Nobody likes me. That's why Sylvia didn't stay. That's why I'm so lonely.'
'If you're lonely,' I told her, trying to make a joke of it, 'you ought to try joining the WAAF. The only time you can be alone there is in the lavatory. But seriously, when I find Sylvia I'll tell her to get in touch with you, I expect she means to all the time, she's just a bit busy.'
I began to edge away from the basket chairs while the string orchestra paused for breath, shuffled its music and then began on *Bitter Sweet*. Miss Simpson's brand of sentimental lassitude was not my cup of tea, but it was difficult to simply walk away.
'Why don't you get another flat mate?' I suggested bracingly.
'I've already got one.'
'Oh. Well then . . . '
'It doesn't work.'
'Why not? Isn't she nice?'
Miss Simpson gazed at me from behind her horn-rims and

finally managed a self-deprecating little smile.

'It's Miss Mather,' she said.

There didn't seem to be any useful rejoinder to that. Confused and very worried about my long absence from the hostel, I more or less turned tail and fled.

I was very sorry for Miss Simpson, but right now I had problems of my own.

With only a ha'penny to my name there was no question of transport back to Regent's Park, and I walked and dog-trotted alternately, thankful that I'd got out of the crowded West End. Lofty's coffee stall was drawn up in its usual place but I ignored it, too intent on solving the problem of getting back into the hostel without being spotted.

I still hadn't come up with the answer when I got there, and stood in the shadows wondering whether there were any likely windows at the back of the buildings. To walk into the guardroom would be tantamount to signing my own charge sheet.

I was still standing there when a small military truck came up the road and turned in by the archway that led through to the courtyard. The archway, adjacent to the guardroom, had been fitted by the Air Force with a pair of strong metal gates which were always kept locked, and as I watched the driver jumped down and went towards them.

It was Maze, returning from her spell as duty ambulance driver.

I glided over to her and touched her on the shoulder. She jumped violently.

'Maze – let me get in the van, quick!'

I crept into the driver's seat then wormed my way into the back. It was dark and very stuffy. I heard her unlock the gates and then after a minute or two get back in the truck.

'What the hell you bin up to?'

'It's domestic night and I had to go out and meet someone who knew Sylvia.'

'Any good?'

'No. No damn good at all.'

She started the engine, drove the truck under the archway then switched off the ignition.

'This do you?'

'Fine. Thanks, Maze.'

She got out, and I heard her go through to the guardroom to report that she was off duty.

And the rest was easy. All I had to do was wait until the courtyard was deserted and then stroll across to the building that housed flat 10. And then be prepared to swear next morning to Flight Sergeant Cutter that she'd forgotten she'd seen me come through after the allotted ten minutes.

I spent the evening sponging and pressing my tie.

The Beaver Club, Miss Simpson had said. A place for young people that she didn't know the address of, and which wasn't on the phone. I checked just to make sure, and she was right. There was no sign of a Beaver Club in the London directory.

Which once again brought me to a standstill in the search for Sylvia. I hadn't got very far, and the recurrence of the running-away pattern was rather disquieting. But then, hell, anyone would have run away from the sticky-eyed Miss Simpson, and as for not turning up at Aunt Mitty's that time, well, there was bound to be a good reason for it. Maybe she had a bilious attack.

I was still trying to work out the next move a couple of days later when a phone call came through for me. I was in the guardroom at the time, pinning up an exhortation to all airwomen to buy National Savings certificates (what with, it didn't say), and I hoped very much that the caller wasn't Miss Simpson.

'What time do you adjourn for lunch?' a man's voice asked. Mystified, I told him 12.30.

'Highly satisfactory,' he said. 'I've booked Spam for two at Gulliver's in Park Road for 12.35.'

'Yes. But — '

'It's David Magnus.'

'I don't know a David Magnus.' Then I began to recognise something familiar about the voice. 'You're not a squadron leader, are you?'

'Not for the next three days.'

'Oh . . . '

'So are you coming?' The voice sounded very brisk and businesslike.

'Yes,' I said finally. 'Yes, thank you, I'd like to.'

Corporal Phillips looked at me with interest. 'Someone nice?'

'Umm. I suppose so.' Surprise made me sound grudging, but the more I thought about the invitation the more it appealed to me.

'Can I have a lunchtime pass, Corp? 12.30 to 1.30?'

'Can't see why not.' She was nice, Corporal Phillips.

So at 12.30 sharp I was off down Prince Albert Road in the direction of Baker Street. It was very warm for the end of May and official permission had been granted for all ranks to discard their tunics. *(Shirt sleeves will be rolled to a height of three inches above the elbows.)*

I didn't recognise him at first as the civilian strolling towards Gulliver's restaurant from the opposite direction, but of course I'd only seen him in the dark before. Noting the grey flannels and the check shirt with the cravat in the neck, my first reaction was relief that I wouldn't be faced with the bind of having to salute. And the second reaction was a sudden feeling of pleasure at seeing him again.

'Hullo,' he said. 'Nice you could come.'

'Nice of you to ask me.'

I hovered for an instant on the brink of adding *sir,* then decided that the wearing of civvies automatically rendered all forms of self-abasement unnecessary. Normal courtesy would be quite sufficient.

We went in, and were shown to a small table in the window where sunlight danced on the knives and forks and made pools of light on the bomb-cracked ceiling. Gulliver's was a small unpretentious restaurant but still beyond my financial scope, although a group of us had once treated ourselves to supper there after pay parade.

'Well now, Kit Coryn,' said the squadron leader. 'I hope I see you well?'

'Very well, thank you. And you?'

He certainly looked very well to me. A smiling, nice-looking chap of twenty-six or so, with thick dark hair that wasn't slicked down with the usual Brylcreem. It was hard to believe that he was the same rank as the WAAF commanding officer.

'Who wouldn't feel well when they've got three days' leave?' he said, and handed me the menu.

There was a choice of rabbit or fish besides the inevitable Spam, but the proprietor produced half a bottle of burgundy which transformed the whole thing into – well, if not a banquet, at least a special occasion.

'Let's drink to peace,' I suggested.

'Let's take first things first,' he replied, 'and drink to the invasion of Europe.'

'When's it due to start?'

'You'd better ask Churchill.'

'I've got a funny feeling he wouldn't tell me.'

'And neither would I,' he said gently. 'Even if I knew.'

We ate in silence, and I wondered whether I was to consider myself rebuked.

'Someone said we're planning to make it the 28th of September because that's the date William the Conqueror invaded England.'

'It'll be before September.'

'And you think it'll work all right?'

He pushed aside his plate, leaned back and lit a cigarette. 'It's got to.'

'I wish I could do more. Typing daily details and ticking names in the ration strength seems a bit ineffectual sometimes.'

'Oh, I don't know,' he said kindly.

'My father thinks I'm a shocking waste of government money. But then he rather goes to the opposite extreme and expects me to win the war single-handed.'

'What's your father like?' He looked as if he really wanted to know.

'Sort of average. Small and thin with stomach trouble. Doesn't laugh much.'

'I've got a feeling that laughter's important to you.'

Over the cheese and biscuits I became aware that we were appraising one another with a sort of cautious curiosity; as if, having played a trial hand as RAF officer and WAAF aircraftwoman, we were feeling our way towards the possibility of another sort of relationship.

Content in my own rather solitary, dreaming world I'd

never so far been particularly keen to acquire a boyfriend; occasionally I'd thought it would be quite fun, but having read through some of the tatty weekly mags that graced the NAAFI had come to the conclusion that it was all too much like hard work. With one voice they stressed the importance of correct appearance as well as the importance of correct behavioural pattern. *Show a lively interest in all that he does. Don't talk about yourself. Be friendly, but don't go too far. No man can respect a girl who doesn't respect herself. Keep a sense of humour. Read the papers. Find out the make-up that really suits you and stick to it. Wash your undies daily. Men don't love girls with whiskers on their legs so whisk yours off with a good depilatory wax of which I will send you the name. Dandruff on the collar spells death to romance, and I'm afraid I cannot possibly answer your problem in this column, Worried Grey-Eyes; send a stamped addressed envelope and I will tell you where to go . . .*

No, no, it was all too much like the sort of WAAF discipline of which I'd already had a basinful. Still, a pity in some way.

'I said — ' he was gently shaking my wrist, 'I've got a feeling that laughter's important to you.'

'Sorry – yes. My sister taught me that.'

'She taught you to laugh?'

'Yes.'

'Lucky sister,' he said.

The coffee came, and the radiant May sunshine twinkled on its rich dark surface. It was much better than the NAAFI stuff; even better than Lofty's.

'My sister's smashing.'

'Where does she live?'

'In London.'

'See much of her?'

'No. The thing is — ' I hesitated, torn between truthfulness and the urge to boast. 'The thing is that we've lost touch a bit. You know what it's like with the war, and everything.'

'Yes. Of course.'

'But I'll probably have caught up with her before the end of the week. Then I could introduce you, if you like.'

He smiled. 'Can't I take one at a time?'

'Honestly, she's terrific, my sister. Very beautiful, with

blonde curly hair and huge blue eyes. Looks the spitting image of Alice Faye. And she's got this marvellous capacity for happiness – a sort of ability to make everything sparkle — '

'She sounds quite a girl.'

'Yes.' I poured out the remains of the coffee. 'She used to be a teacher at a school in Bethnal Green. All the kids adored her but the headmistress was jealous so she sacked her. Last night I was talking to the teacher she used to share a flat with.'

'Doesn't she know where she is?'

'Well, no,' I said. 'As a matter of fact she's lost touch with her, too.'

I sat thinking about Sylvia for a minute, then came back to earth with a jolt. It was twenty past one.

'I'm afraid I'll have to go now. I'm back on duty at half past one, and – oh, by the way, I've just remembered this.' Unbuttoning my tunic pocket I gave him back his laundered handkerchief.

'I told you not to bother.'

'I wouldn't have, if they hadn't been on coupons.'

He paid the bill. 'I'll walk along with you.'

It seemed strange of him to offer, but then, I supposed, no stranger than taking me out to lunch. Probably he just felt like renewing old memories of ACRC. Going through the Park towards the Inner Circle I suddenly asked him if he'd ever heard of the Beaver Club.

'What sort of place is it?'

'I don't know. Something to do with children, I'm told.'

'The only Beaver Club I ever heard of had nothing whatever to do with children,' he said. 'It was spelt B-e-v-e-r, and had everything to do with the drinking of beverages.'

'Oh.' I'd never thought of that. 'You mean, it's a drinking club?'

'Sort of.'

We parted at the gateway of Holme House, and because I didn't have to salute him I seized his hand and shook it heartily. He was very nice, and I liked him.

'Doing anything tonight, ACW Coryn?'

'Well, actually . . . '

'Okay. Just a thought.'

'It's nothing all that special,' I said politely. 'Just something to do with my sister, you see.'

'Yes, I see.'

'Perhaps some other time?'

'Of course,' he said. 'Some other time.'

Then he turned on his heel and sauntered away. I stood watching him for a moment to see if he'd look back, but he didn't. Ah, well.

But Bever instead of Beaver. It was quite a thought, and at the first opportunity I looked it up in the phone book and to my great delight there it was. *The Bever Club, Denman Court, W.1.*

'Sounds like Soho,' Maze said. 'Want me to come with you, mate?'

I said no, but as gently as possible because I didn't want to hurt her feelings. It was difficult to explain the instinct to go it alone, and when I did try she obviously got the wrong idea.

'Are you looking for your sister or going on some sort of holy pilgrimage?'

I told her not to be so daft, but somehow the phrase stuck in my mind.

'Soho's a funny old place,' she said. 'You want to watch it on your own, after dark.'

'I'll be okay.'

'They play funny games down there.'

'Yes. I've heard.'

So I went, alone, and wasted a lot of time prowling through the shadowy twilight looking for Denman Court. Denman Street was easy enough, but its Court was tucked discreetly down a narrow alleyway between an Italian grocer's and a newsagent's shop. And the Bever Club, when I located it, had been bombed.

I stood looking at it for quite a while, trying in the secretive hush to conjure up some sort of tangible link with Sylvia. As well as some sort of tangible link between a Bethnal Green infants' school and a Soho drinking club. Had she really been here? And if so, in what capacity? Secretary, or barmaid, or even some sort of entertainer, perhaps? I remembered how she could sing and dance.

But even allowing for its sad wartime decrepitude, the place could never have been up to much. It was very small – no bigger than an ordinary terraced house, really – and if its name hadn't still been hanging crookedly from the iron bar, no one would have given it a second glance.

I walked up the steps to the front door and when I pushed it it opened, grating on the powdered plaster that littered the floor inside. It was dark, and the smell of damp decay hung heavily on the silence. After a moment or two I could distinguish what looked like the remains of a bar counter on the other side of the room and tiptoed across to it, wincing at the scrunch of broken glass. A couple of tall stools lay upturned on the bar, and peering across it I could just make out the rows of empty shelves on the wall behind.

It was a stricken, melancholy place, and I was on the point of tiptoeing out again when a beam of torchlight suddenly fell across the floor, lay trembling for a moment, and then slowly began to climb the wall beside me. I froze, my heart thumping. I remembered what Maze had said about the funny games they played in Soho.

The beam of light touched the ceiling and then descended again. It snapped out, leaving the darkness impenetrable, and from my corner by the bar I heard the soft sound of someone whistling.

Reason told me that it would be more sensible to deliberately make my presence known rather than wait for discovery, but second by second I kept putting it off. Reason was one thing, instinct another.

Then the light flicked on again and recommenced its journey across the littered floor, and this time it caught the toes of my shoes in its round white stare. It paused, and the whistling stopped. And while I stood motionless it slowly began to travel up my grey issue stockings, up over my skirt and tunic until its dazzling eye made me raise my hand to shield my face.

'Who are you?' It was a man's voice.

I stepped out, away from the light, but it continued to flash across my tunic.

'I'm sorry, I was – looking for someone.'

'In here?' The voice was gentle, quite matter-of-fact.
'Are you an ARP warden?'
'No.'
The torchlight swung in a wide arc and I caught a fleeting impression of wild, blurred colours on the walls, then he came towards me, his feet crunching lightly through the mess on the floor.
'Who are you? And who are you looking for?'
'My name's Kit Coryn, and I'm looking for my sister. Someone told me she used to work here, but I'm not sure that I've come to the right place . . . ' I began to edge towards the door.
'This used to be the Bever Club.'
'Yes, I know. But I expect I made a mistake about her working here. I'd better go now . . . '
'Not for a minute,' the man said, and went behind the bar. 'I've got a lamp here. Hang on a second.'
More than inclined to make a dash for it I waited unwillingly while he rummaged about under the bar, then, wiping a space clear with his hand, stood a paraffin lamp in the centre of it. Propping the torch at a convenient angle he took a box of matches from his trouser pocket and lit the narrow wick. It glowed with light, and the man moved away so that he remained in the shadow.
'There, that's better.' He replaced the glass chimney and turned the wick down to a narrow gleam. I sensed rather than saw him smile at me.
'Ever been here before?'
'No. I've only been in London a few months.'
'You're in the FANYs or something, aren't you?'
'The WAAF.' (Amazing how few civilians could get us sorted out. At least, somehow I imagined he was a civilian.)
'And you're looking for your sister?'
'Yes. But I don't think — ' I halted when he bent down behind the bar again and this time came up with a bottle and two glasses. He poured a liberal splash of liquid into each of them and pushed one of them across to me.
'Salut,' he said. 'Nice to be back in business.'
'Yes . . . But honestly, I don't — '
'No, of course not,' he agreed. 'You sort of girls only drink

cocoa. But this is almost as harmless and tastes very much better.'

Doubtfully I raised the glass and took a sip.

'Italian vermouth. The only case that didn't get smashed when the bomb got us. Jesus — ' I saw him run a long pale hand through his shadowy hair, 'will this damn war ever end? Look at this place – just look at it — '

I did as he told me. Against one wall I could now see a table lying with its broken legs in the air, and in the corner a double bass with snapped strings leaned like a helpless old drunk with her corsets unlaced.

'I keep on saying that I'll make a start on it,' he said. 'But what's the point? I can't replace the stock, the customers have vanished, and ever since Sylvia walked out on me — '

'Sylvia?'

'Yes,' he said broodingly. 'My wife.'

The glass rattled against my teeth.

'Where's she gone?'

I saw him hunch his shoulders. 'Search me.'

So once again I'd arrived too late. Once again the Sylvia-bird had flown.

Tracing a line on the bar top with my finger I thought about the repeat pattern of running away, of ducking out. Why did she do it? I'd always thought that it was only immature people who couldn't cope. And Sylvia immature? Good God, no.

'Look,' I said to the man in the shadows. 'Let's start at the beginning. Why didn't you both go to lunch with Aunt Mitty that day? She was expecting you.'

'Aunt who?'

'Aunt Mitty. She's Ma's sister, and Sylvia arranged to take you round to meet her – it was the Sunday the war started — '

'Would you mind telling me once again,' he said very slowly and quietly, 'exactly who you are?'

'I'm Sylvia's sister. Which come to think of it makes you my brother-in-law.'

'Sorry, dear,' he said. 'Sylvia didn't ever have a sister. And even if she had, you're the wrong colour.'

'But — '

'Sylvia was a West Indian,' he said gently.

Neither of us seemed able to think of anything to add after that, so the man finished his drink then trickled some more vermouth into both our glasses.

'Salut.'

'Salut . . . '

I kept thinking that I ought to go. But didn't.

'My father started this place,' he said eventually. 'Back in the early twenties. Mainly theatricals in those days, then it became a flop-house for artists and writers. Some of them made the grade, others didn't. *He* did, of course — '

He picked up the lamp and held it above his head, and the wavering light illuminated the colours I had noticed on the walls and revealed them as human faces. Big, bold and beautiful, they glowed through the dirt with a strange and terrible life of their own.

'Augustus John,' he said, putting the lamp back on the bar. 'Did them all in a wild weekend.'

'You'd never guess from the outside what a famous place this is.'

'Not any more. It's had it, now.'

'You'll rebuild it after the war. And make it even better.'

'No,' he said. 'Everything's gone. Sylvia, the customers, even the need. Nobody needs a place like this any more.'

With a sigh he pulled the two stools down from the top of the bar, wiped the seats with the palm of his hand and then pushed one of them towards me. We sat down, and he refilled our glasses.

'Now,' he said. 'Let's talk about your troubles.'

'Well, it's my sister, really. Her name was Sylvia too, and someone said she used to work here, but it was a long time ago. About 1939.'

'Sylvia . . . What did she look like?'

'She was very beautiful. Blonde, with blue eyes. People said she looked like Alice Faye.'

'Oh, yes,' he said, his face still shadowed. 'I remember her. She was here with another pretty blonde kid called Daphne. Didn't stay long.'

'No,' I said. 'I'm beginning to find out that she never stayed anywhere long.'

'People don't. Girls least of all. They just bite off the bit they fancy and then move on. They all used to join this place when it suited them for whatever purpose they needed it for, then sooner or later they all moved on. There was a time when Jacob Epstein slept on a rush mat behind the bar.'

'I think I've heard of him. But, about Sylvia — '

'Pretty kid,' he said. 'Pleaded with me to give her a job – washing up, sweeping the floors, anything – she said . . . She chummed up with Daphne — '

'Didn't she sing with the band? Sylvia could knock spots off Alice Faye when it came to singing — '

'It wasn't exactly that sort of club, dear. We didn't have a band.'

Didn't have a band? I thought all clubs had a band. At least they did in all the Hollywood films I'd ever seen.

'You don't mean to say she just did the washing up?'

'That, and other things.'

'What other things? And why did she leave? Where did she go?'

'She left,' he said, 'to go and live with Bernie Patch. He was mad about her.'

I took a mouthful of vermouth. 'Who was he?'

'Bernie was a bookie,' he said. 'One of the richest old men in Soho.'

'Old?'

'That's what I said.'

'You also said *was*.'

'Bernie's moved on, too,' he said bitterly. 'Like all the rest.'

I began to get off the stool, then paused. 'When you say went to live with, do you mean like *that*?'

I saw his teeth gleam in a brief smile. 'I never thought to ask. But I don't suppose he took her along as a playmate for the canary.'

'No . . . '

Perched on the edge of the stool I thought about all the beautiful heroines of the films, and about all the beautiful sentiments expressed in the songs everyone was singing back in the WAAF hostel. Love and desire abounded, together with fickleness, jealousy and vengefulness, yes – but all these passions belonged to the young and the beautiful. It was horrible to think of them raging in the breast of a rich old bookie called Bernie Patch. And even more horrible to think of them raging because of my sister Sylvia.

'Funny we're both looking for a girl of the same name,' the man said. 'Could be a sort of omen.'

'Yes. Well, thank you very much . . .'

The dark shadows pressing close against the circle of lamplight were beginning to give me the creeps. I looked at the dark shape of the man's head and it seemed to have no connection with the long pale hands lying limply inert by the bottle of vermouth.

'Don't go,' he said.

'I really must.' I forced a smile. 'They get nasty in the forces if you stay out too late.'

One of the hands moved across the bar towards my sleeve. I tried to remember how far it was to the door, but I didn't want to run for it unless I had to.

'Don't go,' he repeated. 'You've no idea what it's like, all alone.'

'Please — '

'Listen,' urgently he shook my sleeve, 'listen, I'll help you to find your sister first thing tomorrow, but stay here now. Have another drink — ' He splashed more vermouth into my glass. 'But don't go. I just can't stand the nights, not since the bloody bomb. Salut!'

Refilling his own glass he raised it in my direction, then took a gulp.

'The bomb's to blame for everything. It ruined the club, it ruined my marriage and now it's ruined me.'

'It'll all come right,' I said, edging away. 'Believe me.'

But he continued to hold my sleeve. 'This won't come right,' he said, and moved for the first time into the pool of light.

The blood seemed to drain out of me. I couldn't speak. All I could do was stare at his face.

'The bomb was responsible for this, too.'

The livid scar that ran diagonally from temple to chin had shifted his right eye down on to his cheek, where it lay embedded like a small glittering stone in the puffy morass of distorted flesh. There were other things too, but sick with revulsion and shock I wrenched my arm away and ran blindly for what I hoped was the door. I heard my stool fall over with a crash.

Rushing down the steps I cannoned violently into someone standing under the Bever Club sign. Too dazed to apologise I blundered on, only intent on putting as much distance between me and the terrible shadows of Denman Court as was humanly possible.

Round the corner of Frith Street was a milkbar and I rushed inside and collapsed at one of the tables. And while a juke box pounded out a boogie beat, put my hand over my eyes and tried to blot out the picture of the man's face. It was the first time I had seen at close quarters the effect of a bomb splinter on human flesh, and I was choked with horror and pity and guilt at my own squeamishness.

'Well, well,' said a familiar voice close against my ear. 'You look as if you'd better borrow it back again.'

And for the second time I found myself crying into the squadron leader's handkerchief.

5

We walked back to ACRC together, and, because we suddenly discovered that we'd got a lot to talk about, took the long way up Portland Place to the Park and then went along the Broad Walk until we turned off to look at Chester Terrace standing white and aloof in the late May darkness.

'This place almost makes me believe that houses have feelings,' I said.

He stood looking up at the classical pillars, at the blind windows and the beautiful dignity-in-death look.

'I've done this to houses, too. I've bombed Hamburg.'

'What was it like?'

'A question of concentrating on getting there and back, I suppose. I didn't think much about the people on the ground. I didn't dare.'

'Do you think our grandchildren will learn to hate our generation for all the destruction we've caused?'

'Not if we build it up again. We've got to rebuild, and make it better than it was before.'

'That's what I told the man in the Bever Club, but he didn't seem to have much heart . . . '

'Not surprising . . . '

We walked on, holding hands, and neither did it seem surprising that he should have guessed I was going to try and find the Bever Club, and that he should be waiting outside for me.

And as long as I live I'll never forget that walk through the sleeping Park with only the restless searchlights to keep watch. The air smelt of rich growing grass, and when we sat down by the lake a pair of swans glided out like two stately ghost-ships, stared at us for a moment and then melted silently away again.

We kissed, and the warm closeness of him filled me with a wild happiness so that I didn't give a damn for the war or the WAAF or the poor disfigured chap in the Bever Club, or even Sylvia. Because I'd never held and kissed and loved anyone I loved before, and I just couldn't get over it. I'd often heard other girls say that the first time was rotten, but it wasn't; it was happy and gentle and loving. Loving in every sense of the word.

'It's the first time I've ever done this with a woman in a collar and tie.'

'And I'm wearing Maze's back collar stud.'

'Who's Maze? And what's he or she wearing in the meantime?'

'She's an MT driver and it's her day off.'

'Where's yours?'

'Where's my what?'

'Back collar stud.'

'I lost it down a crack in between the floorboards.'

He rolled away from me and lay frowning. 'As a senior officer I'm afraid that it's my duty to report this frivolous disposal of Air Force property to the appropriate quarter. To – what's her name? – Flight Sergeant Butter — '

'Cutter — '

'Stop giggling, you'll wake her up — '

'I can't, I've got a pain . . . ' he bent over me and I reached up and put my arms round his neck and for the life of me I honestly couldn't get over the sudden amazing wonder of being in love and close to him.

I got back to the WAAF hostel with four minutes to spare.

'See you for lunch tomorrow, Kit?'

'Yes, please. But if I can't get a pass, where can I phone you?'

He gave me a number in Victoria. 'I'm staying in my brother's flat while he's away.'

'I didn't know you had a brother.'

'He's in Burma.'

'There's still so much to learn about you. What's his name?'

'Martin.'
'David and Martin — '
'Go on in, or they'll clang you for being late — '
'Yes, okay. Good-night . . . '
I opened the guardroom door, then closed it again when I felt him touch my shoulder.
'When you talked about our grandchildren a while back, were you visualising just the one set between us?'
'Of course not. I was just speaking figuratively.'
'Of course,' he said, and walked away laughing.

And now, six years afterwards, I'm sitting here in this hotel, thinking about him. Seeing him in the check shirt and cravat, with the lock of hair falling across his forehead. I've still got the little brooch in the shape of an RAF pilot's wings that he gave me . . .

The place is very quiet now. I haven't heard footsteps padding along the corridor for ages. The last of the coffee's gone cold and I suppose that I ought to go to bed. But I can't. Writing all this down has brought the past so close that I can't shake it off, and I feel nervy and on edge at the prospect of seeing Sylvia tomorrow.

So I get up and prowl round the room. Light a cigarette and switch on the built-in radio, which makes me jump with a sudden salvo of Wagner. So I switch it off again, and there's nothing for it but to sit down and take another sheet of writing paper . . . The time is 12.30 a.m.

Three days of leave he had, and we spent as much of it together as possible.

I remember asking Flight Sergeant Cutter if I could have a twenty-four hours' emergency pass, and, when she asked what the emergency was, felt like telling her that I'd fallen in love. After all she was engaged, and presumably in the same state, but faced by her cool and impeccable NCO beauty the words died.

'Trouble at home?' she demanded.
'Well no, Flight. Not exactly.'
'In that case, it can wait,' she said crisply. Then added that she had applied for a runner to be added to the admin.

section, which would mean that I'd be saved the bind of taking the ration strength over to the catering officer every day, as well as other chores of a similar nature.

I thanked her, but privately thought it was a pity. I'd never found walks through Regent's Park a bind.

On the third and final day, David and I had lunch together in Gulliver's. He was back in uniform, ready for the afternoon train back to Waterbeach in Cambridgeshire.

'Shall I write to you?'

'Please.'

'I've forgotten your surname.'

'Magnus.'

'Mine's Coryn.'

'Kit Coryn, 2010057. Yes, I know.'

I walked back to Baker Street tube station with him and we stood by the top of the escalator, constrained and ill at ease.

'Take great care,' I said.

'You, too.'

'No problem for me. I don't run the risks you do.'

'Oh, I don't know. Flight Sergeant Cutter might run you down with her bicycle.'

I giggled, and half choked.

'Look at me, Kit.'

'I can't. We've both got our hats on, and I'll have to salute.'

'Well, take the bloody thing off.'

'I can't. It's not allowed in public places . . .

'Good-bye, my funny darling.'

I made a convulsive grab at his hand and touched my cheek with it.

'Good-bye, David,' I said, and walked quickly and blindly away.

I told Maze about him that night over mugs of tea in the NAAFI.

'I mean, it's not all that serious, it's just that he's nice to be with. You understand what I mean, don't you?'

'Yeah,' said Maze, whose brisk Cockney was becoming laced these days with an American drawl.

I asked her how Sam Corbellini was, and she said fine. But going away soon, by the sound of it.

'They're all going,' I said despondently. 'Everyone says the invasion's due any day.'

'We're going dancing tonight,' she said suddenly. 'So why don't you come?'

I began to make excuses, then remembered that she'd asked me before.

'Come on, mate,' she said. 'Rainbow Corner, seven thirty sharp, and I'll introduce you to him.

'Sounds great.' And I meant it. Because if I couldn't be with David, being with a friend who was in love struck me as the next best thing.

Accordingly we set off for Piccadilly, Maze's alert ferret-face liberally coated in rouge, lipstick and eye-shadow. Sitting next to her on the bus I noticed admiringly that each eyelash had been separated from its neighbour by an application of mascara which ended in a little black ball at the tip.

'He's a right smasher,' she kept saying. 'You'll like him, because he's a right smasher.'

I remembered her telling me that he was like Robert Taylor, only better, and then fell to wondering who David was like. He wasn't really like anyone; he was just David.

Rainbow Corner was in Piccadilly Circus, close to Shaftesbury Avenue. It was the big voluntary club run for all the American servicemen who found themselves in London, and even the pavement outside used to teem with them at all hours of the day and night.

We elbowed our way in, and I couldn't believe it when a short fat chap in tight khaki pants waddled over to us and seized Maze in a crushing embrace.

'Hi, kid!'

'Wotcher, cocker . . . '

Maze introduced me as her mate, and Corporal Corbellini pumped my hand up and down and said he was very, very glad to have me know him.

We went through to the bar where the spirits were plentiful and the company lively. I'd never been in close proximity to a lot of Americans before, and it was interesting what a different sort of atmosphere they seemed to engender. Men of lowly rank who smoke cigars and drink Scotch on the rocks are not easily quelled by the presence of senior NCOs, and there was an easy camaraderie among them that a lot of outsiders envied, and consequently often denigrated. With their crew cuts, their superior uniforms and unending cash they all had a breath of Hollywood about them, although I learned during the course of the evening that a lot of them had rather idealised views of us, too.

'We love all you little people,' Sam said to me very earnestly. 'You're not just walking history books with your kings and queens, you're real, solid little people taking it on the chin . . . '

He had a twinkly, pudgy face and tight curly hair, and he was far from my idea of what Robert Taylor looked like, but who wants a film star's understudy anyway? Still, I understood Maze's proud urge to compare him with one of the gods from the film world, because, as I think I said before, pretty well all our standards were set by Hollywood.

We became involved with a crowd of Sam's buddies, and one of them, a gum-chewing sergeant, taught me to jive.

'C'mon, baby,' he kept saying, snapping his fingers, 'give – *give* — '

Torn between giggles and a grim determination to master it (like square-bashing), I eventually managed to follow his gyrations and we spun round the floor like a couple of frenzied tops. The beat of the music began to get into my blood and I wanted to get lost in it like all the others around me, but I couldn't. Not completely. All the time and in all the heat and frantic pounding noise there was a joyless part of me standing outside and seeing it as the mounting climax to the tribal dance that ends in sacrifice. Maze and Sam, my gum-chewing sergeant and all the other bobbing and bouncing, shuffling and stamping kids in uniform were dancing themselves into a state of readiness for the blood-letting that we all knew would come with the invasion of Europe.

I wondered whether, on the other side of the Channel, the Germans were dancing too.

Fatigued, footsore and full of hot dogs, Maze and I pooled our resources and took a taxi back to the hostel.

'Like him, did you?'

'Smashing, Maze. He's absolutely smashing.'

'Yeah,' she said. 'But he's on embarkation leave.'

'I know. He told me.'
'Oh, Gawd . . . ' Suddenly she put her hand over her eyes.
'He'll be all right. Honestly, Maze.'
She didn't answer, but sat staring out of the window at the dim lights of Baker Street. We passed Lofty's coffee stall.
'All them bloody countries they've got to get through before the war's over.'
'It mightn't take all that long. It didn't take Hitler long to invade them in the first place.'
'Didn't it?' she said listlessly. 'It's so long ago, you forget.'
Trying to coax her thoughts away from the future, I asked what her family thought of Sam. 'I bet they like him, don't they? Even though it does mean that you'll be going to America — '
'Shuddup!' She bawled it with a force that took me by surprise. 'Shuddup about my blinkin' family, can't you?'
'Okay, okay – I didn't mean — '
'Well then, lay *orf!'* When the taxi stopped outside the hostel she threw a two shilling piece into my lap and scrambled out.
When I got up to flat 10 room 4 she was just coming out of the bathroom, her face drained and exhausted beneath the smears of imperfectly removed make-up. I waited for her to make some reference to the outburst in the taxi, but she didn't. So we went to bed in silence, and although I was dead tired it was a long time before I could get to sleep.
On the following evening she came and sat next to me in the cookhouse. It was bangers and mash, and the place was half empty.
''Lo, mate.'
'Wotcher, Maze.'
'Doing anything tonight?'
'I'm on fire picket.'
'Oh.' She dug a pattern in the potato with her fork. 'He's gorn.'
'Sam?'
'Yeah.'
'Rotten, isn't it?'
'Yeah. All his lot's gorn.'
We ate in silence. There didn't seem much worth saying.

'Heard from yours?'
'Yes. Got a letter this morning.'
'Okay, is he?'
'Yes,' I said. 'He seems okay.'
We went on eating, then Maze put down her knife and fork. 'What about tomorrow night?'
'Go out somewhere, you mean?'
'Yeah. Thought you might like to come down my home.'
'Maze,' I said. 'I'd love to. Really love to. And look, I'm sorry I upset you last night — '
'For Christ's sake don't start going on,' she said. 'I just can't stick people always going on . . . '
And then suddenly the weather changed. The sky turned leaden grey and a cold wind rocked the trees in the Park. It might have been autumn instead of early June.
Maze and I set off as planned, and I was looking forward to meeting her family. I'd already pictured them as a happy, unruly brood spilling out of a little terraced house like the ones in Bethnal Green, and had given my shoes and uniform buttons an extra polish in their honour.
'Where are we going, Maze?'
'Silvertown.'
'Sounds nice.'
She glanced at me without speaking. In fact she didn't seem to want to talk at all, and I began to wonder if I was right about her family being happy and all that. Perhaps she'd brought me down here to show me how unpleasant they all were. The idea made me grin.
When we walked out of the station, the grin faded.
'This is Silvertown,' Maze said, and we stood there, two blue figures against a flat expanse of nothing. No houses, no shops, not so much as a lamp post for a stray dog. I couldn't even tell where the streets had been.
Shocked and appalled I stood in the cold drizzle and tried to take it all in. After three months in London I thought I was fairly conversant with the blitz-look, but this was a scene I found difficult to digest. There's nothing harder to grasp than a lot of sheer nothingness.
I turned to Maze, then saw that she had started picking her way across the grey wasteland. She looked small and

obdurate, and I wasn't sure whether or not she meant me to follow. In the end I did, keeping some distance behind as I slipped over loose bricks and skirted round puddles. I stepped over a man's shoe that lay like a small mute protest on the remains of a tiled floor.

She stood waiting for me by a clump of willowherb.

'Come in,' she said. 'Make yourself at home.'

'Oh, Maze . . . '

'The front door was here. And just on the right, about where you're standing, was the front room where we had the pianna and everything nice. In the winter we always had a fire in there on Sundays or if anyone special come. Then further down the passage was the stairs, and the kitchen was at the end, about *here* — '

'I see.' I followed her pointing finger.

'The scullery door was about *there,* and we had a bit of garden out the back where Dad used to keep his racing pigeons. He was a docker, a huge great man, my dad, and he used to get drunk as a lord Saturday nights. But he never raised his hand to any one of us – never. Mum used to call him Ole Sloppy. There was six of us and I was eldest. Then Edie and Lil, then Fred, then Charlie, and then little Greta. Mum fancied calling her Greta after Greta Garbo . . . '

'Go on, Maze.'

'What's the use?' She stood looking at the grey rubbly dust that was turning darker in the relentless drizzle. I stood looking at it too, and began to see the outline of the rooms.

'Wasn't very big, was it?' she said.

'Big enough.'

'Yeah, we all packed in. Stone me, you should have seen Christmas here . . . anything up to twenty-seven of us and Mum boiling a dirty great lump of beef in the copper. Well you see, me Uncle Charlie worked over in Smithfield and he could get a bit orf and we all used to club together.'

'It must have been smashing.'

'Yeah,' she said. 'It's funny how you forget all the rotten parts like chilblains and measles and the times Dad got laid off work.'

We began to walk back through what had been the kitchen and the passage until we reached the spot where Maze had judged the front door to have been. She bent and picked up a bit of plaster, no bigger than a pebble.

'Mum an' Dad's bedroom wallpaper. But you can't really judge it when it's wet.'

I think that if it had been me I'd have put it in my pocket as a keepsake, but Maze didn't. I watched her hurl it at a tin can balanced on a couple of broken bricks. We walked on, heedless of the rain and the dank summer mist curling up from the river.

'Me ole gran lived somewhere about here,' she said, pausing to get her bearings. 'And just round the corner from her was me Auntie Doris and Uncle Jim. It was me Uncle Jim who taught me how to drive a van . . . '

'Did he used to come for Christmas too?'

'Gawd, yes. Auntie Doris used to play the pianna. Never had a lesson in her life but she was smashing at it – everybody used to dance and then Dad used to put Mum's hat on and sing 'Ain't She Sweet?' and all us kids ate jelly and mince pie until we nearly busted . . . '

We walked round in a huge square, Maze every now and then doing a sharp left or right as she turned down the invisible remains of a once familiar street. She showed me the corner shop, her dad's pub, her old school and the little houses where all her mates had lived. And all you could see was grey rubble, sticky with rain. There didn't even seem to be any ghosts.

We reached the station, and she paused to look back for a moment.

'They all copped it,' she said. 'Every bleedin' one.'

I tried to smile at her, but it didn't work. 'At least, you've got Sam, haven't you?'

'Yeah,' she said. 'But how long for?'

And I was woken before first light by the drone of aircraft.

Listening and blinking away the clouds of sleep, it gradually dawned on me that the sound was different from that of ordinary flights of bombers on their way to Germany. The drone increased to a deep and menacing roar that shook the building as wave after wave, squadron after squadron, passed over. I sat up, and saw the pale shape of Maze crouching on the foot of her bed and staring out of the window.

'It's started,' she said.

'What's the time?'

'Dunno. Around four, I think.'

I huddled next to her, and beneath the thunder of planes caught the sound of voices and banging doors as the hostel came to life. The girls from the next room came in and joined us on Maze's bed. One of them, an orderly room clerk, produced the remains of a bottle of gin and we drank it with tepid water from the bathroom tap.

We drank to the invasion.

'Here's to Sam,' I whispered to Maze.

'Here's to yours too. You reckon he's up in that lot?'

'Yes,' I said, and shutting my eyes gulped down the remains of my gin. It tasted awful.

Nobody went back to bed, and I don't think there was much work done during the course of the day which followed. Coffee and tea breaks stretched to unprecedented lengths as everyone hung over the NAAFI radio, and when the first reports of the Normandy landings began to come through everyone started cheering and singing 'Roll Out the Barrel'. And when we got back to the WAAF cookhouse for supper we all had two fried eggs each, an unheard-of bonanza which we took as a sign of the catering officer's belief in imminent victory.

The only sour note was struck by Squadron Officer Gilby, who paused in her writing as a flight of aircraft passed overhead and asked whether I thought French civilians would find Allied bombing any less painful than that of the Germans.

'I don't know, ma'am.' Quite honestly the thought had never occurred to me.

I began to say something to the effect that they probably understood that it was a necessary evil, then shut up. Her clever, sombre face didn't encourage discussion, even though she'd started it in the first place.

So life returned to normal, except for a palpable undercurrent of anxiety that was inevitable with so many young women waiting in close proximity for news of husbands and boyfriends in France. Almost everyone now seemed to have a personal reason for following the war news with breathless attention, and the WAAF hostel rang even more poignantly with songs of frustrated passion and promises of everlasting faithfulness. One girl swore that she was going to devote every evening to reading something dead boring like Shakespeare until her chap came back, although what good she thought it would do him I couldn't work out.

But of course there was no longer the same incentive to jazz it up in the West End, anyway; as if by magic the streets had been emptied of all the young, lively men in uniform. All that were left were the young aircrew cadets – and to jaundiced WAAF eyes they looked callow beyond all hope – and the older, officebound men whose idea of fun was listening to ITMA.

London appeared dull, listless and shabby, and when I received my annual allowance of ten clothing coupons there was nothing in the shops worth spending them on. Their official function was for the purchase of pocket handkerchiefs, but sometimes I dreamed of going to meet David in a smashing civvy outfit all frills and bows and a hat with a veil – in other words, something as different from Air Force uniform as it was possible to imagine. (Maze, who had now cheered up again, said that she was going to marry Sam wearing a crinoline made out of white lace curtains something like the one Lana Turner had on at the Swiss Cottage Odeon last week, only of course hers wasn't made out of white lace curtains . . .)

And so we worked and planned and dreamed and sang songs pierced with love and longing while we waited for the war to end.

I got a letter from David, a couple of paragraphs hastily scribbled that didn't tell me much, yet somehow they brought him close. And the postmark was still Cambridgeshire, which was a relief.

As for Sylvia, she was in abeyance until the night I went to see Aunt Mitty again.

I found her gluing sequins on a pink felt hat.

'Deauville, 1928,' she said, twirling it round on her fist. 'I bought it when Edgar was playing in the band at the casino.'

I said it was very nice.

'A teeny bit past it,' she replied, 'rather like its owner. But there's no point in not *trying* any more, is there, darling?'

She put it on, cramming its cloche-shape down low over her forehead and the two kiss-curls which adorned her cheeks. Its brave raffishness contrasted oddly with her cotton kimono.

'You look wizard, Aunt Mitty. Why don't we go out somewhere?'

'What a ripping idea,' she said. 'We'll go and see if they've got any beer at the Eagle.'

I'd no idea she'd take me seriously, but after replacing the lid on the pot of glue she pronounced herself ready, and there was nothing for it but to accompany her across the road towards Clifton Gardens. But no one seemed to notice her get-up, and I've since learned that Maida Vale has had a reputation for eccentricity for years.

Perched provocatively on a high bar stool she asked me about Sylvia and, a little tight-lipped, I told her about the search that had culminated, for the time being at any rate, at the Bever Club in Soho. She'd heard of it.

She'd also heard of Bernie Patch.

'A famous firm, and highly reputable,' she said. 'I've had the odd Derby flutter with them myself.'

'Do you think it's any use going there?'

'To look for Sylvia? Well, you'd better be careful, darling. After all, it's all rather *personal*, isn't it?'

I agreed, then lapsed into silence.

'Does the idea of Sylvia and a rich old man shock you?'

'Well, not shocks, so much as — '

'Disillusions?'

'I don't know. In some ways I've been trying not to think about it because I suppose I've always seen Sylvia as some sort of heroine and all that, which isn't surprising when you remember her. And I can't help thinking what a stupid waste – supposing it's true, that is — '

'Oh, come off it,' said Aunt Mitty. 'There are some adorable rich old men.'

'And some very nice young ones, who'd give their eye teeth

for a girl like Sylvia.'

'I daresay, and far be it from me to belittle them. But on the other hand I can't see that being old is all that reprehensible.'

I began to say no, not so long as they confined themselves to people of their own age group, then stopped: Aunt Mitty in her sequined cloche and cotton kimono was old, but it didn't stop her flicking appreciative glances at the young Auxiliary Fire Service chap who was sipping watery beer further down the counter.

As she had just said, *There's no point in not trying any more, is there?*

We went back to her room for a cup of coffee and discovered that the kittens had upset the box of sequins all over the floor. I began picking them up one by one.

'In any case,' went on Aunt Mitty, carrying on the conversation from where we'd left off, 'where does Mr Bernie Patch come in relation to the fiancé she was bringing here to lunch on the day war started?'

'I don't know. I thought at first that the man in the Bever Club was the chap she was engaged to, but he wasn't. So presumably she'd packed Bernie Patch in before the Sunday she was due to have lunch with you. I mean, *Bernie* couldn't have been the fiancé, could he?'

'I must say she gave the impression that she was engaged to someone young. What an idiot she was, not to tell his name.'

'She said she wanted it to be a surprise.'

'Or perhaps she was afraid it would be a horrible shock . . . '

'Which brings us back to Bernie Patch.' I put the lid back on the box of sequins. 'I think I'll have a go and see him. He mightn't be too bad, and anyway I can't stop now, can I?'

'Darling Kit,' she looked at me with concern, 'are you absolutely sure that you want to find Sylvia? Are you quite, quite certain it's wise?'

'Meaning?'

'Meaning,' she said, pouring out more coffee, 'that Sylvia may prefer things to remain as they are. After all, it's a very simple matter for her to get in touch with you at Barnard Castle, isn't it?'

That was what the police sergeant had said.

'But supposing she can't? Supposing she's in some sort of trouble — '

'Supposing,' said Aunt Mitty very quietly, 'that she's dead.'

'You said that before. If she was, surely Ma and Pa would have been — '

'Not necessarily. There were hundreds of unidentified casualties during the blitz.'

I picked up one of the kittens, now almost teenager size, and stroked it hard. 'I don't believe she's dead. And what's more, I don't believe she ever got mixed up with a crummy old bookie — '

'You're quite determined to find out?'

'Yes.'

'Then God go with you,' she said simply.

I'd come with the intention of telling her about David, but when it came to it I didn't. However gentle and loving they were, old people always seemed to have this uncomfortable streak of cynicism. I left soon after, Aunt Mitty embracing me fondly and asking whether I could get her some foundation cream from the NAAFI. She'd heard that practically all available make-up was being distributed to the women's services, and quite right too, darling – but if there was by any chance a tiny modicum over, perhaps she might . . .

'Of course,' I said. 'What sort?'

And she looked me dead in the eye and said: 'Well actually, darling, it's called Bloom of Youth . . . '

Standing at the top of the steps to wave good-bye she looked small and frail and ludicrous in her kimono and old pink hat, only I hadn't got the heart to scoff at her. Maybe there's something in the 'While there's life there's hope' philosophy.

On the way back to ACRC I thought it over, and came to the conclusion that I subscribed to it so far as Sylvia was concerned. I didn't really believe that she'd got herself involved with an elderly bookie, but there was a faint chance that he might know where she was. It was up to me to find out.

Walking down Baker Street I stopped at Lofty's stall and the memory of Sylvia was going round in my head like one of the haunting tunes that everyone was singing back at the WAAF hostel.

'Do you know a film star called Alice Faye?' I asked him. And when he said yes, told him that she was the spitting image of my sister.

'Get away?' He leaned his arms on the counter. 'So what are we waiting for? Why don't you bring her round?'

'I will,' I said. 'Any time now.'

When I got back to flat 10 room 4 it was to find that Maze and I had got a new room-mate. She was already asleep, a large alien hump in the bed that had been untenanted for so long. I couldn't see her face.

'Dunno her name,' Maze said in a low voice, 'but she's left her washing dripping all over the bathroom. It's like a blinkin' monsoon in there.'

I went to investigate, and sure enough there were pools of water beneath each garment that sagged from the improvised clothes line stretching from door to window. A drip from the toe of a stocking splashed down the back of my neck as I stood there.

'Blooming sauce,' Maze said hoarsely, 'coming in here and taking over.'

'What's she like?' I asked curiously.

'Big.'

'What else?'

'Nothing else,' said Maze. 'Just big.'

In order to prevent a flood we decided to wake her up and tell her to wring her wretched washing out properly, then came to the conclusion that it would be a bit rotten with her being a new arrival and probably tired and strange and all that.

'So who's going to do it?'

'Who d'you think?' demanded Maze.

So we squeezed the water out of the new arrival's washing, and mopped the floor. Going back into room 4 in the dark Maze fell headlong over the kitbag that had been left sprawling by the door.

'I've got a feeling that I'm not going to like her all that

much. Christ, I haven't half bashed my leg . . . '

When we both got up on the following morning she was still buried beneath the mound of grey blankets.

'*Wakey-wakey!*' roared Maze, shaking her.

The lump groaned, altered its position and then lay motionless again. We called her and shook her, and just as we decided to leave her to it she gave a deep moan and precipitated herself on to the floor, where she stood blinking and gasping like a landed trout.

'Breakfast's from seven to seven thirty,' Maze said.

'Oh God,' said the newcomer confusedly. 'Where do I go?'

We told her the way to the cookhouse, and left her. I had a vague impression of a large and ponderously built girl with a mane of dark hair, and it took me a minute or two to recognise her when she appeared in the WAAF admin. office later and said apologetically: 'I'm awfully sorry to bother you, but I think I'm the new runner.'

'No bother at all,' I said. 'How fast can you run?'

'No more than poor average or I get a stitch,' she replied, taking me seriously.

From the corner of my eye I saw Flight Sergeant Cutter transfer her attention from the fire picket roster to us, so I reached for the appropriate form which when completed and attached to a few more bits of paper would permit the new runner's name to be added to the holy ration strength.

'Name?'

'Florence Hambledon-ffoulks,' she said in the same gently apologetic voice, 'but most people call me Flo.'

We went through all the usual rigmarole of questions, and when we got to the final bit about hobbies and recreation she confessed rather dejectedly that she wasn't much good at doing anything. Mummy and Daddy had always said that she was a frightful mutt.

'But you must be able to do something,' observed Flight. 'Whether you're a howling success at it or not, doesn't matter so long as you're keen.'

Flo thought for a moment, then tentatively admitted that she liked doing microscopy.

'Doing what?' demanded Flight suspiciously.

'Dissecting insects,' mumbled Flo. Then, seeing Flight's

expression, added: 'Mainly freshwater life.'

'We could do with some more volunteers for the hockey team,' Flight said. 'Strikes me as a healthier way of spending your free time than chopping up tadpoles.'

Flo studied the unpolished toes of her shoes, so Flight gave her a pile of folders to take down to the orderly room.

'The sooner you start finding your way round the better. If you want to know anything, ask Coryn here. She's supposed to have all the gen, although sometimes I wonder.'

'Thank you very much indeed,' said Flo humbly, and blundered out of the office.

'Heavenly days,' said Flight, staring after her. 'Whatever sort of stagnant pond did she creep out of?'

'A fairly high-class one, by the sound of her name.'

'High-class or not,' snorted Flight, 'I'm putting it down for Friday the 16th. Now I've finished the list you can type it out.'

It's funny when I look back and remember that I nearly asked Flight Sergeant Cutter if she saw any prospect of the fire-watching chore being abolished. After all, the war would soon be over now that the Allies were sweeping through France, and we hadn't had an alert in London for weeks . . .

I wanted to ask her, but didn't. And so we sailed quietly towards the terror that was due to begin on the night of the 16th of June, 1944. The night that poor Flo was on fire picket.

6

It's 3 a.m. and the hotel's silent as the grave. Even the traffic outside seems to have stopped, so that when I hear the distant scream of a siren it makes my nerves twitch uneasily. I don't know whether it's an ambulance or a fire engine, but either one of them spells trouble for someone.

And the chill banshee wailing takes me back to the night when the flying bombs started . . .

Everyone grumbled furiously at being woken up, and Maze and I tagged sourly on to the crowd of airwomen heading for the blitz bunks. They were nasty claustrophobic places, dusty and dingy, with reinforced walls and blocked-up windows. The only furnishing was rows of two-tier bunks without mattresses.

'No hope of trying to kip,' Maze said. 'The all-clear'll go any minute.'

So we sat down on one of the bottom bunks and waited. And waited.

After an hour had passed I said I wondered how Flo Hambledon-ffoulks was getting on up on the roof with the rest of the fire picket. Maze said she didn't know, but trust her to cop the first air raid for weeks. We dozed, Maze settling her tin hat more comfortably over her curlers.

Next time I opened my eyes I noticed that quite a few bunks were now deserted. I nudged Maze.

'A lot of them are going back to bed . . . '

'Yeah.'

'Shall we?'

'Give it another five minutes. The all-clear's bound to go.'

It was strictly forbidden to remain in the flats during an air raid, and I agreed that having waited for so long it wasn't worth risking a charge when the alert was due to end any minute now. So we waited, dozing fitfully and cursing the discomfort.

At six o'clock we were roused by the sound of a single aircraft passing overhead.

'Sounds a bit shot up,' Maze commented, and shoved her hands up the sleeves of her greatcoat. 'Gawd, it's perishing cold in here.'

'Listen,' I said. 'Where's it gone?'

We sat motionless, and sure enough the irregular stuttering roar of the plane had suddenly vanished. Puzzled and a bit disquieted, we waited, and the silence was broken by the sound of an explosion which rocked the building.

'Told you it sounded shot up,' Maze said. 'It's crashed.'

I wondered if it was one of ours or one of theirs. The thought of David's life being extinguished in a dull crump like that was depressing.

At half past six we decided to chance it and go back to flat 10. As luck would have it we met Flight Sergeant Cutter, impeccable in slacks and tunic, at the door.

'It's been decided that all personnel should proceed as usual,' she said, 'even though the all-clear hasn't sounded. Breakfast will be served in half an hour.'

'Yes, Flight.'

'Oh, and Coryn — ' she said, 'I take it you weren't thinking of leaving the blitz bunk without permission?'

'No, Flight,' I said. 'No, of course not.'

I greatly disliked her brand of unflagging discipline, but had to admit that she was the only female on the station who could look terrific in a tin hat.

We met Flo in the cookhouse. She had just come off fire picket and looked tired and harassed.

'I saw it quite distinctly,' she said. 'It was on fire at the tailend and it suddenly nose-dived. The poor man who was in it didn't stand a chance.'

'Was it one of ours or one of theirs?'

'I don't know,' she said. 'I can only tell Spitfires and Hurricanes. And only then when they're on the ground.'

Poor old Flo. Christened Florence because she had been born there (Daddy at that time being first secretary to the British Ambassador in Rome), her exalted background had no more fitted her for high places in the WAAF than consorting with diplomats had taught her how to cope with the likes of Flight Sergeant Cutter. Dim, dreamy and eternally disorganised, she had a sort of hopeless charm that made people like her even as her chronic inefficiency drove them beyond endurance.

She was, as I've said, a large girl, with a heavy slablike body that resisted all attempts to keep it tidy. In uniform it looked like a sagging bolster, and her patent inability to master the rudiments of square-bashing only made it the more conspicuous: when everyone else turned right, poor large old Flo was bound to turn left and go trudging off in the opposite direction.

Nagged by her parents into applying for a commission she had failed three selection boards, and gently defied all attempts to train her as either a clerk or a medical orderly or a waitress in the officers' mess. By the time she reached ACRC she had come thankfully to rest in what was generally acknowledged to be the humblest job of all; that of a station runner.

'I couldn't tell what sort of a plane it was,' Flo was saying, 'but I rather wondered if it wasn't Japanese.'

'Japanese?' repeated Maze. 'How'd you think a blinking Japanese plane would get over here?'

'I don't know,' confessed Flo doubtfully. 'I suppose I thought it would fly.'

Shortly after that the all-clear sounded.

But the siren went again as I emerged that evening from the Underground at Swiss Cottage, on course for a meeting with Mrs Bernie Patch.

At least, I hoped it would turn out to be Mrs Patch; a telephone call to the book-maker's office had resulted in a man's voice telling me rather sniffily that Mr Patch had passed away some five years ago, and when I asked whether Mrs Patch was still around he told me even more sniffily that he believed she lived in Swiss Cottage. And consultation with the phone book having revealed that there was only one Patch living in Swiss Cottage, it seemed worth taking a chance on it being Bernie's widow.

At first I was going to phone her too, then changed my mind. The matter that I wanted to discuss was delicate to say the least, and it seemed to me discourteous to use such an impersonal medium.

During the course of the last few days I had become convinced that Sylvia hadn't been Bernie's girlfriend in the accepted sense of the word. She had merely been a sort of friend of the family. But on the other hand I was willing to entertain the idea that in the event of Mrs Bernie Patch dying, Sylvia might – in the most romantic and decorous way possible – have become his second wife. As Aunt Mitty had said, there were some adorable rich old men.

Still, I tried not to get excited, or even to consider that there might be a serious possibility of Sylvia opening the door to me, and it was in this frame of mind that I came out of Swiss Cottage Underground and heard the siren wailing again.

No one took much notice until the strange stuttering roar made everyone look up, and there it was, this small stumpy black plane with flames coming out of its backside.

'It's on fire!' I heard someone shout, and we watched it pass over the rooftops. Seconds later the noise of its engine stopped abruptly and the waiting silence was shattered by a loud explosion. Glass tinkled from shop windows.

And the horror was in not knowing what it was.

I saw people drawing together in small groups, and the man selling evening papers asked me if it was ours or theirs. I had to admit that I didn't know, whereupon he cast a withering look at my Air Force uniform and turned away.

Squaring my shoulders I marched after him, tapped him on the back and asked if he knew where Winstanley Mansions were.

'In Winstanley Road.'

'Can you direct me to it?'

He jerked his thumb over his shoulder, and with that I had to be content. And as ambulance and fire engine bells clanged in the distance found my way to the expansive, expensive mock-Tudor mansion flat tenanted, with a bit of luck, by the widow of Bernie Patch. Who, with a bit more luck, might turn out to be my sister Sylvia.

There was thick carpet everywhere, and the front door bell of number 34 was embedded in a brass horse shoe. I stood there for a few minutes before summoning the courage to ring it.

But it wasn't Sylvia who opened the door, it was a pink blancmange-like woman in a gold turban who seized my hand and said: 'Oh God, have they sent you about that terrible explosion just now? It's the third today and I've sat up all night in the cellar without a wink of sleep and the all-clear didn't go until eight o'clock this morning, and now *this!*'

Still holding my hand she swept me through the hall, where my dazed eyes registered a suit of armour, and into a huge and luscious room where mock-Tudor flim-flammery fought strenuously with tributes to the Horse. There were paintings of horses, statues of horses, ashtrays made out of their hooves and rugs made out of their hides. And over the mock-Tudor fireplace hung an enormous painting of a bald baby of a man whom I took to be the late Bernie Patch.

'Look at this — ' ordered the woman, and swept me over to the window where one of the diamond panes had fallen out on to the thick, thick carpet. 'This happened just now in the explosion. What was it? I mean, the general public don't mind putting up with things so long as they know what's going *on!*' She picked up a silver box and offered me a cigarette.

'No, thank you. I don't generally — '

But without waiting she put the open box down by my side then hurried across the room to a glittering cocktail cabinet.

I cleared my throat. 'I'm sorry to trouble you, but — '

'I mean, we all thought the war was all over bar the shouting, and now *this*. I think it's absolutely disgraceful — ' I heard the clink of ice, the swish of a soda syphon. She came back and placed a glass in my hand.

'Sit down,' she said.

I did so. And so we came face to face, Mrs Bernie Patch and I.

Sitting in the overstuffed chair opposite me I saw a plump

overstuffed lady wearing a gold turban surmounting a tight black dress (so plain that it must have cost the earth), the whole lot, including diamond earrings, bracelets and brooches, balanced on a tiny pair of gold mules with high wedge heels. She looked about fifty.

'Here's to victory,' she said. 'Now – what's it all about?'

'If you mean the explosions,' I said, 'I'm afraid that I don't know any more than you do.'

'Then why are you here?'

I took a cautious sip from my glass, then said: 'Well, Mrs Patch, as a matter of face I've come about my sister.'

'Sister?' She looked puzzled. 'Aren't you from the ARP?'

'No (*you pig-ignorant old idiot*), I'm in the WAAF.'

'But isn't that something to do with the Air Force? They ought to know if anyone ought — '

'No, I'm looking for my sister, and someone told me that you might – or at least . . . '

'You're not here about the air raid? About the explosions?'

'No, not really . . . ' I wondered if she might snatch the glass out of my fingers.

'Oh God,' she said fretfully, 'will someone tell me what this is all about? Kept up all night in the cellar and now the windows blown out — '

She took a mouthful of her drink and I heard her teeth rattle lightly against the glass. It struck me that she was nervous.

'I'm sorry, but I've no idea what's going on,' I said. 'I saw a funny-looking plane going over when I came out of the Underground here, and a few minutes later it crashed. Or at least, I suppose it did . . . '

'So what have you come for?' She looked at me accusingly, and I found my gaze caught by the diamond brooch pinned at the neck of her dress. It was in the shape of a horse's head.

'You are Mrs Bernie Patch, aren't you?'

'I am.'

'I'm trying to find my sister Sylvia. I believe she – she knew Mr Patch.'

For a moment she didn't say anything; she just sat there staring at me and it took an awful lot of nerve to stare back at her. She was so smooth and expensive and sophisticated, and

I knew I wouldn't stand a chance if it came to a slanging match. I waited for her to throw me out.

'Little girl,' she said finally. 'You've got one hell of a nerve.'

'I know,' I whispered. And went on waiting.

'Do you know what your sister did to me?'

'No. Well . . .'

Mrs Patch took a slow sip from her glass. I saw for the first time that her fingernails were painted the colour of dried blood.

'She stole from me. She stole my husband, little girl.'

Convention seemed to demand some sort of an apology from me, but I couldn't manage it. I just sat tight and waited.

'And you're her sister?'

'Yes. I'm trying to trace her.'

'I wouldn't bother,' said Mrs Patch with quiet emphasis. She drained her glass then leaned towards me, all signs of air raid jitters gone.

'Your sister is trash,' she said. 'Scum. She stole my husband and left me with nothing.'

Involuntarily I looked round the big room with its lush furnishings, and at the cocktail cabinet loaded with spirits that were unobtainable, let alone too expensive for most people. For a woman who had nothing, Mrs Patch seemed to be doing okay.

'My husband worshipped me,' she said. 'He lavished every penny on me — '

'Did you worship him too?' The words were out before I could stop them. She gave me a curdled look.

'Naturally,' she said. 'But of course. And when this cheap little gold-digger came along and stole him from under my very nose . . .'

She made him sound as inanimate as a diamond bracelet, and I tried not to look over her head at the big portrait of Bernie Patch, the ageing baldy my sister had stolen.

I didn't like Mrs Patch, and I was beginning to think that I didn't care for Sylvia all that much, either. It hurt.

'It stands to reason that I started having him watched as soon as I was reasonably sure that someone somewhere was getting her hands on him. He joined this arty club in Soho –

not that he knew the next thing about art – but as I say, I had him watched and it got results.'

'Couldn't you have asked him?' My voice sounded thin.

'What – and shown my hand?' Mrs Patch snorted with amusement. She got up and refilled her glass. 'My dear little girl, you soon learn to fight dirty when your security's threatened. Have another drink. Although why the hell I'm offering hospitality to the sister of — '

'No, thank you.'

I wanted desperately to leave. The brassy opulence and the horsy knick-knacks were getting me down, but I'd got to find out more about Sylvia now I was here.

'Look,' I said very earnestly. 'I'm very sorry indeed to hear about my sister breaking up your marriage. I think it's inexcusable. But I haven't seen her for six years and I must know what's happened to her. The bottom fell out of my world the day she left home.'

'I take it she ran away?' Mrs Patch was on to that one in a flash, and I cursed myself.

'Leaving home is something everyone does, sooner or later,' I said with dignity. 'My sister was no exception.'

'Little girls who run away to London are looking for the big time,' Mrs Patch said. 'Someone's told them they're pretty, and that in London the pickings are rich for pretty girls. Your sister was just one cheap little go-getter out of a million others.'

'It wasn't like that,' I said.

'Oh yes it was, little girl. Your sister Sylvia got herself a job in a Soho club and she got to work on the big time. And the big time was my husband.'

'It may interest you to know that before Sylvia went to the Bever Club she was a schoolteacher.'

'Then she found out the headmaster wasn't a millionaire.' She had a sly, throaty chuckle.

'It was a headmistress, and she — ' I stopped. The headmistress hadn't exactly cared for Sylvia either.

'Mrs Patch,' I said. 'Can you tell me where my sister is?'

'I hope she's roasting in hell.'

'I believe you, but tell me what happened. I mean, did he ask you for a divorce?'

'Of course he did.' Mrs Patch gave a contemptuous shrug. 'And you can just see me agreeing to one, can't you?'

I nodded, confused and depressed by the parvenu rich and their goings-on.

'Your sister stole my husband,' said Mrs Patch, 'but I had the last laugh. Believe me, little girl. I had the last laugh.'

'Oh?' I stood up, ready to go. Not wanting to hear.

'He came crawling home to die. And he didn't leave her a crumb.' She leaned back and lit another cigarette. 'He left every mortal thing to me.'

'I'm so glad,' I said from over by the door. 'Believe me, Mrs Patch, I'm so very, very glad — ' Then stopped.

From outside the window I heard the strange stuttering roar that was now becoming familiar. It came closer, shaking the building and rattling the ashtrays made out of horses' hooves. With a squeal of terror Mrs Patch bounded from her chair and ran on her little teetering mules to where I was standing.

'Oh God,' she said, 'don't let me die. Not yet . . . '

Torn between panic and a wild desire to giggle I pulled her towards the hall and we crouched in the corner, waiting. The roaring stopped, and in the ensuing silence I could hear Mrs Patch breathing rapidly.

'Please,' she whimpered. '*Please* . . . '

The explosion hurt my ears and I watched the suit of armour topple forward and crash in a tinny heap. Through the open doorway I saw the curtains fly inward in the blast, then heard the splintering of glass as windows and pictures and bottles came crashing down. The place filled with dust.

I became aware that Mrs Patch was crying. With her gold turban askew she stumbled back into the lounge and ran, choking and sobbing, from one broken treasure to another.

'I've lost everything . . . ' I heard her wail. 'Everything's gone – I've lost *everything* . . . '

I turned away, shaking and blinded by tears. During the course of the last half hour I'd finally lost my childhood illusions about Sylvia.

I suppose I should have stayed to help, but I didn't. On the way downstairs I met a couple of air raid wardens who asked if anyone was hurt.

'In flat 34 there's an hysterical woman,' I said. 'I don't know about anyone else.'

And I walked out into the street, picking my way through the debris and wanting to be alone to get over the shock of the bomb and the misery about Sylvia.

I walked all the way back to ACRC and the first person I encountered was Flight Sergeant Cutter.

'Good heavens, Coryn,' she said coldly, 'Why are you covered in dust?'

'I've been in an explosion, Flight.'

'Well surely you could brush yourself down?' she retorted. Then added: 'By the way, there's a phone message for you in the guardroom.'

I thanked her wearily, and went to find it. It was from David, saying that he'd be in London on Sunday and could I get some time off? As it happened I was duty airwoman on Saturday night which would entitle me to have the whole of Sunday free from 8.30 a.m., and I was so cheered by the prospect that I rang the officers' mess at Waterbeach to leave a return message.

As luck had it he was there, and I was able to speak to him. His voice sounded warm and loving and full of concern.

'Are you all right, Kit?'

'Well, yes, but we keep getting funny kind of air raids.'

'Have there been any bombs near you?'

'They don't seem to be bombs. More like planes crashing.'

'Oh . . . ' There was a pause, then he said: 'So they still haven't told you?'

'Told us what?'

'They're guided missiles. I can't tell you much on the phone, but we'll talk on Sunday. Come over to Martin's place in Victoria as soon as you're off duty – it's 27 Brough Street, off Wilton Road — '

'I'll be there — '

'And I'll be waiting,' he said.

I went up to flat 10 room 4 and found Maze and Flo in contemplation of a jam jar full of water in which a large, blunt-ended beetle was swimming energetically.

'It's a *Dytiscus marginalis,*' Flo said, 'and I caught it in the lake. Really rather wizard, isn't it?'

'Dunno so much,' said Maze. 'Suppose it gets out in the night and crawls down me lughole?'

'It's also known as the great diving beetle,' went on Flo. 'It's fiercely carnivorous and flies at dusk. But don't worry, I'll put a book on top when the time comes.'

'Ta.'

'Talking of flying,' I said, 'I've got some gen on those explosions — '

'Yeah, they're called guided missiles,' said Maze. 'It's all round the Naff that they're Hitler's secret weapon.'

I half wanted to tell them about the one that had wrecked Mrs Patch's flat, then decided against it. It was too closely connected with the Sylvia-thing, and like someone with toothache I wanted to hide away in solitude until the worst of the pain had worn off and I could bear it without grimacing.

Being duty airwoman was one of the biggest and most protracted binds of all time.

Mercifully it only came round about once every three months at ACRC, but it meant being on duty from six in the evening until eight o'clock the following morning, and entailed waiting up for the last girl to come in at night and then getting up in time to call the cooks and telephonists and everyone else who was on early shift. In between times you slept, fully clad, on a bed in the guardroom.

That Saturday night I duly presented myself in regulation garb of tunic and slacks, plus tin hat as the all-clear hadn't sounded from the mid-afternoon alert. (Since the onset of the flying bombs, air raids tended to last for so long that most people lost count of whether one was on or not, particularly as bombs sometimes sneaked over during an all-clear.)

The first four hours passes fairly briskly, booking girls in and out on passes, dealing with the switchboard, handing out letters and messages and taking names for early calls. At seven o'clock a girl from flat 14 got a shock from an electric iron and had to be taken to sick quarters, and at half past another one came in complaining loudly that someone had pinched her best stockings.

'Were they issue?'

'Not on your sweet life, they were pure silk!'

'Then I'm sorry, there's nothing I can do. We can only take action over issue clothing.'

'I can take my own action over issue clothing,' she said furiously. 'All I've got to do is pinch somebody else's . . . '

At eight o'clock the duty officer – a nervous section officer with a lisp – put her head round the guardroom door and asked if everything was in order. When I said it was she said 'That's thuper – carry on,' and then disappeared.

At ten o'clock the first trickle of homing WAAF appeared, and had to be booked in; they were mostly the quiet unobtrusive kind for whom a modest evening spent drinking coffee and reading magazines in the Rudolph Steiner Hall was quite sufficient. The next batch had the dreamy, bug-eyed look of cinema-goers, and after them came girls from the station dance, which was held at the zoo. They were a noisy, good-humoured lot who finally laughed and sang themselves off to bed around midnight. The section officer then reappeared, asked if everything was still in order, and upon being answered in the affirmative said good-night and left me to it.

Like a rookery settling down for the night the hostel gradually fell silent. I switched the phone through, bolted the heavy outer door and lay down on the iron bed. And in the quiet, dim light the toothache misery of Sylvia started up again.

I couldn't believe that she'd really run off with Bernie Patch, that awful baldy-baby husband of the awful Mrs Patch. And yet I knew that she had, because everything I'd discovered from every different source added up to an only too composite picture of her; she was a no-good, a drifter, a good-time girl. Mrs Patch had called her a gold-digger, and Mrs Patch was obviously well qualified to recognise a gold-digger when she saw one.

But Sylvia of all people. I tried to push away the things I had learned about her, to smother them with memories of the old days at home; the laughter, the happiness, the old scratchy record of 'The Donkey Serenade', but other faces, other memories, kept superimposing themselves. The steely contempt of Miss Mather, the hurt-dog look of Kay

Simpson, the sad cynicism of the man at the Bever Club, and now the Bernie Patch affair. The policeman round at the station had known a thing or two when he said don't try to find people who don't want to be found. Even Aunt Mitty had echoed the same advice . . .

Shifting about on the hard bed I made another attempt at sleep, then suddenly sat up. Outside the guardroom door, someone was singing. It was a quiet, rather eerie song, and sounded as if it were being sung through the keyhole.

'Who is it?'

The song faltered and lapsed into heavy breathing. I thought I heard a sob.

'Who is it? What d'you want?'

'Och, I canna get in, pet,' the voice said plaintively. 'They've snicket the door and they've locket me oot.'

I opened it, and a short fat WAAF fell in on her knees.

'MacFadden,' I said hoarsely. 'You're drunk.'

'Och, *away* . . . '

'Then get up!'

'I canna . . . '

I rebolted the door, then put my hands under her arms in an effort to haul her up. MacFadden gave a high shriek and collapsed on all fours like a dog. She smelt terrible.

'For God's sake,' I said crossly, 'pull yourself together and get on your stupid feet — '

With me hauling and her pushing we managed to get her upright. She stood there wavering gently, and after a minute began to sing again.

I told her to shut up. Rather to my surprise she did so.

'Have you any idea what time it is?' I demanded. 'It's two thirty, and you're supposed to be in by one minute to midnight!'

I propelled her through the other door. 'Which flat are you in, MacFadden?'

'Dinna ken, pet . . . '

'Of course you do. Come on, I'm not supposed to leave the guardroom — '

Halfway across the darkened courtyard MacFadden stopped abruptly, pointed her nose at the sky and began to howl.

'I want ma mither . . . I want . . . '

Horrified by the noise I clapped my hand over her mouth, about-turned her and ran with her back to the shelter of the guardroom. We half fell inside, MacFadden breathing stertorously. With a huge effort I lugged her over to the bed and she collapsed, sprawling out motionless as a corpse.

Which was an improvement, except that it was my bed.

I looked up her flat number and found that it was 22, which was on the fifth floor. The chances of getting her up there without rousing the entire block were very small, even supposing that I could wake her up and persuade her to walk. So it looked as if she'd be staying where she was until morning.

I sat down on the chair by the switchboard, laid my head on my arms and tried to get back to sleep; and I suppose I must have done, because out of a tangled dream I became aware that someone was shaking me by the shoulder.

'They've snicket the door and they've locket me oot!' roared MacFadden, and I found myself staring into her wicked little bloodshot eyes.

'Go back to bed and go to sleep at once!' Oh Lord, how I wished then that I was Flight Sergeant Cutter.

But she continued to roar, with her cap crammed down over her ears and one side of her collar sprung loose from its stud, and when I tried once again to push her back on the bed she suddenly picked the telephone up and tried to crown me with it.

What happened next happened very quickly. I caught the phone the instant before it hit me, and it landed on the table with a clang. MacFadden reeled away in search of a new weapon, and, colliding with the sports cupboard, wrenched open the door and grabbed a hockey stick. She raised it above her head with both hands and I leaped to catch it from her. We struggled, and although she was small, fat, and fighting drunk her strength was prodigious.

When the hockey stick clattered to the floor she flung herself on me. I lurched back against the table, then put my hands on her shoulders and forced her off. She reeled back, stumbled over the hockey stick and fell backwards into the sports cupboard. Without pausing to think I leaped forward and slammed the door on her, then turned the key.

'Lemme oot!'

'No damn fear,' I panted. 'You stay in there until you calm down.'

It was quite a big cupboard built in the angle of the wall, and as I regained my breath I heard the rattle of hockey sticks and tennis rackets as MacFadden churned among them. Hoping the lock would hold, I sank back on the bed and lay staring at the brown wooden door behind which she was shouting and beating a drunken tattoo.

'As soon as you calm down you can come out,' I shouted, and listened with grim satisfaction as the noise gradually died down.

My eyes closed, and I remember nothing more until the switchboard buzzed at 4.30, which was the signal to get up and start waking all the girls on early shift. Still half asleep I took the torch and the early call book and stumbled out into the courtyard where the chill dawn made me shiver.

Doing early calls was a dreary job because it meant tiptoeing in and out of unfamiliar rooms trying not to fall over things and hunting by torchlight for the white towel draped across the foot of the bed as a sign that the occupant was to be woken up. Everyone cursed you, especially when you thrust a pencil in their sleep-stiffened fingers and made them sign against their names in the book. In flat 14 I inadvertently knocked over the glass containing LACW Tillotson's teeth, and heard them skittering away over the floorboards. I think they ended up under someone else's bed.

Gradually the place crept to life, and by the time I had come to the last flat on the list, lights were on in the WAAF cookhouse and Sergeant Lennard was making the first unofficial brew up.

'Was having a smashing dream when you come in and spoilt it,' she complained. 'Some chap came up for a second wallop of cabinet pudding and guess who it was? Glen Miller.'

As the cookhouse began to heat up and the hot sweet tea coaxed us out of the last pale tatters of sleep I remembered that I had a whole free day ahead of me. And when I remembered that I was going to spend it with David, a sudden urge of happiness pushed aside the nagging misery about Sylvia.

Unfortunately for me, it also pushed aside the memory of ACW MacFadden.

David's brother's flat was very small and strewn with books, its dormer windows looking out over the patched roofs of Victoria. The kitchen was on the landing, and I found David preparing lunch with a tea towel tied round his waist. He was in civvies, but his uniform tunic was on the back of a chair.

'Roast duckling,' he said. 'Or to be precise, one mallard drake which happened to cross my path at Waterbeach.'

'Sounds smashing — '

'Plus new peas and potatoes cooked with a sprig of fresh mint.'

'Can I do anything to help?'

'You might be allowed to stir the gravy when the time comes. In the meantime you can help me demolish the gin.'

He kissed me, and led the way through to the main room. I sat down, happy but a bit constrained. It was the first time we'd met in any kind of private place and I couldn't help eyeing the bed over in the corner. I wanted, yet somehow couldn't help dreading, the opening moves. It could never happen again like it did that night in the Park.

'What's your brother like?'

'Not bad. Five years older than me and wants to be a writer after the war.'

'I've got a sister,' I said, then stopped.

'I know. You told me.'

'Her name's Sylvia.'

'Yes, you told me that, too. Cheers.'

'Cheers . . . '

He sat looking at me thoughtfully and I wished I was wearing civvies too, but we weren't even allowed to leave the camp in them when we were off duty. I felt dowdy and boring in uniform, and conscious that the paybook and identity card in the top pocket of my tunic always made me look as if I had a square left breast.

Gazing back at him I noticed for the first time how tired and drawn he seemed.

'You've been working too hard,' I said, then stopped again. I made it sound as banal as working in a bank. Yet the chunk of silence which ensued made me feel edgy.

'Did you see much of D-day?'

'Only from above,' he said laconically.

'What sort of things did you bomb?'

'Coastal defences. Railways, bridges . . . '

'You were going to tell me about the flying bombs.'

'There's not a lot to tell, really. They're just something the Jerries thought up to annoy us.'

I suddenly felt miffed. 'Annoy is a bit of an understatement when you happen to get mixed up with one. Strikes me sometimes that the safest place to be is in the air.'

'Try it.'

'Quite honestly, I wouldn't mind. My allotted part in the war effort seems to get sillier every day . . . D'you realise the admin. section's now been directed to keep a check on how many toilet rolls are used every week by WAAF personnel, and to report any suspicions of misuse?'

When I caught sight of the old gleam of laughter in his eyes I didn't feel miffed any more.

'What sort of misuse have they in mind?'

'Search me.'

On impulse I put down my glass and went over to him, linking my arms round his shoulders and kissing the top of his head.

'Oh, David, I . . . ' Then remembered that although we'd made love we'd never actually got as far as saying *I love you*. Perhaps we didn't. Perhaps it just felt like that.

'Will they go on much longer – the flying bombs?' I went and sat down again.

'We knocked out nearly all the launching sites in the Cherbourg Peninsula and the Pas de Calais as far back as last year, so the ones that are coming over now are from new bases they've built in a hurry. Once our troops have overrun the area there'll be no more problem.'

He didn't seem to want to talk about it any more so I told him about the flying bomb at Swiss Cottage.

'It shattered all this woman's windows and made a ghastly mess all over her carpets.'

'I'm not surprised.'

'It was an absolutely horrible flat and it had a suit of armour in the hall — '

'It's time to go and prod the duck,' he said, and draining his glass went back to the kitchen. I followed.

Together we peered inside the oven where the drake sizzled and spat, and although I would have given anything to forget about Mrs Patch and her husband and my sister, I was also conscious of a deep and despairing need to tell David all about it.

'And the terrible thing is that my sister Sylvia – the one I've told you about – was apparently the girlfriend of this woman's husband, who was a bookie of all things. Very old and fat and hideous — '

'The book says that ducks should be roasted on a grid on account of their high fat content — '

'It smells heavenly. And the woman – the wife of this old man, who's dead now – was as horrible as the flat. She must have been at least fifty and there she was wearing this gold turban and stupid little gold shoes — '

'I think the potatoes are going to boil over.'

'Turn them down, then.'

'And I'm not sure how you tell when the peas are ready —'

'Taste one.'

He burnt his fingers trying to snatch one out of the boiling water, and swore.

'Why don't you use a spoon?'

'Look,' he said, 'why don't you go and sit down like a good girl and mind your own business?'

'You said I could stir the gravy.'

In the end I did so, while he carved the bird. But it's no use, gin has always made me talkative; it did then, and it still does now.

'David,' I said, 'I'm sorry but I can't help being terribly upset about Sylvia. All the evidence is pointing to her being immoral and despicable and everything and I'm still trying so hard to believe that she's the same wonderful — '

He laid down the carving knife with an exasperated clatter which made me jump. 'For the love of God, would you mind just shutting up about your sister Sylvia? Let's talk about

Beethoven or Betty Grable or Flight Sergeant Butter or anyone you like, but not *her!*'

I felt my mouth fall open.

'The very first time we met you talked about your sister. The second time, ditto. I'm quite prepared to believe she's a paragon of sweetness and beauty and all that we hold dear, but I just don't want to be *told* about it any more – and if you can't pull yourself clear of this paralysing sister-fixation then I suggest that you put yourself in the hands of the first competent shrink in the hope that he can do it for you –'

'But she's all my *past!*'

'Then I suggest you forget about your bloody past and get back to counting toilet rolls!' he shouted.

We stared at one another, appalled. I felt choked with anger and misery and a sense of defeat. I loved David and Sylvia more than anyone else in the world and it didn't make sense that I couldn't talk to one about the other.

'The duck's getting cold,' I said stiffly.

He started to say something, then with a sigh picked up the carving knife again. We carried our plates through to the other room and sat down at the small table. We ate in silence.

A great deal has been written about the premature hot-house blossoming of wartime relationships, but not many people seem to have bothered with the long periods of emotional inertia, the awful feeling of hopeless insignificance that living in momentous times could cast over small human lives. David was tired and strained by an overdose of operational flying and I was lumpish and humourless after only three hours' sleep; we were in love and had quarrelled, but how much did it matter compared to the huge business of demolishing the Third Reich?

'When are you due back at Waterbeach?'

'Tonight.'

The silence fell down again. I wanted to say how nice the duck tasted, but couldn't. (In any case it didn't; it was dry and tough.)

'Wasn't it a pity that Beethoven went deaf?'

He looked startled first, then irritated. 'Umm.'

'It's the only thing I know about him. And I read somewhere that Betty Grable's legs are insured for a sum big enough to equip a new Hurricane squadron.'

'There's no one like dear old Betty.'

'You're so right.' Sourly I squinted down at my half square bosom.

'Now tell me something about Flight Sergeant Butter and you've completed all the alternatives.'

'You're being so blasted stuffy, I just can't take much more — '

'Sorry,' he said. But not as if he meant it.

Finally, it was the air raid siren that settled matters.

'Hadn't you better be getting back to Regent's Park?'

'Yes,' I said. 'When it comes to buzz bombs I'm indispensable.'

So I helped to carry the dirty dishes back to the kitchen on the landing, then put on my cap and said good-bye. 'I'm sorry if I talked too much.'

'You didn't really,' he said. 'But don't you get sick to death sometimes of living in such close proximity to so many other people? Of for ever being bombarded with conversation when all you long for is a bit of peace and quiet?'

'Yes, I do. But on the other hand I can't help thinking that you've got to know someone very well for a very long while before you reach the silent companionship stage.'

'Pity time's so short, isn't it?'

I couldn't think of a good reply to that. I wanted to kiss him, but was damned if I was going to without at least a hint of encouragement.

'Good-bye, David.'

'Be seeing you.'

I felt my face tighten. 'Don't worry if you're busy.'

We didn't kiss, and I walked off to Victoria tube station moody and resentful, and it wasn't until I got to Baker Street that I started to forget about David and Sylvia and think about the WAAF world instead. And when I did so, my blood froze.

I started running, and when I couldn't run any more because of panting slowed down to a frustrated jog-trot. When I reached Abbey Lodge I put another spurt on and finally burst into the WAAF guardroom with my heart pounding and my mouth dry with fear.

Corporal Phillips was contentedly date-stamping shoe repair labels when I rushed over to the sports cupboard and wrenched open the door.

ACW MacFadden fell out, and one glance was enough to tell me that she was dead.

7

When the station ambulance had driven MacFadden away I began to tidy up the pile of fallen hockey sticks and tennis rackets in a mindless, confused sort of way until Flight Sergeant Cutter came back to the guardroom.

'Right, ACW Coryn,' she said, clearing her throat. 'Collect your things and go down to the detention room. You're on a charge.'

'Flight, was she really dead?' All I could see was MacFadden's inert body and grey sweat-stained face.

'I've no information at the moment, so get your things and do as you're told. Corporal Phillips, go with her.'

We walked across the courtyard and up the circular stone staircase without speaking. The usual love songs floated from the open doors of flats as we passed. I tried to remember whether the all-clear had gone, then decided that it didn't matter. The odd flying bomb was neither here nor there, compared with all the trouble I was in right now.

We went into flat 10 room 4. Maze and Flo were both there, and the great diving beetle was still swimming lustily round in its jam jar.

'Hi-ya, Mate,' Maze said, then stopped when she saw my escort.

'Get your things, Coryn,' Corporal Phillips said quietly.

'We were just thinking of going down to the NAAFI — ' Flo started to say, but I forestalled her. They might as well know sooner than later.

'If you were thinking of asking me too, I'm afraid it's no thanks. I'm on a charge.'

'Stone me,' breathed Maze.

I tried to smile at her, then started to pack pyjamas, toothbrush, soap and towel, clean shirt and underwear . . .

'Tin hat and respirator,' prompted Corporal Phillips.

When I'd finished, we went over to the door.

'Cheerio,' I said.

'What you done?' Maze asked bluntly.

'I think I've suffocated someone.'

'Oh, what a nuisance,' said Flo in her ladylike tones. 'Was it anyone we know?'

But Corporal Phillips beckoned me out of the door before I could reply.

The detention room was next door to the guardroom; a dusty, unloved and seldom occupied place with a couple of iron bedsteads and dirty-looking mattresses. I sat down on one of them.

'I'm sorry, Kit,' Corporal Phillips said, and held out her hand.

I didn't grasp her meaning immediately, and, when I did, felt the colour drain from my face. Working in the admin. section myself, I knew the procedure any airwoman held in detention pending a charge was to be deprived of her tie and shoelaces in case she tried to hang herself.

'Okay. No hard feelings . . . ' I handed them over.

They brought me some Spam and a couple of tomatoes later on in the evening and I sat on the edge of the bed and tried to get used to the idea that I was no longer an accepted member of the community. It had all happened so stupidly and unexpectedly, and my abrupt transference to the role of outcast and malefactor appalled and frightened me even more than the thought of poor MacFadden stifling to death in the sports cupboard. I'd never felt so lonely in my life.

I didn't sleep much, and somewhere around dawn heard two flying bombs crash within minutes of each other. Because of the frequency of air raid warnings now, the rule about going to the blitz bunks had been relinquished until further orders, and during the day everyone in London tended to rely on roof-spotters armed with red flags to warn them of imminent danger; a homely arrangement that worked surprisingly well.

Next morning after a breakfast of bread-and-marge and

tea, I was given my tie and shoe laces and told that transport was waiting to take me to Holme House. Maze wasn't the driver, and I sat in the back with an escort sergeant whom I didn't know very well, and who wouldn't talk.

We went upstairs to the WAAF admin. office where Flight Sergeant Cutter, with her cap on, was putting the finishing touches to the paperwork connected with my charge. Then I was lined up with an escort fore and aft (the rear one being poor old Flo), and marched in to Squadron Officer Gilby's office.

She had her cap on, too. Everyone had their cap on but me, and the effect was marvellously demeaning. I might as well have been wearing chains.

'ACW2 Coryn, 2010057,' said the CO, reading from the charge sheet. 'Is that your rank, name and number?'

'Yes, ma'am.'

'You are charged with having knowingly and with deliberate intent confined ACW1 MacFadden 1930276 in a cupboard in such a way as to cause her death. What have you to say?'

I couldn't say anything. I just stared at the gold embroidered badge on her cap.

'Fortunately,' she went on in a dry measured voice, 'ACW1 MacFadden was discovered before it was too late. She is now recovering in sick quarters.'

I heard myself give a long shattered sigh of relief.

'I understand that it was you who let her out?'

'Yes, ma'am.'

'Even so,' said Squadron Officer Gilby, 'I am bound to emphasise the gravity of the situation, Coryn.' She looked up at me for the first time. 'What motive impelled you to shut MacFadden in the cupboard in the first place?'

'She was being a bit – difficult, ma'am.'

'In what way was she difficult?'

I hesitated, then said resignedly: 'She was roaring drunk, ma'am.'

'Coryn was duty airwoman on the night in question,' put in Flight Sergeant Cutter, who was standing to attention by the COs elbow.

'You'd better explain what happened, Coryn.'

'I'd bolted the guardroom door and was lying on the bed asleep when MacFadden returned. I tried to help her upstairs to her flat but she was making too much noise. She went to sleep for a while on the bed in the guardroom, then she woke up and tried to hit me with the telephone — '

'So you shut her in the cupboard?'

'No, ma'am. She fell in it, and all I did was lock the door.'

I heard Flo, standing next to me, give a nervous snort of laughter.

'And in consequence, forgot to let her out.'

'Yes, ma'am.'

'Did it not occur to you to phone the guardroom at Abbey Lodge for help?'

'No, ma'am.'

'That's what the special police are for.'

'Yes, ma'am, I realise that now.'

'But you didn't realise it at the time?'

'No, ma'am.'

'Why not?'

'I was too sleepy and too – too — '

'Too what?'

'Too brassed off, ma'am.'

The CO sat with her chin in her hands for several minutes, then said: 'According to the medical officer's report on MacFadden, she has been in a prolonged stupor induced by an excess of alcohol and lack of oxygen which in turn has been seriously aggravated by a lesion on the back of the head consistent with a fall or blow. Did you at any time strike MacFadden, Coryn?'

'No, ma'am.' I stared into her smouldering brown eyes without blinking.

'Can you offer any theory about the wound on the back of her head?'

'I think she must have hit it when she fell back in the cupboard.'

'Do you remember hearing a bang?'

I closed my eyes in an effort to remember. 'There was a lot of noise going on, ma'am. Hockey sticks falling down, me slamming the door shut and MacFadden shouting — '

'Did she continue to shout?'

'Yes, I think so.'

'For how long?'

'I'm not sure, ma'am. I fell asleep.'

Squadron Officer Gilby sat hunched and brooding while I remained standing to attention in front of her. Looking up, I caught the cool blue gaze of Flight Sergeant Cutter, and for a moment I almost thought she was going to give me a small cheer-up sign like a wink or a smile, but she didn't. Not Flight Sergeant Cutter.

'In view of the fact that MacFadden was undoubtedly the worse for drink,' the CO said at length, 'I am willing to accept that she was proving a source of aggravation and annoyance to you, but on the other hand it is impossible to overlook your grave dereliction of duty in that you did not attempt to seek help. To shut her in the cupboard was extremely stupid, to go off duty and forget that you had done so was little short of criminal negligence, and in order to impress this fact upon you I shall sentence you to seven days' special duties with attendant loss of privileges.'

I moistened my lips. 'Thank you, ma'am.'

'Don't thank me,' she said wearily. 'Thank MacFadden for not dying.'

The week that followed was extraordinary, and a bit like living in outer space.

Special duties, or jankers as they were commonly called, consisted of physical labour cunningly combined with a lot of boredom and a certain degree of unpleasantness, and in my case the punishment allotted was to spring-clean, alone and unaided, the whole of flat 5, which was within convenient sight of the guardroom and was the flat where the WAAF stores were kept.

As in the blitz bunks, the windows had been bricked up and the walls reinforced, and I wandered disconsolately from one dingy room to another, looking at the piles of beds and bedding that would have to be shifted before I could get down to the business of scrubbing the walls and floors. And when the day's toil was over I had to sleep in the detention room, because *loss of privileges* meant no friends, no NAAFI, no books, nothing but your thoughts for company.

It wouldn't have been so bad if I hadn't had that last meeting with David, or, more accurately, if the meeting hadn't turned out the way it did. I kept going over and over it in my mind, sometimes hating him, sometimes hating myself, and all the time feeling so wretched and deprived that I longed to be back in the old days before love had undermined my self-reliance.

Scrubbing down the walls in the room where spare fire-fighting equipment was stored I tried the WAAF comfort-habit of wailing all the sad and beautiful love-songs that were currently popular (*You must remember this, a kiss is just a kiss, a sigh is just a sigh . . .*) and to a certain extent it helped. When I'd finished the walls I started on the floor, getting down on my knees and driving the spiny scrubbing brush along the grain of the floorboards (*No love, no nothin', until my baby comes ho-o-o-me . . .*), and then, when the floor had dried, hauling all the buckets and stirrup pumps and fire extinguishers back into place again. And so on through the flat, sweeping and scrubbing, wiping and wailing (*The pain that I cost you, no wonder I lost you, 'twas all over my jealouseeeee . . .*) until it was time to knock off and report to Flight Sergeant Cutter, who would inspect the day's work with a fastidious eye before telling me to return to the detention room.

On the fourth day her fastidious eye noticed my hands, red and swollen by constant immersion in hot strong soda, and she presented me with a tin of Fuller's Earth from sick quarters. There were times when I distinctly got the impression that she wouldn't mind being a bit more friendly, but it never lasted for long.

The evenings were the worst, incarcerated in the detention room after a plain and solitary supper, and in a spirit of tragi-comic defiance I deliberately misappropriated a whole new toilet roll from flat 5 and flagrantly ignoring the stern warning about misuse of government property pencilled long love-letters to David on it. When I wasn't doing that I lay back on the bed and thought about Sylvia, but the thoughts never got anywhere, any more than the letters ever got posted.

But at the end of the last day when I was officially reinstated among my fellow airwomen I found two letters waiting for me. One was from Ma telling me that Pa was in hospital with his Gastric Trouble, and the other one was from David asking me to marry him.

I suppose gladness always takes precedence over gloom, although to say I was glad about the idea of marrying David is a bit of an understatement, having taken three-quarters of a toilet roll to explain just how much I loved him. So I scratched off a quick letter home saying that I hoped Pa would soon be better, then wrote an even quicker one to David up at Waterbeach saying yes, and then gave myself up to the same rhapsodic dreams-of-the-future in which Maze was indulging in relation to Sam Corbellini.

I was so swallowed up by love that I no longer cared about Sylvia and Bernie Patch, and gave no more than a passing thought to the news that five WAAF had been killed at Adastral House by a flying bomb.

David telephoned and we arranged a brief meeting for the same evening, almost literally between trains from and back to Cambridge, but I felt that even half an hour at Liverpool Street Station would be better than nothing. I wanted so much, among other things, to apologise for always going on about Sylvia, and to promise that I'd never mention her name again.

But things never stay the same for long, and, by the time I reached the platform barrier where his train came in with a tired hiss, the picture had changed.

'Oh, my darling,' he said, 'why the suitcase? Are we running away?'

'I've just had a telegram to say my father's dying. They've given me four days' compassionate leave and I'm going straight on to King's Cross.'

He took my arm and hurried me in the direction of the buffet. It was full of soldiers drinking tea and munching grey-looking sandwiches. We found a corner behind a pillar and embraced hastily, guiltily.

'Being engaged,' David said kindly, 'automatically exempts you from saluting.'

'What a relief . . . '

'And as a simple means of signifying official betrothment I

suggest that you wear this . . . '

It was an antique dress ring set with three small rubies. I tried to speak, but couldn't.

'Does it fit?'

'Yes . . . '

'It was my grandmother's.'

'Oh . . . Does she mind?'

'Good Lord, no,' he said. 'It was her idea.'

We went over to the bar, and when David, poker-faced, asked for a bottle of champagne the barman gave him a sour smile and said that the nearest thing he had to offer was ginger beer. So we drank ginger beer until the barman tumbled to what was going on and reached under the counter to produce a bottle of whisky. He poured us two small tots and wished us all the best – adding, with a nod at the pilot's wings on David's tunic, that his sort deserved the best if anyone did, and that the drinks were on him. Then it was time to walk back to platform 7.

'David, are you sure you want to marry me? I mean, the last time — '

'The last time was a deliberate attempt on my part to show you the other side of the coin. To see how you reacted to the scowling, glowering face instead of the calm saintly one with laurel leaves wreathing its brow. No use, Kit, I'm afraid I do get browned off sometimes.'

'So do I. And I suppose I was that day.'

'We must strive not to get browned off together, then. Give each other formal notice when we feel an attack coming on . . . '

'Oh David,' I said. 'I do love you.'

We stood by the ticket barrier. 'I'm sorry to hear about your father.'

'Yes.'

'Perhaps it's not as bad as they think.'

'No,' I said. 'Perhaps not . . . ' I stood watching him wave from the train, and by the time I was on the way to Barnard Castle it was easier to reassure myself. After all, gastric trouble was a bit of a joke, wasn't it? I mean, no one had ever died of it. Not seriously.

I went straight to the hospital and found Ma sitting by his bedside, and by the look of him I knew for a certainty that he was going to die, after all. He had a strange solemn look about him that wiped away the little-man petulance, the small-town pomposity. He had the beginnings of a sort of nobility which you never see on people in the street.

Ma, on the other hand, looked more palely resigned than ever; she was wearing the inevitable weak-tea-coloured crêpe de Chine and I noticed that her neck was starting to get scraggy. I'd always thought of her as old, but now she was getting *old* old.

We kissed hurriedly, and I took my place on the other side of the bed.

'Is he conscious?'

She shook her head. 'He hasn't spoken since yesterday morning. The doctors say there's nothing more they can do.'

She leaned over and wiped his forehead with her handkerchief; a useless little gesture which moved me very much.

We went on sitting there, watching him, then after a while she asked in a whisper whether I'd had a good journey and if I was tired.

'No, I'm not tired. Honestly.'

'You must be hungry.'

'No, I had a good meal just before I left.'

I wanted to tell her about David, but it didn't seem the right time or place. So we stayed silent, listening to the subdued sounds of the hospital and watching Pa's calm wax features for the slightest sign of change.

He died so quietly that I didn't realise it had happened until the staff nurse came in and gently disengaged Ma's hand from his. She kissed his forehead, I steeled myself to do the same, and like two sleepwalkers we moved away from the bed with its drawn curtains and went down the ward to where the sister offered us a cup of tea in her office.

It was almost dark when we got home and Trix barked at me before she recognised who it was.

'It's Kit, you silly old dog,' Ma said, and when she burst into tears I put my arms round her, and she felt so thin and cold and forlorn that love for her rushed through me and all I wanted was to hold her and stroke her hair and pat her back while I wondered why on earth I'd never had the sense to do it before. When she'd stopped crying I polished her glasses for her and settled them carefully back on her nose.

Then I got supper ready.

'He was a good man,' she said, toying with a thin sliver of cheese. 'And the pain he suffered in the last year was terrible.'

'I didn't realise that gastric trouble could be fatal.'

'It was cancer,' she said.

'Oh, God. Did he know?'

'Yes. But he never mentioned it because he didn't realise that I knew.'

'And you didn't . . . ?'

'No,' she said. 'No, of course not.'

Later that night I lay awake thinking about them both living so closely and yet so separately; each of them practising the same careful reticence for fear of alarming the other. It was pitiful and stupid, and so courageous that I cried more about that than about Pa actually being dead.

Next day I got my compassionate leave extended to a week, and went with Ma to see about the funeral arrangements. I also went with her to buy a black coat and hat, and she was very shocked when I suggested that she should use Pa's clothing coupons instead of her own.

'But he won't need them any more, so why not?'

'Because it would be cheating,' she said.

So we went to the food office and surrendered his ration book and clothing coupon book, and then on to the labour exchange to hand in his identity card, where the woman behind the counter drew a single pen stroke through it as if to say *Well, that's that.* It made death seem very mundane.

But in the evening we sat in the summer twilight and I told her about David. Or at least I tried to, but had to give up any attempt to describe either him or how I felt about him, not through lack of encouragement so much as the knowledge that it all sounded too soppy to listen to. So I just said how much she'd like him and she said yes, she was sure she would. She admired my ring, then asked when we were getting married and I had to say that I didn't know; we hadn't had time to get as far as that.

'That's the trouble,' she said. 'During a war there never seems to be any *time* . . . '

I also told her about my going to see Aunt Mitty in Maida Vale, and persuaded her to invite her to the funeral.

'But we've lost touch,' she said doubtfully. 'And the trains are so unreliable these days.'

The only person we didn't mention was Sylvia; I didn't say anything because I felt that I had nothing either cheering or inspiring to offer in the way of news, and Ma didn't mention her because – well, because Sylvia was one of those topics like religion and sex that she habitually shied away from, I suppose.

And yet, oh Lord, how the place was still full of her even after all these years! Her bedroom was the same – same bedspread, same empty coat-hangers behind the door – and up in the attic I came across the old portable gramophone and the record of Allan Jones singing 'The Donkey Serenade'. I put it on, closing the door so that Ma wouldn't hear, then sank down in one of the old basket chairs as the rasping clip-clop tune filled the cloistered air and vibrated the cobwebs with its cheerful innocence.

There were all sorts of Sylvia's things lying about; her old leather satchel, a pile of film magazines, a dried-out bottle of pink nail varnish. And down the back of the basket chair I came across one of her blue hair ribbons; the bow was still tied, the circle of ribbon still measuring the circumference of her head.

I held it against my face as I listened to the record for the second time, and I began to understand that I had been obsessed by Sylvia when I was a child simply because she was always so nice to me, and now that I was grown up the obsession was with her extraordinary ability to remain a tangible presence long after she had gone away. She clung to the place like smoke, like the scent of musk roses, and in spite of the unprepossessing facts I had uncovered about her in London each step had been permeated with her nearness.

It wasn't that Sylvia was *good,* then, it was that she was so damned *real*. So much more real than ordinary people, I mean.

And sitting there in our old den in the attic I knew that I was going to go on searching for her, and that one day by the grace of God I'd find her.

But apart from the mysterious fiancé of September 1939 the trail seemed to end with the death of Bernie Patch, a couple of months or so before. Mrs Patch had volunteered no likely lead – for which I could hardly blame her even supposing she were able. Then my mind went back to the man at the Bever Club and I suddenly remembered that he had mentioned a friend of Sylvia's who had also worked there. What did he say her name was? Doreen – Diane – Daphne. That was it, Daphne. *She was here with another pretty blonde kid called Daphne*, he said, and then added something about girls just biting off the bit they fancy and then moving on.

What a pity Daphne hadn't left a forwarding address either.

On the day of Pa's funeral a curtain of rain obscured the fells and drenched the wreaths lying upturned on the cemetery grass.

There were a lot of people present, including the entire staff from Pa's shop, and what seemed like dozens of elderly black-shrouded aunts who addressed me as Catherine. And then picking her way between them like Venus beset by storm-clouds was Aunt Mitty in a silvery cloche hat and a purple coat reaching almost to her ankles. She had come up on the night train and her eyes were bright with enjoyment as she tripped and chattered from one group to the next. I remembered what she had told me about Pa being in love with her and only marrying poor old Ma on the rebound, and wondered if it was true.

For her part, Ma got through the ordeal without crying, and when we got back to the house everyone removed their black hats and coats and brought out tins of home-made cakes and scones and pies while Uncle Bob – an auctioneer from Darlington – produced a bottle of brandy and insisted on Ma having the first nip, which made her choke.

And of course they all said what a grand old lad Pa had been, so kind, so patient, so upright, so honest, until Mrs Dinsdale who worked in the cash desk burst into loud sobs and had to be led away by Mr Dinsdale, who worked on the bacon counter.

By six o'clock they had all gone home, including Aunt Mitty who was proposing to spend another night on the train.

'Why don't you stay for a few days?' I demanded. 'It's silly to come all this way just for an hour or two, and it'd do Ma good.'

But she smiled and shook her head.

'There's nothing for me here, darling,' she said. 'I don't belong among all this damp decorum any more than Sylvia did.'

So then it was all over. Pa was dead and buried, Ma was launched on the long straight road of widowhood and I was on the way back to ACRC Regent's Park.

She saw me off at the station, and just before we said good-bye she gave me a shy, wistful little smile and said: 'You know, Kit, your father loved you more than anyone or anything in the world. He always did, from the time you were a baby.'

I stared at her in astonishment. '*Me?* But what about Sylvia? I mean, she was so much more — '

'There you go again,' she said. 'Still on about Sylvia.'

'But if he loved me so much, why didn't he ever tell me so?' I felt curiously cheated. 'Why did he only let me see him as mean and paltry and humourless?'

I saw Ma flinch, and cursed myself for being tactless.

'I suppose he could never find the words,' she said. Then added: 'Any more than I can.'

And that was my parents. As incapable of talking about love as they were about cancer. It made me wish I'd told her more about David, soppy-sounding or not.

I got back to ACRC in time for supper. London looked heavy and listless after the green of the north and I heard the crash of a flying bomb somewhere behind Baker Street.

Maze and Flo were both touchingly deferential because of my father's death, and only resumed their more robust, everyday attitude towards me when I told them about David's letter that I'd found on my return.

It was the longest letter I'd had from him so far, and it ended by instructing me to present myself at the flat in

Victoria at 18.30 hours precisely on Saturday the 1st of July 1944 for the purpose of celebrating the engagement of ACW Kit Coryn 2010057 to Squadron Leader David Magnus 90463.

. *I believe my mother's planning a family celebration – and it's high time you met some of them – but this little knees-up is strictly between the two parties concerned. So I've booked a table at the Trocadero for dinner, and promise, but not on my honour, to return you to base by one minute to midnight . . . Oh, my very dear little Kit, how I'm looking forward to it! We'll hold hands under the tablecloth and sigh over the soup and make wizard plans for the future . . .*

'Stone me,' Maze said, watching me get ready. 'Call them shoes polished? Givvus 'em here, for Gawd's sake!'

I did so, and while I pressed my uniform skirt she got to work.

I never knew anyone who could get a polish on shoes and buttons like Maze. I can see her now, her thin ferret face set in a kind of happy ferocity as she worked the warm melted polish into the leather, left it to dry, and then rubbed it *(you don't rub it off, mate, you rub it in – see?)* with a special soft duster. And it was the same with tunic buttons; only Maze had the patience to pick the dried white powder out of the crowns with a pin . . .

Then Flo insisted on lending me her grey silk stockings, and after diving down to the bottom of her kitbag came up with a bottle of Chanel Number 5 which in those spartan days was on a par with frankincense and myrrh.

'That'll fetch him,' she said, dabbing some behind my ears.

'Strikes me he's already fetched,' Maze grinned. 'Tonight it's just mopping up operations.'

So sparkling and glittering and smelling like a pre-war debutante I set off for the flat in Victoria, and when I rang the bell of David's brother's flat there was no reply.

I rang again, then rang the landlady's bell. After a long time she came to the door and stood looking at me without speaking.

'I'm sorry to disturb you,' I said, 'but can you tell me if Squadron Leader Magnus is in?'

'No.'

'You mean, you — '

'I mean no, he's not in,' she said. 'Hasn't been here for about a week.'

I forced a smile and asked if I could come in and wait, and noting her expression of dubiety added that I was his fiancée.

So she let me in and I hurried upstairs, half expecting to find David sprawled asleep or deep in a book, but the flat was deserted. The bed was made, the ashtrays were emptied, and clean dishes were stacked in the little kitchen-on-the-landing. But there was no sign of life anywhere. Not even a vase of flowers. The nearest approach to anything like that was the blue and red spotted cravat he always wore when he was in civvies. It lay mute and evocative on the chest of drawers and I sat down in the chair and held it in my hands like a talisman. And fear crept over me like the chill of winter.

He didn't come. The only sound that broke the waiting silence was the clatter of pigeon's wings on the roof outside. It began to grow dark, and when I caught the unaccustomed glitter of my WAAF shoes in the half-light I wanted to wrench them off and chuck them somewhere out of sight.

Instead, I folded the cravat very carefully and lovingly and replaced it on the chest of drawers, then let myself out of the house as quietly as possible so that the landlady wouldn't hear. And the terror of what could have happened was so black that when I got to Victoria Station I had to sit down on a seat before I could summon the courage to go into a phone booth and ring up the bomber station at Waterbeach.

It took a long time. First of all I couldn't get through, and when I did I couldn't hear properly. And I didn't know who to ask for.

So I asked for the orderly room, where the duty clerk said he'd no information but would put me on to the ops. room, where a hushed WAAF voice said that she had no authority to divulge personal information about flying crew. I said that I was his fiancée and that we were engaged to be married, but it didn't make any difference. So I asked her to transfer me to the officer's mess.

The line was much clearer when the officers' mess eventually answered, and I asked for the sergeant in charge. Whoever it was who took the call said that the sergeant was busy but I gripped the telephone receiver with both hands and said that it was urgent and that I would hold on. Eventually the sergeant came and when I asked him if Squadron Leader David Magnus was there (*this is his fiancée speaking*) he said hang on a minute please, I'll go and get someone.

So I hung on, and the phone booth filled with the smell of terror and Chanel Number 5, and I shovelled more sixpences into the box as if I were trying to placate some kind of cruel and unheeding God.

At last a young man's voice came on the line to say that his name was Peter someone-or-other, that he was a chum of David's and that he'd heard all about me. My name was Kit, wasn't it?

'Yes, I said. 'I'm his fiancée. And I held on to that stupid word *fiancée* as if it were the last hope of keeping total chaos at bay.

'Listen, Kit,' he said, 'Dave went out on a night raid over northern France last night and he hasn't got back. But don't worry – I repeat, don't worry – a couple of us saw his plane go down and he'd every chance of making a good crash landing . . . '

I knew it. Of course I did. All along I'd known that it was too good to be true. A girl in the teleprinting section's fiancé had been killed the day before they were due to be married, and it could happen to anybody. Now it had happened to me.

'Thank you,' I said. 'Thank you for telling me.'

'Now listen, try not to worry, Kit . . . I hope you don't mind me calling you Kit . . . Dave'll be okay, he's bound to have baled out. The worst that could have happened is that he'll be in the bag for the rest of the war. Which won't be long now, anyway . . . '

'But nobody actually saw him? His parachute?'

'Well, no,' he said. 'But of course, we were all a bit busy at the time . . . '

The line buzzed, and the operator broke in to ask if I was finished.

'Yes, thank you,' I said. 'Quite finished.'

I put the receiver back while David's chum was still telling me faintly and anxiously not to worry, and when I stumbled outside all the fear and foreboding had gone. I just felt as if I were dead.

I walked back through Grosvenor Gardens to Hyde Park Corner, and when I walked up Park Lane towards Oxford Street I remembered the first night when we'd walked home from the Albert Hall together and I'd half resented his intrusion on my precious privacy . . .

It was almost nine thirty when I got to the top of Orchard Street. Unable to stand the thought of going back to camp I plodded on down Oxford Street and Regent Street, and when I got to Piccadilly Circus turned up Shaftesbury Avenue and pushed through the swing doors of the Trocadero Hotel.

The restaurant was full of men in officers' uniforms and women in pearls and smart little black dresses; the band was playing and the air was pleasantly tinted with cigar smoke. And they all stopped laughing and eating and chatting to stare at me as I plodded up to the head waiter and said: 'I've come to cancel the table booked for Squadron Leader Magnus. It was a table for two, but it won't be needed now.'

Then I turned on my heel and plodded out again.

I ended up at Lofty's coffee stall where I belonged, and stood listening dully to a couple of taxi drivers arguing about whether Hitler was mad or wicked. They tried to draw me into the conversation, but I'd no contribution to make. I was beyond words, beyond tears, and even after I'd got back to camp I didn't go up to flat 10 room 4 until I was sure that Maze and Flo were in bed and asleep.

I undressed in the moonlight and crept cold as a stone into my own bed, and the last thing I saw was my tunic buttons twinkling merrily at the foot of it. Nobody could polish tunic buttons like Maze.

Yet somehow life went on. It had to. Breakfast in the cookhouse, then the march through the Park with Flo the admin. runner to Holme House, and the ration strength, the daily details, and the cool, clipped company of Flight Sergeant Cutter. Back to the cookhouse for lunch. Then back to Holme House again, then supper, then a listless visit to the cinema or a ramble round the streets on my own until a final cup of tea in the NAAFI, then bed.

Everyone was very nice to me, although sometimes I fancied that I could read a superstitious fear in Maze's eyes when she looked at me, as if the bad news about David was a type of infection which could spread from me to her. She was getting a few more letters from Sam now, but there was no real news in them except to say that he was still with the VII US Army Corps and that the going was good but mighty rough. Sometimes she offered to let me read them.

Flo, on the other hand, said that she considered herself fortunate with only a great diving beetle to worry about. Still swimming round in its jam jar, it was now known throughout flat 10 as the Air Vice Marshal, and whatever the degree of involvement between the two of them, Maze and I swore it could recognise Flo's kindly moon-face bending over it.

Then I got a letter from David's mother, asking me to have lunch with her. She came up by train from Sussex, and we met at Gullivers because it wasn't far from Holme House and I only had an hour.

I dreaded meeting her in case the poignancy of the situation made me cry, then realised within the first few minutes that she was up against the same problem. So we shook hands and smiled brightly and skirted carefully round the misery that haunted us both. But over the cheese and biscuits she showed me the official letter saying that Squadron Leader Magnus was missing on active service over the Pas de Calais.

'I don't believe he's dead,' I muttered.

'Neither do I,' she said quietly.

I remembered to ask after her other son, Martin, and she told me that he was still in Burma and when I said how awful it must be to have two of them to worry about she smiled and said yes it was, although being in the process of acquiring a daughter-in-law made up for a lot. Which was nice of her. Her smile reminded me of David's and I had to look away.

I walked to Baker Street Underground with her, and when we said good-bye she kissed me. I liked her, and I think we'd managed to derive a certain amount of comfort from one another.

In the emptiness which followed David's disappearance I

suppose it was inevitable that I should start thinking about Sylvia again. And in the same way that I'd come to understand her falling foul of an old acid drop like Miss Mather, and walking away from the gooey sentimentality of Kay Simpson, I was beginning to take a different view of the Bernie Patch interlude.

I was beginning to see how a possibly gentle, peaceable man could flee from the avaricious embrace of Mrs Patch and seek refuge with a girl like Sylvia; and I could also see how a girl like Sylvia would respond with sympathy and affection, loving him for what he was and remaining sunnily indifferent to any charges of gold-digging. In any case, he hadn't left her a penny in his will – Mrs Patch had said so.

No, however bizarre a relationship it may have appeared on the surface, I believed now that Bernie and Sylvia had loved one another, and thinking back to the portrait in Mrs Patch's flat I seemed to remember detecting a hint of sweet sensitivity beneath his bald-baby exterior. I wished he hadn't died, so that I might prove the theory.

But in the meantime I was all ready to start the search again, and the only problem was – where now? My thoughts went back once more to the 'pretty blonde kid' called Daphne, but I didn't know where to start looking for her, either. In any case, because she and Sylvia had been friends back in 1939, there was no reason to suppose that they were still friends now.

It was all hopelessly difficult, and I went back to wandering round on the off-chance that I'd meet Sylvia in the street, or recognise her in a Lyons Corner House, or pass her on an escalator. Because of the flying bombs a lot of people had returned to sleeping down in the Underground stations and on the way home I used to scrutinise their tired white faces for the girl with blonde curls tied up in a bit of blue ribbon who looked like Alice Faye.

Of course I never found her.

It's funny how memory works. I mean, I'm sitting here in this hotel bedroom at the unearthly hour of 4.45 a.m. on the day I go to meet her again, and when I get to the point of reconstructing perhaps the most important moment of all in the Sylvia story – all I can remember is seeing my knife, fork and spoon in their white calico bag lying on the counter in the NAAFI.

I should explain that in the WAAF you were taught from the first twenty-four hours of recruitment that the Air Ministry had issued you with a knife, fork and spoon especially for your own personal requirements, and very speedily you fell into the way of thinking that eating with anyone else's knife, fork and spoon was not only unhygienic but somehow a bit corrupt; so you kept to your own cutlery (known as *irons*), and carted it around with you from place to place in a little white calico bag which bore your name and number in marking ink.

And at seventeen minutes to two in the afternoon of Monday the 16th of July I was in the NAAFI in the courtyard of the WAAF hostel when the flying bomb fell.

There must have been about twenty of us in there, just up from lunch in the cookhouse; the radio was playing a programme of Geraldo's music and, as I say, I was standing at the counter waiting for a cup of coffee and staring idly at my knife, fork and spoon when the familiar noise came stuttering overhead, shaking the pre-fab roof of the hut and clinking the thick china cups and saucers.

We'd heard them so many times before that we didn't panic easily, but when the terrible stertorous rattling of it grew slower and slower and finally stopped, the NAAFI manageress suddenly screamed out: 'Get *down*!'

We did so, diving under tables and lying flat with our heads cradled in our arms. In the full minute of waiting I listened to the band playing 'Pistol-Packin, Momma' . . .

The bomb landed with a crash that blotted out my hearing and I got a confused impression that I was swimming underwater. My mouth filled with dust and grit, and in the shocked silence which followed – even Geraldo was mute – I tried to move and found that I couldn't. I couldn't feel any sensation in my body, anywhere.

Then over by the door a girl began to scream.

8

The reason why I couldn't move was because the table had collapsed on top of me.

It was the NAAFI manageress who got me out; covered in dust she put her arm round my shoulder and kept saying urgently: 'Can you walk? Can you walk all right?' and only when I'd limped a few paces to prove that I could did she turn her attention to the next girl. And when she got to the one who was screaming she slapped her face and told her to shut up.

Because of the thick choking dust it was difficult to see exactly what had happened, but I remember a first impression of shredded curtains flapping at the windows, the scrunch of glass and china underfoot and the sight of a WAAF mopping blood from another one's face with a tea towel.

I limped over the gaping doorway but there was almost as much dust out in the courtyard as there was inside the NAAFI.

Corporal Phillips ran past me shouting to someone that ambulances were on the way, and a girl who worked in the cookhouse blundered into me, dazed and weeping with shock. I became aware that my left leg was aching, but only in a dull sort of way.

Then I heard men's voices, and an RAF sergeant in a tin hat strode over to me and asked if I was all right. I said that I was, so he put his arm round the waist of the girl who was weeping and led her away. And then a fire engine arrived, with a couple of ambulances, and the sound of their bells bells splitting the strange, concussed silence of the place made me realise that being on the admin. staff I too ought to be doing something positive to help.

At which point I looked up at the front block of flats, the one which encompassed both the guardroom and flat 10, and saw with a kind of sluggish surprise that there was now a deep crevasse down one side, and that the courtyard beneath it was strewn with bricks and plaster and beds and bits of blue uniform.

I walked over to it, and through the fog of dust saw a couple of firemen easing Flo out of a niche in the tumbled brick. Her hair was hanging loose and she'd only got one shoe on.

'*Flo*!' I darted forward, and when she recognised me the big dirty tears began to roll down her cheeks.

'The Air Vice Marshal — '

'Take it easy, kid,' one of the firemen said tenderly. 'No high rankin' bleedin' officer's gonna blame you . . . '

They laid her on a stretcher, clumsily because she was so big, and covered her over with a grey blanket.

'But the Air Vice Marshal — '

'Okay,' I said, and as they stumbled with her over the rubble towards the ambulance I went quietly through the hole in the wall that led to the remains of the entrance hall. It was a relief to have a practical purpose in view.

Although the flats on the left side of the block had been demolished the stone staircase appeared intact and I went up it, stepping over lumps of plaster and avoiding the big cracks. On the fourth floor I paused for breath and made the mistake of looking left; there was now a clear drop down to the courtyard where the rescue team was at work. It made me feel queasy.

When I reached flat 10 the full impact of what had happened began to dawn on me. I found some of my own things lying in a welter of dust and plaster in the corridor, and when I walked through the sagging doorway of room 4 half the window frame was lying across my bed. Not surprisingly, there was no sign of the glass jar belonging to Flo's beetle, and I stood in the middle of the shattered room contemplating it all with a dull sense of surprise.

I listened to one of the ambulances clanging away down to

Abbey Lodge sick quarters, and then became aware of another sound which made my heart constrict: a heavy buzzing that was all too reminiscent of a flying bomb seemed to fill the room, and even before I had time to duck I was hit on the forehead by a small hard object which fell to the floor and lay droning and rotating in the dust.

It was the Air Vice Marshal himself. Lost, deprived of his water and covered in white powder, he opened his powerful pincer claws when I picked him up and gave me a savage nip. Carefully I put him in my tunic pocket and retraced my steps. And I was just going out of the door on to the stairs when I saw a pair of grey-stockinged legs protruding from beneath a pile of debris where once the hall cloakroom had been.

I hurried towards them, calling and then scrabbling at the bricks and plaster with my hands. The girl didn't move, and when I'd got her clear I tried to hoist her up with the idea of carrying her on my back. But she was too heavy, so I put my hands under her arms and started to drag her towards the stairs. I didn't know whether she was dead or not; there were scratches on her face, but I couldn't see any other sign of injury. LACW Stokes was a quiet, timid girl from accounts section whose bed was in room 2.

Hauling her out of the flat was easy, but negotiating the stairs backwards was another matter. I had to go down one step at a time, and before I'd gone down one flight my leg was hurting again. But I fixed my slow-working mind on the thought of Flo's delight when she saw the Air Vice Marshal, and went on descending the stairs gently and painstakingly with Stokes's heels dragging at every step.

We were coming down to the first floor when the stairs gave way. There was no warning – or perhaps there was, and I was too bemused to notice it – but all I can remember is one of the cracks on the landing widening and shuddering until the whole thing disappeared with a roar. I held on to Stokes until the light went out.

I came to lying on a stretcher on the floor of the MI room at Abbey Lodge. A medical orderly gave me a mug of very sweet tea and offered me a cigarette. It hurt to sit up, but it hurt to lie down as well, and when I put my hand up to my face it came away sticky with blood.

There were other girls on stretchers too, and one of them was Stokes. She was lying very still, and exasperation filled me at the thought that she might be dead after all the trouble I'd gone to. When she made a little moaning sound, I loved her exaggeratedly.

Then I remembered the Air Vice Marshal. Wincing, I tried to get my hand in my tunic pocket, and when the orderly came back I asked her if I could have some cold water.

'Drink the tea, love,' she said. 'It's much nicer.'

She gave in when I insisted, but when she came back with it it was too late. The Air Vice Marshal lay upturned on the palm of my hand, and whether he'd died of shock or suffociation was anybody's guess. I asked the orderly if she knew whether Flo Hambledon-ffoulks was badly hurt, but she said she didn't; all she knew was that three girls were dead.

When the WAAF medical officer got to me she started with my face (deep cut over right eye), and worked her way down (extensive areas of contusion, some skin abrasion) until she got to my left leg. When she tried to raise it I let out a scream that could have been heard in the street.

Suspected fracture she wrote on the label attached to my stretcher, and I was taken with some other girls and a civilian who'd somehow got mixed up with the WAAF hostel bomb down to the Middlesex Hospital.

I don't remember much about the rest of that day; I can vaguely recall the operating theatre, and being sick afterwards, but mainly I think I slept.

I woke up with a cracking headache and a blurred impression of Maze sitting on the side of the bed.

'Christ, you don't half look a bloomin' daisy.'

'Where am I?'

'Abbey Lodge sick quarters.'

'Why can I only see with one eye? Where's the other one?'

'Under a socking great bandage,' she said. Then added encouragingly: 'Never mind, cocker, you've still got all your own teeth.'

She told me that Flo was okay, and a great surge of

depression hit me when I remembered about the Air Vice Marshal.

'Does she know?'

'Don't reckon so, after concussion.'

'I don't know what she's going to say . . . '

'We'll get her another one. Plenty more where he came from,' Maze said with an effort.

'Yes, but it won't be the *same*, will it?'

I was now completely and utterly cheesed by the way the war seemed to be snatching everyone and everything away from us; even a blasted beetle that bit people was apparently more than we had any right to form an attachment to, and immobilised in that small room in Abbey Lodge I had plenty of time to dwell on my own deprivation. It was eighteen days since David had been posted missing and the dull ache of it corresponded to the dull ache in my fractured leg. I listened to the crash of flying bombs, some near, some distant, without emotion.

Then one afternoon the door opened and Flight Sergeant Cutter came in. She looked intolerably well groomed, and I watched her apprehensively with my one eye.

'Hullo, Coryn,' she said briskly. 'How are you feeling?'

'Fine, thank you, Flight.'

She sat down on the edge of the bed and crossed her legs. Her issue stockings were faded to the beautiful silvery grey that was one of the great snob fashions in the WAAF world.

'I suppose they've told you that you're a heroine?' she said.

I shook my head, still waiting for her to pounce on some misdemeanour like being in contempt of King's Regs by having the top button of my pyjama jacket undone.

'Going upstairs to rescue Stokes was a pretty good show,' she said. 'In fact I wouldn't be surprised if the CO recommended you for the George Medal.'

I continued to stare at her with my one eye.

'But of course it's early days yet,' she said, 'and I expect they'll want to go into the whole thing very thoroughly. So don't bank on it too much, Coryn.'

Feebly I started to explain that I'd only gone upstairs to get a beetle, but she cut me short.

'If you're going to start mumbling on about it then I'll be

sorry I took you into my confidence,' she said, and took her cap off.

My amazement increased.

It's very difficult after all this time to convey the extraordinary sense of intimacy incurred by Flight Sergeant Cutter removing her cap. It's true that she didn't wear it in the admin. office, but at all other times during our association it was placed squarely and formally upon her beautiful head, and now, with it tossed carelessly aside on my bed, I felt that I'd entered a new and giddy world that made nonsense of social barriers. I stopped worrying about my top button.

'Also,' said Flight, opening her Air Force blue shoulder bag, 'I thought you might like to have this back. It was found sticking out of a pile of rubble.'

It was the photograph of Sylvia that I'd kept stuck on the wall above my bed in flat 10.

I thanked her confusedly.

'Not at all,' she said. 'Sylvia was a great friend of mine.'

I lay back on the pillows to ease the sudden pounding in my head. Then sat up again.

'My sister?'

'Yes. I'd never have connected you both, even though the name was the same, unless I'd seen her photo over your bedspace. I don't mind telling you it shook me rigid, seeing Sylvia in connection with — '

'With such a model of mediocrity?'

'Oh, don't be too hard on yourself, Coryn,' Flight said magnanimously. 'At least you're displaying a little more *esprit de corps* than you used to.'

'Thanks, Flight . . . '

I lay back again. And if it had been a surprise to learn that I was considered a heroine for inadvertently rescuing Stokes, it was downright stupefying to discover that Flight Sergeant Cutter of all people had been a friend of Sylvia's.

Then I sat up.

'Flight,' I said. 'I don't wish in any way to appear familiar, but would you mind telling me what your Christian name is?'

'Daphne,' she said. 'Why?'

I fumbled for my handkerchief because my one good eye

was watering with the strain of staring at her.
'You're Sylvia's friend Daphne. And you both worked at the Bever Club?'
'Yes,' she said. 'Two little girls from the provinces determined to see life. I saw as much as I wanted in a very short time.'
'And Sylvia?'
'Sylvia was – different. I suppose she was less rigidly conventional than I was.'
'Tell me about her.'
'Tell you what about her?'
I thought I sensed a slight evasiveness in her voice, a tinge of the same old evasiveness I'd heard in all the other voices, but I swept it aside in my delight.
'Tell me everything — '
'I don't know everything.'
'Do you know where she is, Flight?'
'Yes, of course. Don't you?'
'No.'
'Do you mean to say your parents didn't tell you?'
For some reason my heart began to thump unpleasantly.
'No.'
She recrossed her silvery-grey legs and sat looking at me thoughtfully.
'Flight – where is she?'
'In Germany,' she said.

His name was Kurt Wenz. And she met him when she took a secretarial job at the German Embassy after Bernie Patch died.
Shocked and baffled, I asked what on earth had possessed her to take a job there, of all places; surely she must have been aware that peace was running out between us and Germany, and Flight said yes, of course she was, but being Sylvia she probably thought she could help to spin it out for a bit longer. It was the first joke I'd ever heard Flight make, but I didn't even try to laugh.
I asked her if she'd ever met this Kurt Wenz and she told me that she'd been Sylvia's witness at the wedding, a hastily conducted affair in a register office that took place only a

couple of days before diplomatic relations ceased between Britain and Germany, and von Ribbentrop's Embassy closed down.

'Which explains why she didn't turn up for lunch at Aunt Mitty's on the Sunday war was declared.'

'Aunt who?'

'It doesn't matter,' I said, and lay back with my head turned away.

'Don't be too browned off, Coryn,' Flight said. 'They loved each other very much, you know.'

'Was he old and fat?' I asked bitterly.

'On the contrary,' she said. 'He was young and good-looking. Very good-looking indeed.'

'But he was a Nazi . . . To think that she married a hideous, murdering Nazi . . . '

'Not all Germans are Nazis. As a matter of fact Kurt was a doctor, and I remember him saying how much he wanted to get away from diplomatic pen-pushing and return to practising medicine. Don't forget that doctors the world over are pledged to save life, not take it.'

But it was poor comfort.

'I know how you feel,' she said with a sigh, and put her cap on ready for departure. 'But Sylvia did write home for her parents' blessing, and they never replied.'

So Ma and Pa had known all along! No wonder Ma had said *You'll never find her* . . . The bitterness increased.

'Serve her right,' I muttered. 'Sylvia was a no-good, and this finally proves it.'

'Sylvia was okay in many ways,' Flight said from over by the door. 'And with someone decent and sensible like Kurt to rely on she's probably very much less irresponsible now. The night we had a farewell drink together Kurt told me he'd already accepted a new appointment in Germany as senior medical officer in a big rehabilitation centre, and he was tremendously enthusiastic. So was Sylvia. Well, a big house went with the job, and lots of servants too, apparently — '

'Bully for her.'

'And if you're sufficiently interested,' she continued in a slightly more steely voice, 'I can probably let you have the address so that you could write to her. After the war, of course.'

'Of course,' I said. 'Thank you, Flight.'

She stood looking at me for a moment longer, then said: 'Don't judge people until you know all the facts, Coryn. But if you want my opinion, I think the worst thing that could be said about poor old Sylvia is that she never developed a really strong sense of *esprit de corps* . . .'

What an epitaph. What an end to the search for the golden-girl sister who could sing and dance like Alice Faye.

After Flight had gone I lay staring at the battered photograph that she had returned to me, then crumpled it up in a ball.

There's only one more sheet of hotel writing paper left. All the rest lies in a rough pile by my elbow, covered on both sides with urgent scribble. My hand's stiff with cramp, but I've told the story as I remember it. Why? God only knows. You tell me.

According to my watch it's now five thirty a.m. Too late to go to sleep, but all the same I lie down on the bed and close my eyes. The holy pilgrimage, as Maze called it, is finally over; today I'm going to see Sylvia, and the thought fills me with terror.

The war's been over for five years now, but the memory remains like the taste of ashes. There are no more bombs, and the concentration camp victims have been herded into bigger and better huts and rechristened Displaced Persons. Some of them came from the address Flight Sergeant Cutter gave me, the address where Sylvia's husband was appointed medical officer, and she was wrong when she told me that all doctors are pledged to save human life: Kurt Wenz was one who was not, and he was executed after the Nuremberg Trials.

For a long while after the Allied troops had uncovered the horrors of the concentration and extermination camps I was convinced that Sylvia was as guilty as the rest of them; guilty by default, if not for taking an active part. I hated her as something rotten and contaminated, and looking back on the summer of 1944 hated myself as a naïve and immature little idiot.

But little by little the old doubts have crept back again,

dissolving the hatred and clouding the issue, and now here I am in Düsseldorf with only a couple of hours between me and Sylvia. And I'll know the truth about her the minute I look into her eyes . . .

In the meantime I turn on my side and resolve to think of other things, and once again my mind drifts back to the RAF station at Regent's Park, to the WAAF hostel in the block of flats where grey lisle stockings dried in rows on the radiators and the stone staircase rang with sad songs – *'JEAL-ouseee!'* – and the clerks in the orderly room used to paint their nails with the pink correcting fluid used on stencils and the girls in the cookhouse sent a snap of themselves to Frank Sinatra c/o Hollywood, USA . . .

Soon after I got back from sick leave – and I never got the George Medal, by the way – I was posted up to Lancashire, and as if to set a seal on the finality of the London interlude I had a letter from David's mother. It was a very nice letter, and she enclosed some old snaps of him as a little boy that she thought I might like to have, but there was a melancholy tinge of good-bye about it. More than six weeks had gone by since his disappearance and he was officially listed as missing believed killed.

And what else? Maze finally made it as a GI bride, and she and Sam Corbellini send me a Christmas card from the Bronx every year; and the last I heard of Flo Hambledon-ffoulks was that she was helping, none too efficiently, in a Belgravia gown shop for outsize uppercrust ladies. I never saw Flight Sergeant Cutter again after I got sent up to Lancashire, but I've often wondered if she spotted Kurt Wenz's name among the list of war criminals that was published back in 1946 . . .

Which brings my thoughts back to the present. The hotel is beginning to come to life with the creak of floorboards and the subdued sounds of plumbing. In the next room I can hear a man gargling. So I get off the bed and go through to the shower, where the warm water washes away the gritty tiredness of a sleepless night.

At six thirty I'm downstairs drinking coffee in company with another early riser, a businessman in rimless glasses, and at seven o'clock I'm in a taxi going to 368 Mullerstrasse. It's a hell of an hour to call on anyone, but she said in her letter to come any time. I watch the early morning streets flick past and try to work out what to say to her when I first see her. What's the most sensible thing to *start* with, I mean.

We've passed a lot of new blocks of flats, but the taxi stops outside a big florid building pock-marked by bomb fragments. Some of the ground-floor windows are still boarded up. Clutching the small canvas airbag that holds the things I've brought her from England, I go in, and my heart starts pounding at the thought of how close we are.

There's no lift, and I pause for breath on the third floor; it's a crummy-looking dump with dustbins on the landings and her name is outside a door on the top floor, tucked away under the eaves where someone's left a bucket to catch the rain. I put the airbag down and prepare to knock, then see that the door's on the latch. So I go in, slowly and quietly, and there she is.

It's an attic room, not very big, with cracked walls and a bare floor, and she's lying on an old brass bedstead and she's sound asleep. I walk in and stand looking down at her and she's thin and pale and her bright hair has gone a bit colourless, yet she's still the same. She's still my sister Sylvia. And while I'm looking at her through a haze of stupid tears she opens her eyes and smiles.

'Hullo, Honeybee.'

'Hullo.'

For a moment I can't think of anything else to say, so I just stand there clutching the airbag and trying to smile while she lies contemplating me at leisure. Then suddenly she sits up and holds out her arms and we embrace and it's like all the warmest and happiest bits of my childhood all streaming back to me. I can hear the helpless, fall-about laughter, feel the comfortable summer sun on bare arms and legs and smell the dry formal smell of old school text books. I suddenly remember her dressing up in one of Pa's suits and tipping his bowler hat to imaginary customers: 'A pound of sago and a quarter of ninepenny tea? Certainly, madam . . . Nothing but the very best, madam . . . ' and then Pa appearing, glazed with outrage round the door. I remember the Palais Glide, the quick-steps and slow-steps up and down the hall to the braying of the old gramophone, and Ma telling us that we should have a little thought for other people, particularly on half-closing day . . . It's all there in the tight, convulsive embrace, and even while I note with dismay the new sharpness of her bones I'm amazed and gratified to discover that her skin smells just the same; sort of creamy, lemony smell that I envied like mad when I was around fourteen. And I know that I did right to find her, to refuse to accept permanent discouragement during all the long years of war and after, when sometimes it seemed as if fate had made up its mind that we weren't ever to meet again. I'm glad that I went on and on; that I never gave up.

Then we both regain the power of speech, and start babbling in unison.

'How are you? . . . Oh, my God, how *are* you?'

'Look, I've brought you some things — '

'You've grown up so *pretty*!'

'Well, I had my hair done specially just before I came . . . But Sylvia, what's it *been* like, all this time?'

'Wait while I make us some coffee — '

'I got a bottle of gin on the plane — '

'Marvellous. Gin and coffee — '

'Ma sent half a pound of butter and some chocolate – hope it hasn't melted — '

'How is she?'

'Not too bad. She sold the shop of course, after pa died — '

'Tell me about it — '

'Later — '

'Okay. First of all, let's find some glasses . . . '

She leaps off the bed, and her legs are thin and white under the little faded nightie. She rummages in the battered cupboard and finally produces two cups. We pour some gin into them, and as there's nothing else add a dribble of water from the tap in the corner.

'Cheers!'

'Cheers! Here's to sisters!'

She hugs me again, and although I'm feeling pretty dizzy with relief and gratitude and a huge, headlong happiness I'm conscious that there's an extra depth of emotion in her; a kind of desperate fervour that's making her shiver and giggle and sob all at once. We take a swig of gin and her teeth rattle against the cup, and it occurs to me then that one of us has got to pull herself together and take command of the situation. To show a little of poor old Cutter's *esprit de corps*, in other words.

'I've also brought some digestive biscuits,' I tell her, and dive for the airbag again. 'Things like that aren't rationed any more and I remembered that you always used to like them. So brush your hair back and put something round your shoulders because you've gone all goosy . . .'

She does as she's told, combing her hair back behind her ears with impatient fingers, then breaking open the packet of biscuits. She takes two.

'And now tell me everything that's happened, during the war and after.'

'No,' she says. 'You first.'

'Mine doesn't take long to tell. Service in the Women's Auxiliary Air Force, then marriage and two children.'

'Are you happy?'

She looks across the rumpled bed at me, the skin stretched taut over the bones of her face but her eyes as deep blue as ever. And the smile in them is the same, except for a touch of something I can't put a name to.

'Yes,' I say. 'I'm very, very happy.'

'Can I have another biscuit?'

'For God's sake – they're all yours . . .'

She sits munching. I take another sip of gin and water, which I'm not exactly enjoying although it helps somehow.

'Mine's long and a bit difficult to tell,' she says finally. 'And I don't know how much you know.'

'I'm up to the outbreak of war and you marrying Kurt Wenz.'

'Kit, do you really want to know?'

Something makes me start to think about it rather carefully. 'In as much as I'm hungry to catch up with everything that concerns you, yes. But if it could be construed as an invasion of privacy – no, of course not.'

She smiles at me, and it then occurs to me that she's probably asking for a little encouragement to get started.

'I do know about Kurt. About him being at that camp, I mean, and about him – well, all the Nuremberg — '

'He died,' she says very quickly. 'He wasn't executed – he died. I was interned with him when the Americans took over. It was a place near Munich and we had only the clothes we stood up in. There was hardly any food – we'd had no proper food for weeks – and because of all the bombing and shelling there was no water supply. He died of typhus, like thousands of others.'

'Oh.' It's hard to know whether I feel glad or sorry. Kurt Wenz had been one of the more obscene examples of Nazi ideology; he had also been my sister's husband and my brother-in-law.

'Like all the rest of us, he got caught up in history and found himself doing things that were against his nature merely in order to survive. I knew him and understood him, and now he's dead and out of reach of them all, thank God.'

She bends her head and her hair flops over her face again. I don't say anything. But I make a note of the words *I understood him* and wonder whether understanding had become a substitute for loving.

'You'll never know what it was like, Kit, when it all began to disintegrate. In Germany we'd grown so used to being ordered about, and then at the very time we needed the security of being told what to do there was no one in charge. We were left to face the final part all on our own, and those of us not buried under tons of rubble didn't know whether to stay put or try to find somewhere where things might be better. No one knew what was going on anywhere else, but the main dread was the Russians. In our case we were lucky to be liberated by the Americans, but Kurt's sister was in Berlin and she was – well, in the end they shot her.'

'We read about some of it at home.'

'They raped her in front of her children and she went out of her mind, and so they shot her. Just as if she'd been an animal. And then they bayoneted little Lisa and Karl and the baby Emmi.'

I put out my hand and take hers. It feels very cold, although the sun is beginning to find its way through the skylight above our heads.

'There's nothing I can say.'

'No. It went beyond words a long time ago.'

'Sylvia, listen to me — ' I start to say, but she gives my hand a quick squeeze before releasing it. She tucks her hair back behind her ears again.

'Come on, let's have another gin. After all, this is the reunion of a lifetime and I want to hear all about home. What's dear old Ma like these days, and is Trix still alive?'

'Trix went to join her ancestors last year, but Ma's fine. Everyone's fine, and I'm longing for you to see them. Oh, Sylvia, you can't imagine what a job it was, finding you — '

'Is England still the same?'

'More or less. A bit battered, but they're getting ready for the Festival of Britain. We've bought ourselves a pre-war Morris 8 and I've learnt to drive, the Labour Party's been re-elected, and at Regent's Park zoo there's . . . Oh, by the way, I was in the WAAF with a friend of yours called Flight Sergeant Cutter — '

'You don't mean *Daphne* Cutter?'

'I've got some snaps here somewhere. Some wartime ones, and some of our wedding, and — '

And suddenly the sense of oppression has lifted and it's like a crazy sort of Christmas. Here in this threadbare German room with the sagging bed littered with more presents from home – a sweater, some cigarettes, nylon stockings, paperbacks, Yardley's soap and a pair of blue earrings which I knew would suit her – my sister Sylvia sits crouched in her faded cotton nightie and laughs and cries and we drink gin and water out of cups and sing bits of 'The Donkey Serenade' and the sun grows in strength and blazes its full force down through the skylight. It melts poor Ma's half-pound of butter, and although butter is still one of life's most precious commodities we laugh like a couple of lunatics.

Then Sylvia tries the sweater on over her nightie and

wonders if she'd look better with her hair done up on top and all I know is that she's exactly the same as she always was, and that I was right ultimately not to believe any of the rotten things people told me about her. Even marrying a man like Kurt Wenz can be explained somehow. Later.

'Sylvia — ' I try to keep my voice steady. 'There's something I want to ask you.'

She looks at me brightly, with her head on one side.

'Will you come back to England with me? We've made enquiries at the Foreign Office and they say that provided your passport's in order there's nothing to stop you coming home for a holiday. And then, when you're there, we could start exploring the possibilities of your becoming a permanent resident again.'

The bright look fades. Her eyes become shadowed.

'I don't think it's possible, Honeybee.'

'Why not?'

'Well – money for one thing. And then — '

'You don't have to worry about money. I didn't tell you before, but I've got an open return ticket for you in my bag.'

Her face seems to crumple for a moment. I suddenly see what she'll look like when she's old. She sits cross-legged on the bed, staring into her lap and smoothing a piece of tissue paper with pensive fingers.

'Do come Sylvia. Please.'

'I'd love to,' she says very slowly. 'But it's difficult because of other things as well. When are you thinking of going?'

'As soon as possible. I can't leave home and the kids for too long.'

'Imagine you having children,' she muses. 'I'd adore to see them.'

'All I want is a chance to introduce you. Come home with me, Sylvia.'

She gets off the bed and rambles round the room, rumpling her hair abstractedly.

'I'd love to, Kit, believe me I would. But I've got a job, you see, and I don't want to lose it because of the money. Also because I – well, I don't want to let them down.'

'But surely they'd be willing to let you take a fortnight's

holiday? They must see that you're tired and ill — '

'Compared with the vast majority of people here I'm fit as a flea. But it wouldn't be easy to take time off just at this particular moment, what with one thing and another.'

'You make it sound very mysterious. What sort of job is it?'

Even as I say the words I find myself brushing away memories of the headmistress at St Ebenezer's, Bernie Patch and his widow lady and the horrors of the Bever Club.

She turns to face me from the corner where the tap drips into a small cracked sink.

'I work for a *Tierartz*. I'm a vet's assistant.'

'Good God.' I gaze back at her in blank surprise. 'Do you enjoy it?'

'Yes,' she says. 'I've grown to like it very much.'

'Look – couldn't I go and see them? Or at least, if I went with you and you told the vet that I was your sister and we hadn't seen one another for years, surely they'd agree to your taking a holiday, even if it was only a short one. Not even Krauts could be heartless enough to say no . . .'

The gin I've been drinking has taken effect. It's made everything seem very clear and very simple. All the same I'm not sorry when she starts to make some coffee; measuring out the grains with care and tipping them into an enamel pot. She searches for matches, and light-heartedly I go and help her. I poke about inside the battered cupboard, then pull aside the old curtain covering the alcove, and the first thing I see behind it is a pair of men's trousers hanging there by their braces. Quickly I let it fall again and the gin helps me to pretend that I haven't noticed anything.

'Of course, I *want* to come back with you,' Sylvia is saying. 'Perhaps I could manage just a couple of days, although the whole idea's crazy — '

'It's not in the least crazy. You have every right to see your family, and as for staying on in Germany, well, let's face it – the past is over and done with — '

'Yes, but — '

'Shall I wash the cups, or are there some others?'

'I'm not sure . . . '

And now she seems to have changed completely. To have lost all her happiness and her confidence. She's become small, harassed and grey-looking, uncertain even of her own few pitiful possessions. So I go and fetch the two cups we've been using and wash them out, and I know that if we're to get anywhere at all I'm the one who's got to take charge of the situation. Once I was the little sister, but now I'm grown up too; being a wife and mother, let alone an ex-leading aircraftwoman from the administrative section of the Women's Auxiliary Air Force, have taught me how to cope with just about everything.

'You're coming,' I tell her as she starts to pour the coffee. 'You're going to make your bed and get dressed and then we'll both go round to the vet's place and explain that all you want is a week's holiday – without pay, if necessary – and then we'll catch the next flight back to Northolt. It's all quite simple.'

'But I've got other things to see to — '

'Go ahead, see to them. Drink your coffee, get dressed and see to them. And if you're short of cash I can let you have some.'

'Are you sure?' She looks at me doubtfully.

'Positive. I've got about fifty pounds in unsigned traveller's cheques. All I need is enough to settle the hotel bill — '

'You see, I owe a couple of weeks' rent . . . '

The hot, bitter coffee makes my eyes sting. 'You're still having a pretty lousy time of it, aren't you?'

'If I am, it's of my own making.'

'Never mind, it's all going to be different from now on. So let's start by getting this vet sorted out — '

'It'd be much better if I went on my own,' she says quickly. 'People are still a bit sensitive about – about — '

'The so-called conquering races? Okay, I take your point, but I could wait outside — '

'For Christ's *sake!*' She bangs down her cup and the agony in her face suddenly warns me that I've got to handle the situation far, far more carefully. Once again the gin's made me too talkative; altogether too busy.

'Sorry, love, I'm rushing things.'

She closes her eyes, opens them again and says very quietly: 'Just let me do it my way. I'll go and see the people I work for, I'll collect my clean laundry and if you can really lend me the equivalent of five pounds I'll pay the landlady. I'll meet you back here at six o'clock this evening.'

'So late?' Then I glance at my watch and see that it's already close to midday. 'All right then, but don't forget the plane leaves at nine.'

'You wouldn't rather go tomorrow?'

Instinct tells me that she's on the point of changing her mind. 'It would make things much easier for me at home if we got back tonight.'

I watch the conflicting expressions in her big hollow eyes; doubt, worry, uncertainty . . . fear. Then she blinks them all away and smiles.

'Remember the days when you used to tell me that I looked like Alice Faye?'

'Not half.'

'Do I still?'

'Sylvia,' I say earnestly. 'I swear to God that you're still the dead spitting image.'

9

And the doubts and worries seem to disappear. She suddenly begins to laugh again, throwing off the sweater and the old faded nightie, then putting the sweater on again and tucking it into the top of an old black skirt. She's too thin to need a bra and I notice that her panties are held up by a safety pin. She thrusts her feet into a pair of cheap shoes and my heart contracts when she sweeps her hair back with a couple of impatient strokes of the hairbrush and ties it with a bit of blue ribbon.

I help her to make the bed, and while she's sorting through her belongings which seem to be kept in a suitcase I give her the book of traveller's cheques, then realise that although they're not signed she still can't cash them.

'I'll have to do it because they need to see my passport. I'll draw twenty for you — '

'No trouble, Honeybee,' she says, putting the cheque book in her handbag. 'I can get someone to do it for me without bothering the bank. And I told you, I only need five just for a loan until I get squared up — '

'Don't worry so,' I tell her. 'We're not rich, but we can manage all right.'

So we leave her suitcase and my now empty airbag stacked ready for six o'clock.

'Sure you don't want me to come with you?'

'It wouldn't be very exciting for you, and besides, I'd be quicker on my own — ' Cheerfully she slams the door.

'Don't you ever lock it?'

'No point, when you've nothing much to lose.'.

We part at the foot of the stairs, Sylvia kissing her hand as she hurries off. Then I remember something, and go dashing after her.

'Is your passport in order?'

'Yes. I've always kept it going, in case . . . '

The clouded look reappears for an instant, and standing there in the noise of the traffic and the hustle of passers-by I take her arm and say stumblingly: 'Everything *is* all right, isn't it? I mean — '

'Of course it is,' she says fondly. 'And now it's going to get righter and righter, isn't it?'

I watch her run across the street, wave to me when she reaches the other side, then turn a corner and disappear from view.

As for me, I now propose to spend my one and only day in Germany meandering contentedly round the sights of Düsseldorf.

The bombing must have been very bad. Easily as bad as ours. There are still mounds of rubble here and there but rebuilding is going on at a furious rate with pneumatic drills splitting my eardrums and cement powder flying like pollen as the concrete blocks rise on all the main streets. Maybe it's the spring sunlight dancing on the bright window boxes or maybe it's just because I've found Sylvia again, but there's an atmosphere of exhilaration. There's hopefulness in the twinkling shops, and I'm tickled pink to see that some of the trams have little cafés in the front half; people are sitting at little tables drinking beer and eating cakes as they glide through the city and everywhere there's a sense of purpose, of energetic resolution, that I can't help admiring.

I have lunch in a *Bier-Restaurant* and try, unavailingly, to converse with the elderly German couple who sit at my table. But I don't know their language and they don't know mine, so all we can do is smile and nod because the war's over now and there's no need for any more hatred, and believe me I feel like nodding and smiling every time I remember that tonight at nine o'clock I'm catching the plane back to Northolt and that Sylvia will be with me.

After lunch I find my way back to the Europaischer Hof

and pay my bill with the one 100 mark note I've got left, then go up to my room and pack my things. When I get to the pile of manuscript I wrote last night I almost chuck it in the waste-paper basket, then hesitate, because someone who understands English might find it and it's a bit, well – personal, and because after all the story isn't quite finished yet. It doesn't finish until the plane takes off from the airport tonight with two English sisters on board.

So I bundle it into my valise, say a mute good-bye to the blandly anonymous room where I spent a sleepless night, and then take a taxi back to 368 Mullerstraase. And when I climb up to the top floor, her door's locked.

It's only a quarter to six, so perhaps she hasn't finished doing all the things she had to do. I lean against the wall and wait, and at five past six go all the way downstairs again and look along the street to see if she's coming. She isn't.

So I go upstairs again, and then gradually it dawns on me that something's wrong. She said she never locked her door. And with increasing agitation I see that the little card with her name on has been removed.

I rattle the handle, then put my shoulder against the door and push. Nothing happens. I bang on it with my fist and the answer is silence. Standing there on the sad landing with the bucket waiting to catch raindrops I go on banging and rattling and calling her name until a fat old girl with plaits round her head bounces out of the place next door and shouts: '*Nein* – nein — ' and then burbles on, and of course I don't understand a word.

But the fear rises in me more and more and I shake off her restraining hand because I'm convinced now that something utterly dreadful has happened.

'*Zimmer zu vermieten* – young lady gone away . . . ' insists the old girl, and a bit of guttural English brings me to my senses.

'Young lady not gone away *yet,*' I tell her with emphasis. 'Going tonight. With me. I am her sister.'

We stand there, breathing into one another's faces, and I see her searching for the wherewithal to express herself in some way I'll understand.

'Young lady gone,' she repeats at length. 'Good-bye. All finish.'

Stupefied, I watch her go through the motions of shaking hands and waving farewell, then a sudden thought occurs to me. Perhaps she's gone straight to the airport. Perhaps she misunderstood me when I said we'd meet back at her place at six o'clock. In which case she's probably got her suitcase and my airbag with her.

I ask the old girl if I can borrow the key to Sylvia's room, and go through a pantomime of unlocking the door.

'Nein,' she says, shaking her head. 'Key gone with man belonging — '

I take it that she means the landlord. It's now six thirty, and when I hear footsteps running up the stairs I rush to the top of the landing. But it isn't her. I hear a door bang further down, then silence.

'Gone,' repeats the old girl, still wagging her head. 'Gone – all gone . . . ' And she goes back into her own place and shuts the door.

And so I'm left alone outside as the light begins to fade and the silence settles deeper, then I sit down on the valise and rest my back against the wall and I feel as if I'm the only person still on earth.

At half past seven I scribble a note to say I'm at the airport and shove it half under the door where she'll see it, then walk slowly downstairs to find a taxi. Half way down I hear footsteps coming towards me and hope fills me, but only for a second. It's a slow, heavy tread, nothing like hers.

A man passes me, wearing a leather cap with a big peak. He gives me a quick glance from under it, then looks away. And I've almost reached the ground floor when I hear his footsteps halt and then the rattle of a key in a lock and some weird instinct makes me turn back and run, as quietly as possible, back up the stairs again. And my heart's pounding with the effort when I reach the top floor and see that Sylvia's door is open and that the man is in her room.

Attack seems the best form of defence.

Standing on the threshold I grip my handbag tightly under

my arm and say: 'Do you mind explaining what you're doing in my sister's room?'

It's a pretty daft thing to say because even if he felt inclined to explain it would probably be in German and I'd be none the wiser, but hearing the sound of my own voice, chill and peremptory, has the effect of increasing my indignation.

The man is on his knees, dragging out a cardboard box from under the bed. It seems to be packed with objects wrapped in newspaper. He removes one of them and then slowly regains his feet, levering himself up by pressing with his elbows on the side of the bed. He's a big man, not far off six feet, and his shabby brown suit doesn't fit very well. He's not all that young, yet a quick glimpse beneath the sheltering peak of his cap shows a smooth, rather shiny face that somehow looks as if it hasn't been lived in all that long.

'I'm afraid you are mistaken, Fräulein. This room belongs to a friend of mine and he will be returning here this evening.'

'But that's nonsense!' I'm disconcerted when he answers me in English, but it doesn't stop the indignation. 'I came here this morning and my sister was asleep in that bed. I was here with her almost until lunchtime. We talked and made coffee and arranged to meet here again at six o'clock this evening to catch the plane back to England. We left our bags right there, by the — '

I look at the place where we put them, close to the door. They're not there now.

The man doesn't say anything. He just looks at me carefully, politely, then begins to unwrap the newspaper parcel he's holding. Inside it is a small narrow box which he opens, and I feel a nasty little twinge of apprehension when I see that it contains a hypodermic syringe. He takes it out, and then, pointing it at the skylight, slowly depresses the plunger.

'I want to know where my sister is,' I say in a voice high with suppressed panic. 'My sister is an Englishwoman and she lives in this room. She has a job somewhere in Düsseldorf and she's coming back with me to Northolt tonight.'

I'm not even sure he's listening. All his attention seems to be focused on the hypodermic, and just in case I'm in the presence of a homicidal maniac I'm glad I'm nearest the door.

'I want to know where my sister is,' I repeat. 'And I want to know what's happened to our luggage — '

'I have no knowledge of any sisters who may live here or anywhere else,' the man says finally. His English is good, but he speaks with a German accent. 'I can only suggest that you have made an error, Fräulein, in coming to the room of my friend. Perhaps you should contact with the police.'

Without haste he replaces the hypodermic in its box, closes the lid, and then pushes the cardboard box back under the bed with his foot.

He's talking rubbish, of course. This is the room I was in this morning; it's the same sagging brass bed, in fact I think I can recognise a few digestive biscuit crumbs still clinging to the woollen blanket. The battered cupboard is the same, so are the two cups and the coffee pot although I can't see the bottle of gin anywhere. With that in mind I go across to the curtain that screens the alcove and jerk it aside.

'Does your sister wear men's trousers, Fräulein?' He tilts his head to stare at me from under the peak of his stupid leather cap. Everything about him is stupid, and fills me with rage. I forget about feeling frightened and apprehensive.

'Of course she doesn't! But even if she did it would be no affair of yours, and I'm warning you now that I intend to find out why she didn't come back here tonight. My sister is the widow of a German but she still holds a British passport and I have every intention of seeing that she leaves Germany as and when she wants to. And furthermore I am not a Fräulein, I am a *Frau* — '

The next thing that happens surprises me very much.

At one moment the man is placing the small box containing the hypodermic in an inside pocket of his jacket, and then, almost without appearing to move, he's outside the door. I hear the rapid scuttle of his feet on the stairs and I suppose it's no more than blind instinct that makes me rush after him. The front door's still swinging as I leap through it.

It's dark outside now, and the sudden drop in temperature is a reminder that winter's only just passed. But the lights are bright, and I see the man walking swiftly to the end of the street with his hands in his pockets and his head bent. I follow him, and now it's no longer a case of blind instinct but of a steadily mounting conviction that something strange is going on so far as Sylvia is concerned, and that he knows far more than he's prepared to admit. I break into a run, intent on catching him up, then decide that it might be more practical to continue following him. Not knowing any places connected with Sylvia except the room in the Mullerstrasse, I can't afford to ignore the possibility that he might lead me to her.

He crosses the street and for a moment or two is lost from sight behind a tram. I hover uncertainly and get hooted at by an irate Volkswagen, then hurry forward again as I see the man disappearing down a main thoroughfare where people are pausing to look in the big shop windows. I catch a whiff of good cooking from a restaurant and realise that I'm getting hungry. By the time we reach the second set of traffic lights I'm also getting tired, but the man has slowed his pace now and walks with the careless ease of someone unaware of pursuit. I begin to wonder whether I'm being silly to follow him all this way, then indignation flares up again: who's taken our luggage? Who locked the door of Sylvia's room and removed the card with her name on it? And above all, what's happened to her? I don't believe she's at the airport.

I almost lose the man as he turns down a side street and have to put a spurt on because I'm getting too far behind. Then he turns into another street, and abruptly the scene changes. The bright lights and agreeable bustle have given way to an area of shadowy gloom. The streets are very narrow, more like alleyways, and there is the old damp smell of bombed buildings that I remember from the Regent's Park days. Here and there light spills from an uncurtained window and from one house I hear the sound of a baby screaming. There's no one about, and I put on another tired spurt because the man is more difficult to see in the thickening shadows and suddenly I bash my toe on a bit of broken kerb, nearly recover my balance and then finally sprawl headlong. Winded and despairing, I hear the contents of my handbag tinkling like Christmas tree ornaments all around me.

I get up slowly, and find that my knees and the palms of my hands are stinging. My toe hurts, too. I brush myself down, collect my handbag and as many of its bits and pieces as I can find, and when I discover that my prey has now completely disappeared in the sombre obscurity that surrounds us I feel a rush of self-pitying tears.

There's the remains of a low brick wall close by and I limp over to it and sit down. My knees are still stinging but it's too dark to explore the damage. I take my shoe off and rub my injured toe. And I listen hard, straining to catch the least sound of footsteps that will give me the hopefulness and the courage to go on trying to follow the man in the leather cap. But there's nothing. I can't even hear the baby screaming any more and the sound of traffic from the main thoroughfare might be a million miles away.

Still, I can't sit here for ever. The tears have receded and all I know is that having got myself into this muddle I've got to get myself out of it. I'll try to find my way back to the Mullerstrasse to see whether by any chance Sylvia's returned, and if not I'll get a taxi to the airport. If I've missed the plane I'll just have to hang around until the next one because without the traveller's cheques I haven't got enough money for another night at the Europaischer Hof. My mind's made up, but when I stand up again I start limping in the other direction: the direction I was going in before I fell over.

I come to another lighted window and look in through it as I pass. A family is sitting at supper, with the father in shirtsleeves and saucepans on the plastic-covered table. It looks warm and golden and very loving in there, and for a moment I'm tempted to knock on the door and ask if I can join in. Maybe it's just as well that I can't speak German.

And then I come to the dimly lighted archway which leads into an even smaller alleyway, and I walk down it and to my great joy see a little pale quadruped with a long tail held aloft tripping daintily ahead of me. At home we've got a cat called Emily, and filled with a sudden rush of homesickness I follow it. It stops at a door with a dim blue light over the top of it, and looks up at me; I think it's a ginger cat, but everything's so strange and unreal in these sepulchral shadows.

I stop too, prepared in my awful loneliness to knock on the door and say *Your cat wants to come in,* then I see the brass plate displayed in the centre of the door where the knocker would normally be. *Tierarzt,* it says. I repeat the word out loud, and my tired, fumbling brain insists that there's something familiar about it.

The door's not locked, so the cat and I go in.

We're in a small dingy room lined with folding chairs upon which are sitting an assortment of men and women and they're all clutching animals. Some of the animals are in baskets, some in boxes with holes punched in, while others are on leashes or lengths of knotted twine. One old woman has a heavy crucifix on her bosom and a parrot snuggled motionless on her shoulder. And then I remember: *Tierarzt* was the word Sylvia used. *I work for a vet,* she said. My heart starts to thump.

The cat passes the length of the chairs, courteously touching each pair of patient legs with its arched back before disappearing through an open door at the far end of the room. As for me, I stand blinking on the threshold for a moment, then sink unobtrusively on to the one empty chair that remains. After the first mildly curious glance no one takes any notice of me; but I feel out of place without an animal and do my best to look like a woman with a pet mouse in her pocket.

I'm studying the alsatian dozing on the floor opposite me when a voice calls something that sounds like *'Der nächste, bitte.'* It's a voice I know very well indeed, and there in the doorway that the cat has gone through stands Sylvia, wearing a white overall and with a white turban covering her hair.

A man with a brown wicker basket gets up, but before he can reach her I've bounded out of my chair.

'Sylvia – what happened to you, for God's sake? I waited and waited — '

She jumps violently. Tripping over feet, both human and animal, I grab hold of her arm and shake it. The man with the wicker basket gives me a shove in the back, suspecting that I'm trying to take his turn, but Sylvia speaks to him in rapid

German. He disappears into what is presumably the vet's consulting room.

'Oh, Honeybee, I'm so sorry — ' She turns to me, and we step out of sight of the waiting room. 'Listen, I did try to tell them, but when I got here there was such an awful rush of work. Three emergency operations, the phone wouldn't stop ringing, and then it was time to get ready for surgery – you know how it is . . . '

'No, I damn well don't!'

Now that I've found her I don't feel relieved so much as angry and betrayed. I feel as I did when Flight Sergeant Cutter broke the news to me that Sylvia had married a kraut.

'No, I don't know how it is, except that I've spent hours waiting, and then charging about in the dark looking for you because you haven't even bothered to get a message to me —

'But I couldn't – there's no phone at my place — '

'*Your* place? Are you sure it's yours? Someone I met there said the room belonged to a friend of his. A man friend — '

For a moment she looks as if I'd hit her. What little colour she has drains from her face and I can't bear the expression of fear that flickers in her eyes.

'I'm sorry,' I say, turning away. 'I'm tired, and a bit fed up at the way it's all turning out.'

'Did you say anything to the man you met about my coming to England with you?'

'Yes, of course I did. Why?'

'No particular reason,' she says. Then adds quickly: 'It's all my fault, but please, Kit, be patient with me for just a little while longer . . . '

Glancing at my watch I realise that I've no option. It's now ten to eight. I know the airport's a long way from the city, so unless I can persuade her to drop everything and get a taxi with me right now we'll miss the plane anyway. And it's at this point that I remember about my valise: I left it outside the door of the room in the Mullerstrasse.

Some sort of deep and terrible moaning noise suddenly fills my ears. Sickened, I stand listening to it, and I'm so fed up that it might well be coming from me. But it isn't. It's coming from behind the wall on my left. The door on my right is half open and through it I can hear the murmur of voices and the hiss of a steriliser, and I know then that it's the moaning of some big animal in unendurable pain.

I try to say something to Sylvia but the blood seems to drain out of my head, and when the moaning climbs the scale and becomes a tortured scream I'm fleetingly aware of the floor tilting wildly before a ringing stinging darkness blots everything out.

I seem to come out of the faint in sections. The moaning's stopped, and I can hear Sylvia's voice and the trickle of water coming from a long way off. Then I become aware that I'm sitting slumped in a chair and that something's hurting. When I open my eyes it's to find Sylvia crouching at my feet with a bowl of water, gently sponging the dried blood and grit and fragments of torn stocking from the raw surface of both my knees.

'Poor little Kit, why didn't you tell me?'

'Must be where I fell over in the dark . . . '

The disinfectant bites, and I float away on a dream of long-ago summer and my sister Sylvia dressed in a bedspread and a crown of buttercups and daisies while she mops my tears and then ties the handkerchief round my injured kneecap. How extraordinary that it should all be happening again . . .

'Never mind, soon be better.' She smiles up at me, and looking dazedly into her eyes I see that they are full of the same memory. It's comforting to think that we can still be united by recollections of our early days – somehow it proves that everything between us must ultimately be okay – and then I become aware that someone's standing behind my chair. I can sense him, hear him breathing, and when a man's hand holding a glass of water appears from behind my shoulder I know with a curiously sinking heart exactly who I'm going to see.

He's still wearing the peaked cap, and he comes round to where Sylvia is bandaging my knees.

'By the way, Kit,' she says. 'This is Bruno, our odd-job man.'

I sip the cold water and it clears away the last hint of dreaminess.

'We've already met,' I tell her. 'In your room, which incidentally he insists belongs to someone else.'

She laughs, but it's strained and unconvincing somehow. 'One way and another I've got quite a bit of explaining to do, haven't I? Just hang on until we've finished surgery and then we'll sort things out — '

She gets up from the floor, and the bowl is brimming with swabs of dirty pink-stained cotton wool. She carries it towards the door.

'We shouldn't be more than half an hour, then we'll have some supper.'

'Yes, but . . . '

I want to follow her, to argue, to get this ridiculous situation cleared up, but a sense of weary oppression prevents it. So I'm left sitting in the chair, with the man called Bruno hovering to take the glass of water from me, when the animal-moaning starts again. It makes my scalp prickle.

'What in God's name are they doing to it?' In some ways I don't want to know, yet I won't know any peace until I do.

'That sound you hear?' He looks surprised. 'It is the old man who lives in the next room. Before the war he was a 'cellist of very famous quality but now he is old and blind and forgotten — '

'You mean that's someone playing a *'cello?'* The idea astounds me. 'But it sounds just like — '

The man puts down the glass of water and then drags another chair close to mine. He lowers himself into it.

'What we are listening to,' he says placidly, 'is his death music.'

'In England,' I say, dignity fighting with a sense of horror, 'we would refer to it as a swan song.'

'As you will, Fräulein. As you will.' Without haste he takes my hand, raises it to his lips and kisses it.

'You are very pretty.'

'I'm aware of having looked better.'

Removing my hand from his grasp I sit back in the chair and contemplate my legs, which are stretched out in front of me with the feet propped up on a wooden box. My stockings are rolled down to my ankles and both knees are lightly but voluminously bandaged. They don't hurt any more, but the effect is hardly one of spell-binding glamour.

And then for the first time I start contemplating my surroundings. It's a big, strange, broken room that we're in, shadowed except for the harsh light that pours from a single unshaded lamp bulb dangling from the ceiling at the far end. The walls near me are bruised with dirt and here and there plaster has fallen away to reveal bare brickwork underneath. There is a carpet, and one or two random pieces of furniture like the chairs we're sitting in, but the place is untidy with boxes and piles of newspapers and such irrelevant objects as a lawnmower and a baby's cot. It has a damp, closed-up smell which is challenged only timidly by the scent of disinfectant coming either from my knees or from the vet's surgery in the room opposite. Everything about it combines to give me the creeps. The old man's 'cello music has subsided into a low throbbing and I know that the moment I touch home soil I won't be able to believe that any of this really happened.

'Poor little English knees,' says the man in the peaked cap. 'Running through the streets with them to find her sister, and then down she goes – *bop!*'

'But I was right, wasn't I? You ran away, I followed you and I found her.'

'Life is full of extravagant coincidence. That power which erring men call chance, as your John Milton said, and so here we are.' He doesn't seem at all disconcerted at having been caught out.

It's very tempting to demand that he should start explaining some of the weird carry-on I've got mixed up in, but something warns me not to. The person to ask is Sylvia, and if only she'd come out of that damned vet's surgery perhaps I might be granted the luxury of five minutes' quiet and uninterrupted tête-à-tête with her.

'You like this room? Perhaps you wish that I would show you round?' His voice breaks in on my thoughts.

'No, thank you. Well . . . ' I haven't the slightest desire to see any more of this dismal hole, but neither am I particularly keen to go on sitting here with him.

'It would be good for the knees to take a little exercise now they have recovered from the shock. Otherwise the skin will stiffen and there will be additional discomfort.'

Suddenly he removes his cap, and his big smooth face beams across at me like a bright sun. There's a gap between his two front teeth, and his hair (what there is of it) is a rich chestnut colour.

'Come,' he says, and helps me to my feet, and after the initial sensation of skinless flesh being forcefully detached from its bandaging, I find walking no problem.

Beyond the reach of the single light bulb the shadows disclose a stone staircase, down which a cold draught blows on my bare legs. We go through a door at one side of it and within a very few minutes I lose all sense of direction in the confusion of passages, alcoves, steps up and down and rooms that suddenly end in a sheet of corrugated iron. At one point he opens a cupboard door and I find myself staring giddily down into the cold and dimly lit street, and realise that this must have been two or more houses which have been made interconnecting by bomb damage. The old sweet damp smell of rotting plaster is very pronounced and every now and then I seem to catch the subdued sound of other people who are hidden from view; whisperings, rustlings and furtive little scratchings like those of mice in the wainscot. The shadows lie thick as velvet and I steel myself in case we suddenly come upon the old blind 'cellist. But we don't. We don't see anyone. And I can't make out whether this bloke Bruno is expecting me to admire the place or disparage it, but after following him in silence for what seems like a very long time I finally observe that it would make a good place for a game of hide-and-seek. At which he bursts into a loud guffaw as if I've said something funny.

And then we're back at the point where I first saw Sylvia. The waiting room is empty now, and something prompts me to look round the door of the surgery. It's poor-looking but very clean, with shelves of bottles, a big old-fashioned geyser over the sink, and a high enamel-topped table. There are signs that the place has just been washed down and I notice a man's white coat hanging on a peg close by. It looks as if he's only just taken it off because it's still swinging gently. I suppose it belongs to the vet.

'Come, Fräulein.' Bruno cradles my elbow. 'Come now, we find the others.'

The kitchen is the only room I haven't seen, apart from those which contain other tenants. Another stark, unshaded light bulb illuminates cracked walls and flaking ceiling, but from an old iron stove of heroic proportions comes the smell of cooking and the scrubbed table is laid with knives and forks, plates and a basket of rough cut bread.

'Darling, I do apologise for all this,' Sylvia says. Divested of white overall and turban I see she's still wearing the black skirt, and tucked into it the sweater I brought from home. She comes over to the table with four glasses and then proceeds to open a bottle of white wine.

'At least we've got something reasonably decent for supper tonight,' she says. 'And Hans brought some *Apfelstrudel* this morning.'

I suddenly find myself resenting her cheerful assumption that I'm staying to supper. I'm very hungry, but would far rather get a snack at the airport. I tell her so.

'But that's ridiculous, we wouldn't dream of letting you!'

'Sylvia,' I say, pulling a chair out from the table and sitting down. 'Just tell me one thing to start with. Who's *we?*'

'Hans, Bruno and me. We sort of live here.'

'But you didn't say anything about sort of living anywhere else this morning. You led me to believe that you lived alone and permanently in that room in the Mullerstrasse and I believed you, in spite of your not knowing how many cups and saucers you had, and in spite of men's trousers hanging behind the curtain. You even said you owed a couple of weeks' rent — '

'Yes, I know,' she says, and pushes a glass of wine across to me. 'I was planning to explain things in more detail if I came back to England with you — '

'If? Do I gather that you've changed your mind?'

She looks at me steadily, unsmilingly. 'It was a lovely idea, but that was all. No, I can't come. Not possibly.'

'But this morning — '

'This morning was different. We were excited, and got

carried away.'

I didn't, I feel like saying. Instead, I ask: 'Is Hans the vet?'

'Yes. He'll be here in a minute.'

'Is he afraid you won't come back?'

I don't know why I said that, but I notice her flinch. I also notice that the man Bruno is over by the stove with his back to us, and his immobility tells me that he's listening to every word.

'Of course he isn't.' She speaks a little impatiently. 'He knows perfectly well that I would never walk out on him whenever I felt inclined.'

For my part, I feel inclined to say something about all the walking out she did back in England; but I don't, because it wouldn't get us anywhere. I just heave a sigh and ask when she thinks circumstances will allow her to take a holiday back home with her family. I also take the opportunity to pull my stockings up and re-suspender them while Bruno's back is still turned.

'We'll see if we can fix something tonight,' she promises, then raises her glass. 'Here's to sisters.'

The wine is cold, light and refreshing but it doesn't cheer me up. I feel bogged down in evasions, half-promises and silly suspicions of skulduggery induced no doubt by the weird place we're in. I just long to know whether she's coming or not, and if she isn't to catch the next plane back to England, home and beautiful banality. I glance at my watch and see that it's nine o'clock, and the thought of tonight's Viking speeding down the runway and setting course for Northolt fills me with a renewed bout of homesickness.

I gulp the rest of the wine and stand up.

'If it's all the same to you, I think I'll get back to the airport. But before I do that I'll have to go back to the Mullerstrasse because I left my valise there . . . '

Such is my mood, I feel pretty sure that someone will have pinched it before now; I ask Sylvia if I can have the remainder of my traveller's cheques, if she's still got them, but before she can reply someone else walks into the room.

He's very tall, with long legs and narrow hips, and I would put his age at somewhere between thirty-five and forty. He's wearing a black polo sweater and I find myself standing by the table staring at him as if he's someone utterly unique. Perhaps he is, because when I can drag my eyes away I see that Bruno has turned round and is looking at him with a strange intentness; as for Sylvia, she's holding her wine glass in both hands like some kind of chalice and she looks like a woman upon whom the sun is shining for the first time in weeks. The effect he has, not only on us but on the room itself, strikes me as extraordinary; everything seems charged with a new energy, a splendid sense of certainty. I find myself staring at him all over again, and as I do become conscious that he's the most outstandingly handsome man I've ever seen in my life.

'Kit,' Sylvia says finally. 'This is Hans.'

I find myself staying to supper after all. Not only that, I seem to have made some sort of tacit agreement with Sylvia not to ask questions, not to criticise, not even to pass comment on the situation I've become involved in. The whole mad bundle of tricks has been temporarily shelved, suspended, put on ice, and temporarily (but only temporarily) I'm resigned to just sitting and watching and trying to work things out for myself.

The first thing I work out is the reason why she didn't really want to come back to England with me. It's not difficult, because it's sitting right opposite me at the table. Only thing I can't understand is the reason for her evasiveness. Why couldn't she just tell me there and then, straight from the shoulder and no nonsense, that there was this chap Hans, who . . . But in a way, of course, she did. *I can't let him down,* she said, *It's all rather difficult* – and I must have made it a damn sight more difficult, playing the busy bossy little sister who wouldn't take no for an answer. But none of this explains the strange business of the Mullerstrasse room, or the reason why Bruno ran away from me . . .

During the meal it becomes apparent that Hans doesn't speak English and the conversation switches from German to English and back as Sylvia and Bruno share the translation chores. She and Hans discuss the evening's surgery; clinical facts, I gather, interwoven with anecdotes which she translates for my benefit about the frequent apparent mismatch of animal and owner. I hear about the large man shedding tears over a defunct hamster, the tiny spinster in charge of a brutal mastiff. I say that it's surprising to find people preoccupied with animal welfare at a time when there's so much else to claim their attention, and Hans leans across the table towards me and the power emanating from the man is almost sufficient to persuade me that I understand German.

'He says that in a world where most people have been robbed of their closest kin,' Sylvia says, 'animals fill the gap most easily because they offer the maximum sympathy while making the minimum demand. A goldfish in a bowl offers compassion easier to accept than that of a fellow human being because the goldfish, by virtue of its very simplicity, is bound to be dispassionate.'

'Goldfish are cold-blooded.'

'So are many human beings, Fräulein,' Bruno says. I remember some of the things the Allies uncovered during the invasion of Europe and grimly agree.

'In the meantime, Hans is happy to be cashing in on the prevailing trend?'

He smiles at me, and shrugs. '*Als Ueberlebender des Massenmordes tut man was man kann,*' he says, and somehow I get the gist of it in all its subdued bitterness: 'As a survivor from the holocaust, I merely do what I can.'

Yet we seem to be laughing quite a lot, even though there's a sort of undercurrent of watchfulness (presumably they're all watching me), and when they open another bottle of wine the cavernous kitchen with its frozen teardrop light bulb has become quite cosy.

'Hans is half Polish,' Sylvia explains. 'He studied to become a veterinary surgeon in Berlin but went back to Poland to his father's people when the Nazis came to power. After the invasion he was lucky to be drafted into the *Wehrmacht* because of his mixed nationality. He had a rough time of it, though. North Africa, Russia, and then Normandy. By the end of the war he was the only surviving member of his family.'

I sense that there's a lot more to it than that. The carefully chosen words are so bare, so matter-of-fact, but when I murmur something conventionally sympathetic she translates it into German. Hans replies briefly.

'What did he say?'

'He says that you've got to be either very tough or very unscrupulous to survive.'

'Which is he?'

'Both.'

'Still – it's all over now, isn't it?' I strive to sound politely comforting.

'No,' Sylvia says very quietly. So quietly that only I can hear. 'No, it isn't quite over, yet.'

I make a note of the words and resolve to ponder them later.

'Tell me what happened to you, I say to Bruno, who so far has contributed little to the conversation. As we demolish the second bottle of wine I find my aversion to him decreasing slightly. In spite of his strange smooth face he has an almost homely aspect; homely compared with Hans, anyway.

'My story is similar in outline,' he says laconically. 'And I too survived.'

I'm suddenly tempted to tell them how I survived the flying bomb at the WAAF hostel, then decide it's time we gave the subject of survival a rest.

'When things got moving again Hans settled in Düsseldorf and started this practice,' Sylvia says, slicing the last of the *Apfelstrudel*. 'Six months ago I answered his advertisement for secretary-cum-assistant and now we have Bruno to help out as general factotum. The premises may not be impressive, but as they're due for demolition they're very cheap. Other people set up home in odd corners for a while, then move on somewhere else when they've got themselves sorted out. There's still a lot of sorting out to do, and we've all learned not to ask questions.'

Silently I compare the bright brash Düsseldorf of high-rise hotels and glittering new shops with this furtive, sepulchral world of bombed back streets, and then try to relate them both to the similar yet vastly different circumstances back home. And although I've never been more sharply aware of what the Germans have suffered, somehow I still can't shake off the moral rectitude of *Well, whose fault was it in the first place?*

It took me a long time and a lot of personal misery to finally get in tune with the war, and although the whistle blew for peace five years ago I'm still not finding it easy to forgive and forget. God knows why my reactions seem to lag so far behind. I'm not proud of it.

'Life must be very difficult,' I say finally, 'for the guilty as well as the innocent.'

No one speaks, but once again the atmosphere is full of that strange watchfulness. Then Bruno pushes away his empty plate, reaches for his peaked cap and walks out. Sylvia gets up to make coffee and I'm left sitting at the table with Hans. He's studying me carefully, as if I were some small animal brought to him for diagnosis. I try to study him back, but feel my gaze shifting evasively. It only becomes fixed when Sylvia comes over and stands behind him with her hands resting lightly on his shoulders.

'Dear old Honeybee,' she says, smiling at me over the top of his head. 'It's so wonderful to see you again.'

'Is it?'

'You'll never know.'

'So what's going to happen? Are you coming back with me or not?'

Instead of giving me a direct answer she says: 'You must have seen enough now to realise that there are problems.'

'No problems are insoluble. Go on, ask him now if you can take a week off.'

'Please be patient with me, Kit, and I promise that I'll tell you first thing in the morning. In the meantime we're all going to sleep here tonigh and the sooner you get your head down the better. You look all in.'

'I am.'

'Didn't you sleep well last night?'

'I didn't sleep at all.'

'Because you were too excited?' Her smile's so warm and so gentle and so like it used to be. They're both smiling at me now, her chin no more than an inch from the top of his head.

'I don't know,' I say wearily. 'I'll tell you first thing in the morning.'

The kitchen stove has gone cold and the blind man's 'cello has finally ceased its velvet moaning when Sylvia shows me to a small room up a flight of stone stairs. I may have seen the room when Bruno showed me round, or I may not – I can't remember. I can't even work out if the stone stairs are the ones that led out of the first big room I was in; I'm too tired and too bemused. My raw knees have stuck to their bandages again and it hurts to walk.

It's a fairly makeshift bed under its duvet, and the spare light shows that the window has been fastened over with a big sheet of tin. Sylvia offers to lend me a nightie but I tell her I'll be okay in my petticoat. Fondly she kisses me good-night, and when she's gone I feel so cold that I creep under the duvet fully clothed except for my shoes.

In spite of being so tired I don't think I can have slept for long. Maybe it was too much wine or too much black coffee, but I'm lying here in the darkness struggling with a monster tangle of disconnected thoughts. It starts with worrying about my valise – although there's nothing of particular value in it, I was a fool not to insist on going straight back to collect it – and then I start thinking about that little attic room with the ornate brass bed in which I found Sylvia fast asleep. Is it her room, or isn't it? What happened to her suitcase and my empty airbag that we left by the door? Why all the mystery, and why is she so evasive about coming home? I swear I can read in her face the temptation – almost the *longing* – to come back with me, yet there are all these veiled hints about problems. What problems? Why is she so reluctant to ask for a week's holiday? The set-up here seems friendly enough – then I start remembering the little flickers of fear in her eyes, the sudden defensiveness which makes it so difficult to be more insistent with her.

There's still a lot of sorting out to do and we've all learned not to ask questions. That was what she said, and it was obviously meant as a hint that I should stop prying into her affairs

. . . And yes, I can well understand that all over Germany there are people trying to pick up the threads again, that things are complicated, not always what they seem; that people themselves aren't always what they seem.

Then suddenly I know. Maybe I knew it in the first ten seconds, but still the knowledge shocks me and rocks me so much that I sit up in the darkness with my heart thumping and my mouth dry as a pebble. *It isn't quite over yet*, Sylvia said when we were having supper, and now I know exactly what she meant.

Because Hans the vet is her husband, and his real name is Kurt Wenz.

10

It fits. I remember Sylvia sitting on the brass bed in the Mullerstrasse telling me that Kurt wasn't executed as a war criminal but died in one of the transit camps set up by the Americans. I remember, too, how quickly she said it; how anxious she was to change the subject. It also explains the room she said was hers. She borrowed it from someone – Bruno, for instance – just long enough for us to meet there, and for her to give the impression of a decent little sister living solo and doing her brave little best to earn an honest living. She hadn't foreseen that I'd ask her to come back to England, and when it became obvious that I was going to hang around until she did there was only one course of action open to her and that was to beetle off, as we used to say in the WAAF. And so she beetled off to the place where she really belonged. This place.

So where does Bruno fit in? How much does he know? Probably he's got secrets of his own to hide, which would account for his being a part of this weird, shadowy world where no one asks questions any more.

I sit huddled in the dark, sick with horror yet afraid to put the light on.

And I can't stop thinking about Hans. Or Kurt, as he really is. When Flight Sergeant Cutter broke the news to me that she had been a witness at Sylvia's wedding I remember her saying that Kurt had been young, thin and very good-looking. He's still thin and good-looking, in case she's interested, and if the intervening twelve years have taken away some of the youth I've a feeling that they've merely swopped it for an additional dimension, an extra helping of deadly dangerous enchantment which even I, a fairly stolid type of kraut-despiser, find difficult to dismiss. Hell, what I mean is, he's dead sexy.

Then I start remembering all the things I've ever read about Auschwitz, Buchenwald, Belsen. The walking skeletons, the lampshades made out of human skin, the ovens, the experiments carried out on human guinea pigs by the camp doctors. I think if you asked the average person which aspect sickened them the most nine out of ten would say the camp doctors, and now here I am under the same roof as one; somehow he's managed to evade death by execution and by typhus and he's creeping back into the medical profession by setting up as a vet.

It's so dark in this room. Not a glimmer of light can filter through the tin-covered window and when someone starts knocking softly on the door I break out in a cold sweat. I can't answer. I just sit here. The knocking is repeated and I think I can make out a shadow of two feet under the door.

'Who is it?'

'It's me, Fräulein,' says Bruno, then opens the door and comes in. The dim light outside cuts a mournful swathe across the bed and I shunt myself up closer to the pillows, the duvet drawn up to my chin.

'What d'you want?'

'Nothing, Fräulein, except to give you this.' And he puts my valise in the middle of the swathe of light.

My pleasure and relief are out of all proportion; I hug the thing to me as if it were some kind of ally.

'Where did you find it?'

'Where you left it.'

'You didn't go back there especially?'

'Why should I not? There is nothing better to do.'

Nothing better to do, when it must be long gone midnight? What strange, eerie lives they all live in this God-forsaken hole.

His face is in shadow under the leather cap, and I suddenly feel touched and grateful that he should go to all that trouble just for me.

'Thank you very much, Bruno.'

'It was my pleasure, Fräulein.'

I want to remind him again that I'm a Frau, but don't. He remains motionless by the bed and I do the same under the duvet. Although I very much want him to go, I also have a growing compulsion to discover how much he knows about Hans's true identity. But I'll have to tread carefully.

'It's been very exciting, seeing Sylvia again.'

'So?' I feel him peering at me intently. 'You find her much changed?'

'Yes and no. Time and wars are bound to change people.'

He sits down on the side of the bed and asks how my poor little English knees are feeling. A bit stiff, I say, but much better. He nods understandingly, silhouetted against the hazy light from outside the door.

'Did you ever know Sylvia's husband?'

'Yes, he says. 'But only a long time ago. We met briefly again in the American transit camp a few days before he died.'

'What did he die of?'

'Typhus. Didn't you know?'

I sidestep that one. 'What sort of person was he?'

'A pretty nice fellow, he seemed to me.'

'And very good at his job, I gather?'

If Bruno's aware of the bitterness in my voice he doesn't betray it.

'He was a very competent doctor, yes. But of course we are speaking of the early days when he was at the beginning of his career.'

I become aware that his hand has crept nearer to the one I'm still holding the valise with. As unobtrusively as possible I withdraw it under the duvet.

'One thing I don't understand,' I say brightly, 'is the muddle-up over the room in the Mullerstrasse. I honestly thought it was Sylvia's and I'm sorry if I was rude to you when we first met.'

I wait for him to say something in reply, but he remains silent. I wonder if he's offended because I won't let him hold my hand. 'Purely as a matter of interest, who does the room belong to, Bruno?'

'It is not simple,' he says finally, and I think oh God, here we go again. 'At the end of the war every German was a refugee in his own country, and in the cities we lived like rats in the sewers. Those days have passed but the memories have not, and we still have the instinct to provide ourselves with an extra little hole in the wall in case something should happen to the one we are occupying now.'

'What sort of thing do you envisage?'

He shrugs his shoulders. 'Demolition, like this place. Or maybe the return of the owner who has been reported dead.'

'Like Sylvia's husband?'

'Sylvia's husband will not return,' Bruno says gently.

I wish he'd go away, but as he shows no sign of doing so I decide that we might as well have another question or two.

'Why do you keep hypodermic syringes under the bed in the Mullerstrasse room?'

'Medical supplies can still be very difficult to obtain, especially for animals. Now and then we are forced to do a little business with the black market.'

In other words, they're stolen. I can see his point about old habits dying hard. His hand moves towards the duvet and I feel my injured knees begin to prickle.

'Bruno,' I say, 'just tell me one more thing. Do you think Sylvia will every marry again?'

'Not while she still loves her husband — '

'You make him sound as if he's still alive — '

'You do not permit me to finish my words, Fräulein. Not while she still loves her husband's memory.'

To my relief his hand suddenly stops its travelling and he stands up, so I'm unprepared when he bends over the bed and kisses me. His mouth just misses mine but it's warm and moist and very soft. Almost as if he's got no teeth.

'Good-night, little Fräulein,' he says, and the door closes quietly behind him.

I lie back in the dark and my heart starts thumping again. I don't want to put the light on, then remember that there should be a small pocket torch in my valise. I unzip it and grope inside, rustling among all the sheets of paper I wrote on last night. I find it, and its thin beam stabs the darkness. Lying back on the musty pillows I let it play round the walls, and when I notice the chair at the foot of the bed I get up and hurriedly jam the back of it under the doorknob in case anyone else should decide to pay me a visit. Although my nightie's in the valise I'm far too cold to undress; my only need is to get through this awful night without any more thinking or any more horrors.

Rolled tightly in the duvet I'm just drifting to the edge of sleep when there's a soft thump on the bed, and when something furry touches my face I nearly die. Gasping, I grope under the pillow for the torch and its light shines straight into the enigmatic green stare of a cat. And I recognise that it's the one I followed here earlier on.

In a furious whisper I tell it to shove off, but it obviously doesn't understand English because it starts to purr. Lulled by the sound and comforted by the bit of extra warmth I cuddle it close to me, and when I fall asleep I dream that I'm back home with Emily and the rest of the family.

In comparison with my chill, blacked-out bedroom the kitchen, when I find my way to it next morning, is radiant with sunshine. There are signs that the others have already breakfasted, and when I apologise for oversleeping Sylvia comes over from the stove and hugs me. Maybe it's the golden light – could even be a reflection from the jar of daffodils on the table – but she looks much happier than she did yesterday. And it's nice to be alone with her.

She pours coffee for us both, then sits down opposite me, and I see now that the happiness has something a little wild and precarious about it.

'It's all fixed, Honeybee! We talked it over last night and if there's room on the plane there's no reason why we shouldn't go tonight. In fact the sooner the better — '

'Oh, *marvellous!*' I suddenly feel a terrific sense of liberation.

'Just one thing, though. Is it all right if Hans comes too?'

Oh, God. I don't know what to say. And it must show in my face because she seizes my hand across the kitchen table:

'He's always longed to see England. And if you haven't got a room for him to stay at your home maybe there's a cheap hotel or something — '

'But what about his work? The surgery — '

'Oh, that's easy!' She laughs merrily. 'All we have to do is put a notice on the door saying call back later.'

'Yes, but . . . '

Please, God, tell me what to say. What to do. But He doesn't, so I just sit there and smile numbly while she rushes on about how lovely to have a holiday back home and to be able to introduce Hans to the family and the English countryside and country pubs because he's always been terrifically pro-English . . . '

'It may be a bit difficult,' I finally hear myself mumble, and realise with fresh despair that we seem to have changed roles; yesterday it was me saying that everything was so simple, and now it's my turn to be evasive and cling desperately to dark hints about difficulties and problems.

'*Please*, darling — ' she says. 'He's got a passport and everything.'

'Well, if that's what you really want.' I can feel my face setting in a sulky-child pout, then decide that I might as well play it that way. 'But I rather took it for granted that you'd come on your own. We all want to have you to ourselves for a while, and I know poor old Ma'll be very disappointed.'

'Hans will love her,' she says vehemently, and it's obvious that we're both equally desperate to get our own way.

'But she's old now, and easily upset — '

'But why should Hans upset her? Oh, Kit, you've no idea how much this would mean . . . '

Oh yes, I bloody have. It would mean aiding and abetting a Nazi war criminal to escape the death penalty. Most of them, according to the papers, make for South America, but to take refuge in England would probably succeed by virtue of sheer effrontery.

'I don't know,' I say crossly. 'I'll have to ring home first.'

'No, don't do that,' she says very quickly. 'It wouldn't work.'

'Why not? Most people would prefer to be warned about

an extra guest — '

'They wouldn't understand. Before they even met him they'd be raking up the past and hating him just because of his nationality.'

'So what would we do – pass him off as Irish?'

A smile flickers momentarily, and then her face has set back in its old tired lines. The happiness has been extinguished like someone snapping off a light.

'He probably wouldn't stay with us for more than a day or two,' she says wearily. 'He couldn't leave Bruno to cope here all alone for very long.'

'I was going to ask about Bruno — '

'He can deal with all the simple things. He could keep the practice ticking over so that Hans could have a few days' rest. He's so tired . . . '

'Oh, Sylvia . . . ' Crossness collapses into despair.

Of course, if I'd got an ounce of *esprit de corps* I'd have the whole thing out with her here and now. I'd tell her that I know the truth, and that I have no intention of sheltering a creature like Kurt Wenz. After all, I fought in the last war (well, I was in it, anyway), and the honest thing would be for me to tell her that I'm leaving this place here and now and that I'm going straight to the authorities with the information in my possesion; after which she has the choice of coming home with me alone, or not at all.

But I know I won't. I won't because it's Sylvia, and because she would probably face a long prison sentence for complicity, and finally it's not all that easy to go bounding off to the authorities when you don't know enough of the language even to ask the way.

All I can do is to stall until the right course of action presents itself. I just hope to God it won't be long.

So we drink our coffee, then she grabs my arm as we hear footsteps coming down the stone passage.

'Listen Kit, don't say anything about this to Bruno yet. Hans is planning to tell him at lunchtime.'

Yes, it all fits. They'll ditch Bruno just as they're going to ditch the veterinary practice and everything else. And I'm just going to sit here and watch because I don't know what else to do.

But it's Hans who comes in, not Bruno. Seeing me, he smiles good-morning and once again I can't get over the sheer presence of the man; for most people extreme good looks would be more than enough, but he's got this extra quality that defies description. Still, I remember reading somewhere that Satan made far more charismatic impact than Jesus.

Sylvia starts speaking to him in rapid German, and from the way she glances at me every now and then I know she's telling him about our recent conversation. He glances at me too, and occasionally interrupts her with a question. They seem tense and anxious, and believe me I'd give anything in the world if it could be different; if only I could smile and indicate in sign language that he was welcome to come home with us. But all I can do is sit here sipping the last of the coffee and trying to look as if the whole thing is no concern of mine.

'It's all going to be okay.' Sylvia finally turns to me. 'Hans is coming over with us and we're going to find him a nice little place where he can stay and where I can join him in between catching up with all the family and everything.'

'I see.'

'Darling, don't look so *worried* — ' But in truth she's the one who looks worried. 'Hans is going to explain to Bruno while I start doing a bit of packing. It won't take long.'

'The plane doesn't leave until tonight.'

'I know, but it takes nearly an hour to get to Lohausen and we've got to get tickets and things. It might be a good idea to set off early — '

'Sylvia.' I stare at her very hard. 'Are you quite sure you're doing the right thing?'

As if by instinct she and Hans move closer to each other and I read antagonism in his eyes.

'Quite positive, Honeybee,' she says gently. And I know she's aware that I've discovered the truth.

It's now close on midday and I still don't know what to do.

I wander back to the room I slept in, smooth the bed tidy and tell myself that I should be honest and say out loud that I know Hans's real identity and want no part in his escape from

Germany. But I'm also trying to work out if I want to go further than that; if I want to be instrumental in his arrest, trial and execution. When I think back to the newsreels of Belsen and Buchenwald I'm quite certain that I do; then I start thinking about Sylvia again.

To be honest, I also start thinking about myself. About what could happen to me if Hans discovered that I was even toying with the idea of turning him in.

Sitting on the bed in the gloomy electric light I open the valise and riffle through the sheets of hotel paper so closely covered in my urgent scrawl. God knows what induced me to pour out the story of my life and I'll chuck it as soon as I get home. No, maybe I'll wait until this particular episode's finished; whichever way it goes, I've a feeling that it's not going to take very long.

I lock the valise, leave the bedroom and wander quietly along the labyrinthine passages. A strange woman passes me on the stone staircase. We stare unsmilingly at one another and I know that I can't take much more of this sepulchral place with its secretive, rodent-like population. On the top floor I pass an open door and see Hans with his back to me packing a canvas bag with clothing. It's a very small untidy room and I'm surprised by the little truckle bed shoved against the crumbling wall because it's miles too small to accommodate him and Sylvia. I glide past before he sees me.

Downstairs in the kitchen I come face to face with Bruno. He's sitting at the table wearing his leather cap and eating a meal of white sausage and *Sauerkraut*. He beams amiably.

'Good-day, my dear Fräulein.'

'Hullo, Bruno.'

'Did you sleep well?'

'Yes. Oh, yes . . . '

'And the knees? How are the little English knees?'

'Fine. No problem.'

'Tomorrow morning early Hans and I go to Frankfurt,' he said, prising the top off a bottle of beer. I stand watching it foam into the glass. 'We go to buy some good drugs cheap for our little sick animals.'

'I rather gather you won't be going now.'

He stops chewing and looks at me intently. 'How so?'

They haven't told him. I know they have no intention of doing so.

Forcing myself to return his gaze I suddenly feel my heart bumping up in my throat. Until two seconds ago I still couldn't decide on the right course of action, but now every nerve in me is sending the message loud and clear: play innocent, play stupid, and stay out of trouble. What they get up to is no concern of yours, dear Kit, because you've only got one option open to you and that's to get home to husband and children as fast as possible and all in one piece.

'No, no,' Bruno says. 'We go to Frankfurt tomorrow. All is arranged.'

'Yes. I was thinking about something else.'

But he continues to watch me carefully from under the peak of his leather cap. I flinch and move away.

'Frankfurt was a fine city before it was bombed.'

'So was Coventry.' I stand by the window looking out into the narrow street. An old woman passes, her lips moving as if she's talking to herself.

'War is stupid,' Bruno says through a mouthful of *Sauerkraut*. 'It makes much suffering and much pain.'

'Especially for the innocent.'

'Ah. But who do you class as innocent?'

I turn round from the window. 'Let's start with all the children who died in the extermination camps.'

He nods slowly, sadly, and I have a sudden mad urge to confide in him. To ask for his help.

But he speaks first. 'Are they planning to leave me?'

Dear God, he's one jump ahead. I stand looking at the big smooth sad face partly shadowed by the cap, and think that he could well epitomise all the rootless, helpless and hopeless people who have been cast up in the wake of the havoc. Then my nerve fails.

'I – I don't know — '

I force myself to go on looking at him, and as I do the little hairs on the back of my neck seem to crawl. The low, terrible supplication of the old man's 'cello has started again, so near that I think he must be in the next room.

'So. He is not yet dead.'

'Doesn't anyone ever go in to see him? To see if they can help?'

'How can you help an old, sick blind man who wants only to die?'

'I don't know the answer to that, either.'

And at that moment Sylvia and Hans come into the kitchen, and my relief is as huge as it's cowardly. I slink over to the chair by the stove but no one takes any notice of me because they're all busy speaking in German; at least Sylvia and Hans are, and it's Bruno who's doing the listening. They're obviously asking him to do something and Hans offers him a piece of paper torn from a pad and I catch the word Frankfurt.

Bruno says nothing for a long moment, then asks a brief question. And they both smile at him and Sylvia goes into another quick torrent of, presumably, explanation. Slowly Bruno pushes his plate away and stands up. His chair makes a harsh scraping sound. He looks at them dejectedly, like a dog, then pulling his cap further down over his ears takes the piece of paper and goes out.

Motionless, we listen as the sound of his footsteps ends in the bang of a door.

And I know exactly what Sylvia's going to say before she says it.

'Bruno's gone to Frankfurt to get some things for the surgery.'

'Uh-huh.'

'We've got a very good supplier there – not exactly black market, but – well, he's cheaper than all the others, and of course most of the people who come here with their animals are very poor.'

'When will he be back?'

'It'll take him quite a time. Anyway, we told him not to hurry. He's got an old aunt living there . . . '

She can't keep still. First she clears Bruno's plate and glass away, shoving them into the chipped sink and pouring water over them. She comes back to the table and twitches the daffodils into place in their jar. She sits down, tapping her fingers, and then springs up again. She jerks a question at Hans, who replies without looking at her; he's looking at me, and I can't read the expression in his handsome eyes.

'Honeybee,' Sylvia says, 'Hans and I think it would be a good idea if we left now.'

The 'cello music stops in mid-phrase. Fleetingly I wonder why.

'Leave now – where for?'

'The airport, you fathead!' she laughs joyously, but I catch the hysteria. 'Hans has arranged everything here. A locum friend of his is going to take over surgery hours and Bruno understands about our holiday and is quite happy to cope with the more mundane things . . . So don't let's bother with lunch here; we can have it at the airport. We're both packed and ready – are you?'

'Yes,' I say. 'I only travel light.'

'By the way, I must let you have your airbag – the one you left at the Mullerstrasse room — '

'Keep it. Along with the book of traveller's cheques.'

And I just can't stand the way she's scuttling about; it's not Sylvia, the Alice Faye girl with the golden hair and dancing blue eyes and happy laughing warmth you could bask in . . . This is a thin, drawn, haggard woman with sharp kneecaps poking through cheap stockings; there's a thin, cheap air about the whole of her, a tinny desperation that's somehow come about because of the beautiful male bastard she's determined to protect from the fate he deserves. She would lie for him, die for him, and the whole aspect of this cringing and essentially un-English sort of love fills me with a dreadful sickness.

'Sylvia,' the words seem to come of their own volition: 'I know the truth. I know that Kurt Wenz isn't dead.'

She stops her stupid scuttling and gives a little cry.

'How – what do you mean?'

'I mean that I know he didn't die of typhus. I know that you're using me to help him escape to England, and I just can't go along with it.'

And I suddenly feel better. Not in the clear, because I'm only too aware that anything could happen to me now. I could end up at the bottom of the Rhine or under a truck, but I do feel better. More honest.

'Have you said anything to him?'

'How could I? I don't speak kraut — '

Her face seems to disintegrate. It creases into wrinkles, with closed eyes and a downturned mouth.

'Who d'you think is Kurt?'

'Him over there.'

Our voices are very still, very quiet, as I indicate Hans with a nod of my head.

'Sweet Christ in heaven,' Sylvia whispers finally. 'It's not him, it's Bruno.'

Everything blurs. I'm no longer capable of comprehension. Then I come out of the sickening whirl to hear Sylvia screaming at Hans in German. He leaps for the door and I hear the pounding of his feet along the stone corridor. Then she turns to me.

'Did you tell him we were going to England?'

'No. Well — ' I vacillate helplessly. 'I didn't directly, but he may suspect — '

'Get your suitcase. We're going right now!'

I run to do as I'm told. I pass Hans on the stairs dragging a canvas holdall and the suitcase Sylvia had in the Mullerstrasse room. It bangs against my leg but he doesn't seem to notice me. By the time I'm running downstairs with my valise and my handbag they're both at the door leading into the street. The door I came through with the cat.

Hans opens it and peers out cautiously. Then he jerks his head and we follow him, half running and half walking, and it seems appropriate that the sparkling sunshine should now have become doused by bulging clouds. Hans reaches the archway first and motions us to a halt while he looks out into the street and fear trickles down my spine at all these cops-and-robbers precautions. I wish with all my heart that I could dismiss them as unnecessary. We hurry on without speaking, our footsteps sharp on the cobblestones, and although the area seems deserted I feel conscious of being watched. It takes a lot of willpower not to glance over my shoulder.

I'm out of breath by the time we reach the big streets and conscious of Sylvia panting by my side. But the noise of traffic and the profusion of ordinary-looking Düsseldorfers has a calming effect and I feel almost cheerful when I see Hans trying to attract the attention of a taxi. It sweeps past, then he grabs my arm and I suddenly find myself being hauled on to a tram. The three of us manage to sit together, and for a moment no one speaks. We're too busy trying to relax and look ordinary before the curious gaze of our fellow-passengers.

But as soon as I get my breath back there's a question in urgent need of an answer.

'Sylvia — ' I pull her sleeve, whispering hoarsely. 'Why are we running away from him? He's a war criminal, so why don't we just turn him in?'

Her lips are working, her eyes scanning the street scene flickering past. 'It isn't easy.'

'Why not?'

'Could you hang someone you'd been married to?'

'I could if — '

'But it wasn't *like* that!' She drags her gaze from the window and although we're hissing the words in one another's ears I sense the interest around us. Hans leans across me and murmurs something to Sylvia in German. Probably it's a warning.

I try to remain quiet but can't, and, when the tram squeals round a corner and I'm pushed hard up against Sylvia, demand to know whether she's still married to him. Tight-lipped, she nods, and I'm swept by fresh incredulity. It's no use, I'll never understand. I don't even know where to begin trying.

But it seems now as if Sylvia's impelled to talk. Clutching her suitcase on her lap she starts whispering rapidly, the words spilling out, running together and tickling down my ear. Our shoulders bump together in rhythm to the tram's swaying and on the other side of me I feel the thin taut body of Hans.

'It was so perfect in the early days. He was a keen party member and although he had a genuine vocation for medicine he always intended that his work should be of direct benefit to Germany. He loved his country, and that's no crime. When he was recalled from his job with the German Embassy in London he was sent to a medical unit dealing with infantile paralysis – what d'you call it now? – polio . . . He was put in charge of work on a new serum to protect children, and when he discovered that there were special centres where experimental work could be carried out – well, he decided to ignore some of his principles and — '

'And so he used little gypsy and Jewish guinea pigs?'

'Faced with a situation from which there was no chance of withdrawing, so would you. He worked fanatically hard, sixteen and eighteen hours a day, in the hope that he could perfect the serum with the minimum amount of – of human involvement, and because I couldn't see any alternative either I — '

I cut in; and her tired yellow curls blow away from her ear as I put my mouth close: 'So you helped him?'

'I helped check results in the lab and we were on the verge of breakthrough when the war ended. We managed to escape from the Russians into the western sector. There was starvation, typhus, casual rape and murder. Kurt's name was on the list, but when he got taken by the Americans he escaped. Three months later we met up in a transit camp and we were horrified when we learned that someone had apparently been hanged in his place. But in those days you didn't waste time being sorry for other people. When you've been stripped to the bare bone your only problem is how to keep alive.

'You've also seen people as they really are. And I saw that Kurt was prepared to survive no matter what the price. I didn't love him any more. I tried to, but maybe no love on earth can stand what we went through. He was obsessed by the fear of discovery. A plastic surgeon worked on his face but because of the chronic shortage of medical supplies – even ordinary disinfectants – he developed septicaemia. I didn't love him but I felt sorry for him. He didn't deserve all the things he suffered – all the pain . . . '

Conscious that Hans is excluded she reaches across my lap to him. They sit with their hands linked on top of my valise and it's funny how he doesn't seem powerful and dynamic any more. It must have been my overworked imagination because now I see him as I'm sure he really is: still wonderfully handsome, but as nervous, worried and fallible as anyone else.

'When did you two first meet?'

'All that part is true. Hans really is a vet and I really did answer his advertisement for an assistant. Kurt wasn't fit to work, either mentally or physically. Even with his face – how it is now – he didn't dare to go out, so I had to earn our keep. Our marriage was finished – he knew it was – but he wouldn't let me go. He had a chance to get away to Canada at one point but he refused to go unless I went with him —'

'But all you've got to do is go to the authorities — '

'For God's sake, I've already told you that's out of the question. In any case, they could probably prove that I was implicated too — '

The tram sways round another corner and I find myself pressed hard up against Hans with Sylvia's rapid, vehement whisper following.

'I just don't want any more trouble. All my life things have gone wrong for me – I've been through enough. All I want is to get away. One day I want Hans and me to be married, but to begin with I just want us to be left alone in peace.'

'Does Bruno – Kurt, I mean – know my address in England?'

'No,' she says quickly. 'I didn't even tell him you were coming. I planned to keep it secret because to be quite honest I hoped you'd just — '

'Just clear off and mind my own business.' The knowledge is bitter.

'I didn't think you'd wait for me so long in the Mullerstrasse. And I didn't know Kurt was going to call there — '

Hans prevents her from saying any more by indicating that it's time to get off the tram. I've no idea where we are, but the big streets have long ago given way to desultory suburbs. I suppose the tram doesn't go any nearer to the airport than this.

Shoving past the other passengers we alight and the clouds

are now spitting a spiteful rain. It feels colder, much colder, and I clutch at my coat collar with one hand and lug the valise with the other.

'Suppose the plane seats are all booked,' I say to Sylvia. She shrugs.

'Let's take one thing at a time. At least we've got rid of Kurt.'

We hurry past small houses and fields and every now and then the urgent patter of our feet is drowned by the swish of passing lorries. We don't talk any more; just concentrate on reaching the airport. It seems a hell of a long way, and when Hans looks behind and sees a taxi coming towards us he steps into the road and waves it down.

It stops, and my hand is already on the passenger door when it flies open and the first thing I recognise is the leather cap with the pulled-down peak. Sylvia screams and starts running, her suitcase banging against her side. I feel a violent shove in the back as Bruno – Kurt – pounds after her, and, in the first seconds of realising what's happened, I know there's nothing I can do. The taxi is still at the kerb with the engine throbbing and I stand mesmerised by the two figures running ahead.

A big lorry dripping wet sand passes and drowns the noise of the shot, so that at first I imagine he's tripped over or something. He seems to fall very slowly, first to his knees and then full-length, and when I turn round to look at Hans I see the gun and the drained white mask of his face.

When we reach Kurt he is already dead. His cap has come off and the raindrops are bouncing on his smooth hairless face and filling his open eyes with tears. Hans, the taxi driver and I are all kneeling by him and it seems strange that traffic should go on passing with no more than a curious glance at what's happened. Either they don't believe it or the war made them indifferent.

Then I look up and see Sylvia.

She's standing some way off, looking back at us. She's dropped her suitcase. Then she starts walking back, diffident and wary, and I want to go and meet her, put my arms round her shoulders, but I haven't got the strength to get up. Hans has opened the dead man's jacket and unbuttoned his shirt by the time she reaches us. She doesn't look at either of them. They and the taxi driver mightn't even be there. The only person she's looking at is me, and with the rain soaking her cheap clothes and flattening her hair in dark rat-tails it seems as if everything she could possibly feel is concentrated in me. But it's a long time before she says anything.

'Now perhaps you'll go.' She speaks through clenched teeth. 'Perhaps you'll go back where you came from and leave me alone. Because I don't want you. If I did, I'd have got in touch with you years ago.'

Her voice is quiet, easily drowned by the swish of tyres on the wet road, but her face is filled with implacable hatred that I don't seem able to breathe properly. I certainly can't speak.

'Go away,' she says. 'I never could stand you, and I still can't.'

They took Kurt's body away in an ambulance and now I'm sitting here alone in a bleak room in what is presumably a police station. I don't know where they've taken Sylvia and Hans.

Only one of the *Polizei* can speak English. He asked for my name and address, and for my passport, then informed me that I was under arrest pending enquiries and that I was allowed one telephone call. Some while after that I was given a cup of coffee.

Since then, nothing's happened. I just go on sitting here and all I can see is Sylvia, shop-soiled and rain-soaked, spitting hatred at me on that long road out to the airport. So now perhaps I've learned to leave well alone; to stop crashing about in other people's lives like poor old MacFadden crashing about in the sports cupboard that time. I try to work out how I feel about it, but I can't.

Then the *Polizei* stumps in again.

'Telephone. Your telephone call is through.'

I go with him across a big echoing hall and into an office where another uniformed man is sitting behind a desk. Formal and unsmiling, he indicates the telephone receiver lying by a pile of papers. I pick it up, dimly aware of the polished jackboots standing to attention by my side.

'Hullo?'

There's silence for a moment, followed by a crackling sound and then finally a faraway voice: 'Kit, is that you? What's happening?'

I press the receiver closer to my ear, and all that's happening is that I'm starting to cry. I thought I'd no feeling left, but the sound of his voice is making the hot blinding tears gush out. And when the kraut copper unobtrusively withdraws his hand from his breeches pocket and slips me a clean white handkerchief I hear myself give a long high wail at the memory of other places, other days.

'Kit? For Christ's sake, what are they doing to you?'

Words come at last. 'Nothing. I'm just crying a bit because it's nice to hear your voice and the chap standing next to me's just lent me a handkerchief . . . '

'Listen Kit – I can't make out what's happening over there but I'm getting the plane out tomorrow — ' He goes on to say other things; sensible, proper things like don't panic, keep up your *esprit de corps,* and then there's silence.

'Darling — ' I replace the receiver very slowly, conscious now that the two *Polizei* have been following the proceedings to the best of their ability. Covertly, a little sheepishly, they smile at me and I do my watery best to smile back.

Tomorrow David will be here to help sort things out.